*"Few Americans born after the Civil War
know much about war. Real war.
War that seeks you out.
War that arrives on your doorstep - not once in a blue moon,
but once a month or a week or a day."*

Nick Turse

★★★★★★★

ELLA

A Tale of Love, War and Redemption

★★★★★★★

4-24-23

DAVID HESS

Acknowledgments

While this book is a work of fiction and the characters are products of my imagination, I hope to pay homage to the men and women who served and died during the American Civil War. I also wish to especially acknowledge the bravery of the men in the 151st Pennsylvania Volunteer Infantry Regiment.

And as always, thanks to my wife who never gives up believing in me.

Table of Contents

Part One
PONY LAKE

INTRODUCTION
★★★★★★★
1861 - 1862

In 1861, Pony Lake was the gathering place for the people of the small town of Herronville, Pennsylvania, in Pike County. During the spring and summer months, folks would go there to swim, picnic, and fish in the small lake, which was teeming with large pickerel, perch and sunfish. During the cool fall evenings, they would gather around the fires built from the fallen oak and maple leaves and sticks found in the woods and in which they would roast potatoes while drinking cider. Winter was the season to skate and ice fish. Those fishermen who braved the ice and wind would take their catch home where their wives or mothers would prepare a hearty meal of baked perch and potato pie.

Everyone loved Herronville and Pony Lake. Artists would come on the train from New York City to paint scenes of the lake during the summer, spring, and fall. Only the heartiest of them could endure setting up an easel in the cold to sit and paint or sketch a winter scene. Many of them stayed at the inn located in the town. Others stayed in the lofts of the barns of the local farms or took lodging in the houses of the residents, often paying them with a portrait of their family, a drawing of the lake or the town.

The town sat on the Delaware River, and while the river attracted many visitors, it was Pony Lake that most of the visitors and citizens came to see and enjoy. During picnics at the lake, many young boys and girls discovered their first love. Some of those romances blossomed into relationships that lasted a lifetime. A generation later, their children also shared a nervous first kiss at the lake as they strolled on one of the many paths that circled the lake and wound through the soft boughs of white pine trees. It was an idyllic setting for all aspects of life in the small village.

In 1862, when the United States Government needed more troops to fight in the War Between the States, everything changed in Herronville. The young men of Pike County, feeling the call of duty, along with men from several other counties, formed a voluntary infantry division. The unit was filled with farmers, railroaders, teachers, and others who had no military experience but were willing to fight and die for their country—at least most of them were. There were also a few who did not believe in the war or the cause that the North was fighting for. Despite their individual views, they were all sent to Harrisburg, received some very basic training, and sent off to assist in the Battle of Chancellorsville. The unit was nicknamed "The School Teacher Regiment," in spite of the fact that, most of the men were not educated.

While they played only a minor role at the battle of Chancellorsville, several men contracted malaria and one man's eyesight was damaged after he washed in a contaminated pool of swamp water. Shortly after, the men became a major force in the battle that changed the tide of the war—Gettysburg. They were moved north to the battlefield that would be forever remembered, not only as the turning point of the war but also for the carnage left behind after the battle was fought. The unit fought for three days at Gettysburg defending units on Seminary Ridge where their commander, G.F. McFarland, was shot in both legs. He later lost one to a surgeon's knife. They retreated and regrouped on Cemetery Hill, where they suffered enormous casualties, losing 75% of their men.

In late July, several weeks after the battle had ended, the survivors of this regiment were physically and emotionally reduced to a group of dazed and maimed catatonics. Most were never the same again. They were about to disband to begin their lifelong curse of reliving the war in their minds. Now that they were no longer needed as cannon fodder, the unit was sent to Washington, D.C., where the government expressed its gratitude by pinning a medal on each of their uniforms and thanking them for their service and sacrifice.

It was a cold November day, winter already beginning to bare its teeth, when they were discharged. Their commander advised them that they could return home to their towns and villages, where anxious families awaited them. But they were strongly warned not to go anywhere near the southern enemy territories, adding if they were captured, they would be imprisoned in one of the notorious Confederate prisons.

One man, who never did believe in the war or its cause, had survived with nothing more serious than an infected eye. It came from something as simple as washing his face in a contaminated swamp in Chancellorsville, leaving him partially blind.

After being discharged in Washington, he mounted the horse he had taken from the battlefield, to begin his journey home to Herronville. He traveled with several other soldiers who were also fortunate enough to have survived the Battle of Gettysburg. His unit had been almost totally annihilated in a war that he did not believe should have happened. The other men who were attempting to make their way home with him, dropped off one-by-one, leaving him to ride on by himself.

1.
Nicholas Haff
★★★★★★★
1864

It took Nicholas more than three weeks to get to Herronville. During that time, the battle-beaten horse he was riding struggled to complete the journey. When they finally reached the border of Pennsylvania and Maryland near the village of Emmitsburg, they stopped for the night. In the morning, the poor beast was too weak to get to his feet. Nicholas said a few comforting and apologetic words as he knelt and looked into the suffering animal's eyes, then he pulled the trigger putting him out of his misery. The horse had belonged to a Confederate cavalry soldier who had been shot off his back. Unfortunately, though not physically wounded, the brave horse had experienced too much war, exhaustion, and disease.

He continued his journey alone, walking and hitching rides on the backs of passing wagons whenever possible. As he trod along, he thought of his home and Pony Lake. But most of all, he thought about the girl he believed he loved–Ella, Ella Samter. His thoughts of her were interrupted when he realized that he would soon be passing Gettysburg. His body shivered when he remembered those who had died alongside him on those fields that surrounded the quaint little town, and he feared walking past the still fresh and bloody battlefields. Mentally distressed and exhausted, he took his bedroll and walked off into the woods to find a place to rest, hoping that his mind would cleanse itself of the memories that lingered like a crown of thorns.

Before this final journey home after his participation at

Gettysburg, he would often lie restless with his bedroll under his head in the fields and swamps near the battlefield of Chancellorsville and fantasize about Ella. He had never kissed her, but many times he secretly held her hand under the stars as they sat on the banks of Pony Lake while the older folks talked about their crops and animals. He dreamt of kissing her and more. They would stare into each other's eyes, and as they held hands, she would eventually give out a quiet sigh, a smile and pull her hand away and whisper, "We better not do that; our folks will see us." She would then smile and turn her head slightly to the side and look out at the lake. Their conversations were slight, but he hung on every word that she said, and he felt alone when she excused herself to return home with her parents. He always feared that they would never again sit on the bank of the lake, and he would never have that wonderful feeling again, the feeling that he believed was love. These were the memories he shared with himself as he tried to forget his situation. He thought of her soft touch rather than the screams and moans of the battlefield that he knew were sure to come at any time. But now, as he lay several miles from the battlefields, he could not focus on his thoughts of her. Instead, they would appear for moments, and, in a flash, he was on the battlefield again, recalling the atrocities he had witnessed.

The young rebel boy who looked younger than he, had made it through the lines of Northern soldiers and was prepared to kill anyone with his rifle. Instead, he was beheaded by two swipes of an officer's sword. He watched as the officer kicked the boy's head to the side and ordered Haff to continue firing at the charging rebels. With great clarity, he saw the man next to him, an old man who had volunteered to fight in the war even though he was not drafted, die as a Southerner's bullet found its mark in the middle of his forehead.

He sat up and shook his head, hoping that the memory of Ella would return and that he could fall asleep. Then as he began to doze off, he awoke with a scream, seeing in his mind the first man that he knew he had killed.

He was a young man with no rifle, sword, or weapon of any kind. He had run at Nicholas, yelling something that he could not understand. He drew his pistol from his belt and fired point-blank into what he hoped was that young man's real face and not the double image caused by his only useful eye. The sudden splatter of blood covering his face confirmed that his shot had hit its mark. He stood over the dead man looking off at the approaching formations of Rebels, who were firing at close range and mowing down his comrades as if they were stationary targets. It was then that he lay on the ground in the blood of the man he had just killed and feigned death. He had seen enough; he could fight no more.

When the images of death and chaos stopped appearing in his mind, he slept for several hours. Sometimes Ella would appear, and beautiful thoughts and half-remembered fragrances replaced the horrors that haunted his mind.

In the morning after he awoke, he folded up his bedroll and walked through the woods to the small pond he had seen the day before to wash-up. Then he slowly headed north toward Gettysburg and the now-vacant battlefields hoping that his mind would allow him some peace.

2.

Ella Samter

★★★★★★★

1863

Ella Samter had never been a particularly pretty little girl, and as she matured, she did not turn into a swan. She relied instead, on being kind and giving to everyone around her. She visited neighbors when they were ill, cooked them meals, cleaned their houses, and took care of their animals that needed tending. She was a generous person, but her parents feared she would never marry. By the time she came of age to consider marriage, there were very few eligible men in Herronville, or for that matter, in Pike County because of the war. But she was content living with her parents in the house that her grandfather had built after he arrived from Germany in 1821 on the Amaranth. Ironically, this was the same ship that Nicholas Haff's grandparents came on. She was happy to tend to her flower and vegetable gardens and the animals owned by her father. She always kept thoughts of Nicholas in the back of her mind. She just knew that he would come back, and they would marry.

When Ella was young, she seemed to be liked by the other children at Pony Lake, but she shied away from them when they played games, such as Graces or Cup and Ball or any of the other games that children play. She always felt a bit unsure of herself and often felt socially clumsy. Ella would rather be alone than to ice skate or play hide and seek with the other children. However, from the time she was very young, she would become excited when the cute boy who lived on the next farm would come to the lake or even ride his father's giant draft horse past her house.

His name was Nicholas Haff. She would follow Nicholas with her eyes as he rode by on his buckboard carrying supplies from the general store back to the family farm. She often waved at him, hoping that he would nod his head and maybe even smile at her. She would watch him until he made the turn at the corner and disappear up the road, still hearing the clip-clop of the big animal's hooves. Sometimes, when she saw him coming down the road, she would quickly run out the front door hoping that he would stop and talk to her at the front gate of her house. When he did stop, she offered him a cool drink of lemonade or a cold glass of water from the well in her backyard. She beamed with pride, telling him that she had personally squeezed the lemons and made the lemonade. This ritual went on for many years until Nicholas marched off to war in the autumn of 1862.

After Nicholas and the other men left, Ella had no one. Her only girlfriend, Emma Mathers, who used to live near her, moved to Barnsdale, which was twenty miles away. So, she knitted, crocheted, and wrote letters to Nicholas. These letters were never sent but neatly bundled together with a red ribbon and placed in a box that she hid in her dresser drawer. She hoped that one day, she would be able to give them to him in person when he returned.

The young girl was much too shy to send the letters and to let Nicholas know how much she liked him. So she would walk to the banks of Pony Lake and, with her pencil and paper, write him letters that were more of a make-believe conversation with him. They were the kinds of conversations they used to have when he would reach over to her and hold her hand in the darkness. She then took the letters home and placed them in her little wooden box. Smiling and blushing, she visualized him reading the daring words she had written. Often, Ella would take the small box to her bed and hold it to her chest and tell herself that the next day she would walk to Nicholas's house and ask his mother if she would tell her where to send the letters. Her brave excitement of the night would wane in the morning, and the box filled with the heartfelt letters she had written, would be placed back into her drawer under her chemise. She would then pick up her mirror and scold herself for being such a foolish girl, after which she would reassure herself that one day, she would hand the box over to Nicholas.

Each night, before falling asleep, she got on her knees and prayed. "Please Lord, bless my mother and father, our home, the animals in the barn and, most of all, Nicholas, please keep him safe and out of harm's way." With a great surge of guilt, she also asked the Lord to allow her to dream of Nicholas.

Ella Samter was aware for many years that she loved Nicholas Haff.

3.

Return to Gettysburg
★★★★★★★
1863

It was late in the evening of November 18, 1863, when Nicholas arrived in the area of the battlegrounds of Gettysburg. He could have covered the fifteen miles faster, but his fear of seeing the blood-soaked fields again caused him to move slowly. He politely turned down rides from many of the folks who drove their wagons by, tipped their hats to him, and offered him a break from the road. He explained that he was not going too far and would rather walk. Several of them asked him if he had fought at Gettysburg. He pointed to the medal on his chest, acknowledging that he had indeed fought. Then they would thank him and hand him some smoked meat and bread before they moved on.

As he approached the town, smoke from the campfires wafted up through the trees. The smoke burned his nostrils and made pus ooze down his cheek from his infected eye. There were small glowing encampments filled with groups of people, filling the streets of the little town. In the distance, he saw the yellow flames of smaller fires flickering on the battlefield, and people gathered around them to feel the warmth. He took a deep breath and moved to the side of the road so that he could avoid the crowds of people as much as possible. Taking a seat on a rock near the sodden bank alongside the road, he wondered why such a crowd would gather in the battle-beaten village. The vision in his remaining eye was poor at night, and his blinded eye was still painful from the infection. The doctor had told him to flush it with clean water whenever he had the chance, but by the time he got to the fight in Gettysburg,

11

he was already experiencing double vision, which was becoming a way of life for him.

He lay back onto the cold earth and watched the fires and the people milling around and then looked up at the stars and the moon. He wondered if Ella was looking at the moon, the same moon that he could see. He thought of that many times during his campaigns and would smile, thinking that she was also gazing at the yellow globe.

Nicholas slept very little the night he arrived in Gettysburg. The ground was harder than he had ever remembered it to be, and the noise of the people clustered on the road near where he lay, was enough to keep him from falling asleep. They were talking loudly with great zeal in their voices. Others whispered with glee while some giggled with delight. Whatever they were excited about would have to wait until morning, as he struggled to fall asleep. When he did finally sleep, it was sporadic and restless, and all too soon, the sun rose in the east. The sky brightened enough so that when he sat up, he could see that the crowds had grown even larger than when he had moved into the woods the prior evening.

Smoke continued to fill the air, but now, along with the smell of smoke, the delicious odor of frying bacon and ham, mixed in with the increasingly louder sounds of the people, all talking at once. He tried to make out the words wafting in the breeze from the clusters of men, women, and children. "Lincoln!" "Train..." "What time?' "Will he be safe?" He could make little sense of it, and with his eye oozing, he was hesitant to approach anyone for fear of offending them or scaring them off. He sat and ate the last bit of smoked meat that had been given to him by a woman in a passing wagon the day before. He made his bedroll, slung it over his shoulder, and walked cautiously toward the crowd. Standing on the incline of the bank, he spied on them. Even though his double vision was causing him much difficulty, he was learning to manage it. In a short time, he observed a Union soldier in uniform, standing amidst the crowd of civilians. He decided to approach him to find out why such a gathering was taking place. He wiped his eye with his sleeve and then his sleeve onto his pants before slowly walking toward the soldier. As he wove his way through the crowds, he excused himself while attempting to get closer to the soldier. He finally reached the man who was quite a bit older than he at first thought, maybe forty or fifty, with a graying beard. His uniform was as unkempt as was his own, and he smelled of whiskey. The soldier did not notice Nicholas standing next to him. As he was about to speak, the man lifted a bottle to his lips, took a long drink, and in a loud and beautiful deep voice, began to sing a song familiar to Nicholas. The soldier stared into the sky when he sang, singing as if to no one, but he was standing on the edges of the blood-soaked battlefield. *"We live in hard and stirring times..."*

Slowly the crowd around him began to hush. With growing deference, they listened intently as the craggy-face soldier held his bottle at his side and continued to sing the popular Stephen Foster song:

"...Too sad for mirth, too rough for rhymes;
For songs of peace have lost their chimes,
And that's what's the matter!
The men we held as brothers true
Have turned into a rebel crew;
So now we have to put them thro',
And that's what's the matter,
The rebels have to scatter;
We'll make them flee, by land and sea,
And that's what's the matter!"

The men and women cheered him as he raised his near-empty bottle to his mouth, took one last drink, and with a sadness in his voice, looked at the ground and said, "That's what's the matter!"

As he peered into the crowd, his eyes locked onto Nicholas's face. "Hey, lad, what are you doing here?" he said with a laugh, "The battle is over, and the rebs are on the run! Lee, Longstreet, Stuart, Hill, all of them run back to the South. Run like rabbits. I was there when Armstead attacked with Picket. He was waving his

13

hat in the air and his sword too. Daring us, brazenly daring us to surrender! We shot him full of holes! They say we shot him three times—I know it was more! Lots more. I was there!" He paused and looked at Haff, and with a hint of boastfulness, he declared, "They said he was going to live! Well, I'm here, and he's as dead as all of those others that followed him toward that wall! And now, that ugly monkey they call the President is going to be here today to tell us all about how brave we was. Gonna tell us that the war will be over soon! He's been saying it for three years! 'Gonna get a new Commanding General!'" He gave a belly laugh. "Who this time? Little Mac again? He couldn't command my ass! But I'm gonna drink the rest of this whiskey and stay right here to hear him. Maybe I'll get close enough to him to tell him he's full of pig shit!"

Nicholas did not respond. He knew what he needed to know. He, too, would wait for the President. He would not talk to him or call out to him. He was much too shy to do that. But maybe if he got near enough to him and could make eye contact, Lincoln would see his eye, and perhaps that would be enough for the President to understand the pain of those who were injured and of the families of those who died.

4.

Jonathan Kuhn

★★★★★★★

1863

During the early 1860s, the telegraph office was located on Solly Alley in Herronville, and even though it was a small building on a side street, it was the busiest business in town. The town folks would regularly stop at the office and visit with Jonathan Kuhn, a forty-five-year-old widower and the owner of the office, to get the latest news from the battles taking place in the South. He would post the daily events on a billboard outside of his little office. One morning in late February, he received a telegram indicating that from April through July, 1863, a new campaign was possibly going to be launched which meant that his little building's billboard would soon be surrounded by citizens reading his postings and inquiring of their loved ones from Pike and surrounding counties.

Presently, visitors to the office were only interested in the outcome of the battles. However, Jonathan knew that in a short period of time, citizens would be more concerned with casualties rather than the battles themselves. Kuhn's actual duties did not include taking the bad news to the families of those killed, but when no one came by to read his board, he took it upon himself to knock on the door of the family to break the news that a soldier or a relative had been killed in battle. It became an increasingly sad chore as the war progressed, and the farmers, teachers and, other young men of the county marched off to war in 1862 and never returned. Those that did were ghosts of their former selves.

It was a cold and snowy evening in March of 1863 when

Ella Samter answered the heavy knock on the door. She found Jonathan Kuhn from the telegraph office standing on the stoop with his hands in the pockets of his heavy woolen coat. "Is your father about?" he asked. "It is important I speak with him."

"Please come in, Mr. Kuhn., It is terrible cold out tonight. I will get my father,." she said, slamming the door to keep the gusting wind from entering. "Please have a seat near the fire."

"Excuse me, Miss Samter, I don't want to track snow onto your clean floors. I will stay here by the door," he said. "You are looking very pretty tonight and smell sweetly of lavender."

Suddenly feeling uneasy with the conversation, Ella excused herself and said to Jonathan, "I'll run upstairs to tell Father that you are here. Are you sure you wouldn't like to have a seat in the parlor?" He respectfully declined and watched Ella as she went up the stairs to tell her father that Mr. Kuhn was waiting downstairs to talk to him.

Her father immediately rushed down the steps of the steep staircase. He greeted Kuhn with a one-handed wave while holding onto the railing with his other. As he got close enough, he extended his hand to welcome Kuhn. Then Mr. Samter asked with concern, "Hello, Jonathan. What brings you out on a night like this? It surely can't be good news. What is the matter?" Jonathan fixed his eyes on Ella, who was standing in the parlor, listening to the conversation. His eyes told Mr. Samter all he needed to know. He turned and gave Ella a quick glance. "Honey, please go with your mother in the kitchen. I believe she could use some help cleaning up supper plates." Ella nodded and reluctantly walked into the kitchen, looking back as the two men began to speak in a whisper.

Jonathan shook his head from side to side, "Not good news, I'm afraid, Alfred. The Pike County unit is being sent to Virginia from its headquarters in Washington. It seems that there will be a major battle brewing soon, and our boys will be in the fighting—right in the midst of it. I am fearful that there will be many of our boys and men not coming home, and it has me sick to my stomach thinking about it. Today as I read the telegraphs, I came across the name of William Schultz, the son of Floyd Schultz, who was killed somewhere in Virginia, and I shook like the last leaf on an oak tree. I just know that more will be arriving back here on the train, arriving dead or maimed for life. I have already taken it upon myself to tell several people in surrounding counties of their sons' deaths. I fear that I won't be able to deal with all that is coming. These men won't be unknown to me as the others were. They will be our own boys, Alfred, boys from Pike County, boys that grew up at our feet at the lake and played in our streets, and men whose barns we helped to build, and some of the boys that your wife helped to deliver." As he began to sob, Mr. Samter put his arm on Jonathan's shoulder and guided him into the house, encouraging him to sit near the fire.

Mr. Samter sat across from Jonathan and, in a kind and understanding voice, spoke to him as if he were his son even though only several years in age separated them. "Jonathan, listen to me. You are a kind man, a very kind man. And while I know it is not your official duty to deliver the horrible news to families, I cannot think of anyone besides you who I would want to approach my door with the gut-wrenching news of the loss of my son if I had one lost in battle. You are loved by everyone in the town, and you would do the town a great disservice if you were not to perform that duty.

On the other hand, maybe there won't be a major battle. Telegraph messages have been wrong before. Maybe with the grace of the Lord, the one you received today about the new campaign will be wrong again. But if it isn't, you need to pray for the strength to perform that duty entrusted to you. I always say that the Lord gives us a reason for everything. By His divine providence, you are the one that has been chosen by Him to deliver the news to the families of those killed or wounded in this horrifying war that has been brought upon this great nation. But you, Jonathan, you can maybe make a difference to many."

Jonathan sat staring into the fire, uneasy. His eyes began to move back and forth from the fire to Mr. Samter. "Thank you for your kind words, Alfred," he answered, his sobbing having subsided as quickly as it had started, and the accompanying tears already dried up. "And I hope you are right that my new telegraph information does not come to fruition, that our boys do not become engaged in a bloody battle. But I am fearful that they will. And if they do, I will need help at my office.

"While I know that you are a busy man with your animals and farm duties, I will not ask that you help me, I understand. So, I have come to ask a huge favor of you." Mr. Samter did not respond, and after an uncomfortable pause, Jonathan continued to speak. "As I have indicated, I will be needing help in the office, and I have come to ask your blessing to have Ella come to assist me. She wouldn't have to deliver any death notices, and I assure you that the conduct of the men who come to the office is kept clean at all times. I have often admired Ella and, well, now that all the men are away at war, and the town doesn't have its gatherings as before, well, I thought that she might be happy having a daily routine of sorts." What had started as a request on Jonathan's part had turned into a plea for help that sounded a bit odd to Mr. Samter, and he stirred uncomfortably in his seat, staring with a hint of suspicion in his eyes. Jonathan was feeling warm not only from the fire, but from the questions that he was sure were about to come his way.

"So, Mr. Kuhn, you are here to ask if my daughter, my only child, would be allowed to come to your office to do a man's job, in an office visited by older men every waking minute of the day, a place where I have heard, and have to admit I have had conversations unfit for the ears of a mule take place there. You want **my** daughter to go in there on a daily basis to work? That is what you are asking me? And you sit in my house and tell me that you will protect her from this. I feel that you have come here with intentions other than for Ella to be your assistant, Jonathan. So, tell me if I am wrong. I feel that maybe you are enchanted with my young daughter and that maybe you feel that if I were to give my permission for her to work with you, you might have a chance at courting her. Am I on the right road with my thinking, Jonathan?"

No words or utterance came from Jonathan, and after many minutes he mumbled, "That is a possibility. I find your daughter to be most becoming. But, please do not think that I have come here under false pretenses, I **do** need help, and there **will** be many casualties coming our way." He paused as if replaying the scene in his mind then added. "But, I believe I have overstepped my limits and should leave..."

As he stood up to leave, Mr. Samter cut in. "Hold on. Please remain seated." Jonathan sat back down and stared at the wide planking of the floor. At the same time, the other man ran the possibilities over in his mind as to what was best for his daughter. "Okay, Mr. Kuhn, I will give you permission to have Ella as your apprentice; however, any thoughts of courting her will have to stay in your mind for the time being. And I will come by on a daily basis to check on her and the conduct of the men that come and go. You are to place signs on the door and walls concerning the use of foul language and the conduct of those who patronize your office. Is this understood, Jonathan?"

Without raising his head, he reviewed the terms in his mind that Ella's father had put forth. He rose from his chair and said, "I agree to all of your terms. Thank you, and have a good evening. Please give my regards to your wife and to Ella." Mr. Samter sat and watched with a wry smile as his visitor walked quickly to the door and let himself out into the cold evening. He wondered if maybe something good would come of this for his daughter.

5.
Alfred Samter
★★★★★★★
1838 - 1840

Alfred Samter was a respected cattle farmer in Pike County. He and his wife Eugenia and his daughter Ella lived in a home that was built by his father in 1821 shortly after they settled in Herronville. He loved his family, but he was particularly fond of his daughter. He took her everywhere with him. People would often comment on his devotion to her. Even so, he and his wife feared that her gangly appearance would not entice any young men in the area to propose marriage. It seemed that there would be no grandchildren in their future.

Other than his family, religion was the main focus of his life. In fact, he helped to build the little Methodist Church that graced the corner of Main Street and Chestnut Avenue. He prayed hard that his family would be healthy, and when the time came for them to meet their maker, the Lord would welcome them all with open arms, and they would be a family for eternity. He often told his wife and daughter that as they sat in their parlor after dinner and sipped tea while he read bible verses to them. One of his favorites was the following:

"But if anyone does not provide for his relatives, and especially for members of his household, he has denied the faith and is worse than an unbeliever."

After he recited it, he would look at Ella and Eugenia and say, "So always believe in me; I am your provider, and you are my faith." His family loved him without question. He was the perfect father and husband.

In 1838, a year before his daughter was born, he and his wife were married in the parlor of the minister's house. That was before he helped to build the church. The minister, a man by the name of Seth Kunstler, was a nice man, but some said that he was a bit 'simple.' Before the church was built in 1840, he would preach to his small congregation in the barn behind his house, and his wife Marella would provide refreshments to the congregation after services. Although the sermons were oftentimes long and tedious, Alfred would never complain, believing that the word of the Lord was to be taken without complaint. He would sit through most of them, trying to keep his head from bobbing, but he would often skip out to help Marella prepare the snacks and drinks in the kitchen of her home. The Reverend appreciated that he helped his wife.

As the years rolled on, Alfred and Marella became very close friends. The minister would often have Alfred, his wife, and little Ella over for dinner at their quaint home. They would pass the evening playing cards while having tea and coffee as the child nodded off on the giant feather tick bed.

Marella and Alfred became well known in the community for the wonderful snacks they prepared together on Sundays after church. Often, when the Samters visited the minister's home, Rev. Kunstler would pipe up and say, "Alfred, why don't you and Marella go to the kitchen and make us all some of those tasty snacks like you prepare on Sunday?" And with that, Alfred and Marella would be off to the kitchen to whip up a delicious treat made with honey and other sweets, leaving the minister and Eugenia to talk about the town and sometimes scripture.

One particular night after a hard-fought game of Faro, Alfred and Marella moved to the kitchen to prepare and supply refreshments. They had long known they were attracted to each other. So, it was not a surprise to either person, that when he bent over to get a fork he had dropped on the floor, he felt Marella's hand softly touch his neck. He froze for a moment, then stood up and looked toward the doorway that led to the parlor where his wife and the good minister were engaging in idle chatter. He moved Marella out of the view of the minister and embraced her, kissing her soft lips. It was not a kiss like he and his wife did as a habit at bedtime, but rather his lips pressed against hers firmly. He felt her fingers dig into his back, and the guilt he experienced at that moment was fake. In his heart, he had waited for this moment and knew that during all those Sundays, it was inevitable that this would eventually happen. Now, while he kissed her over and over, his mind moved like a locomotive planning where and when he and Marella could meet in private. Marella looked into his eyes, her own filled with passion and her lack of guilt.

"Alfred," Eugenia called. "Is the tea ready yet? I am quite thirsty."

Alfred and Marella jumped apart and quickly straightened their clothes. Alfred picked up the tray with the tea and sweets, and they casually walked back into the living room. Marella, looking a bit flushed, busied herself pouring the tea. Eugenia and the Reverend did not notice anything amiss.

The long-time infatuation and that first kiss forever distanced Mr. Samter from his wife. Her hopes of ever having another child were quickly waning. There was no more intimacy, and even conversations were reduced to family business. When not tending to his cattle, Alfred spent much of his time at the minister's barn and helped the minister and his wife plan the construction of the new church. It would be called The House of Purity of the Lord. After its completion, the minister hung a plaque hung on the back wall of the church. Alfred's name was the first name engraved on it, along with all those who helped to build it. The plaque read 'With Thanks to our Pure Angels.' Alfred was always very proud of his name being on the plaque. The second name was Marella Kunstler, the second Pure Angel.

6.

Kindness in Gettysburg

★★★★★★★

1863

Nicholas walked through the crowd and was headed back into the woods when he was stopped by a young woman cooking a breakfast of bacon, eggs, and potatoes. She asked him if he would like to have breakfast with her and her family. His stomach rumbled from his lack of nourishment, as the only food he had eaten in the last 3 days was dried meats given to him by people as they passed him on his journey north. It was out of character for him to accept gifts from strangers. Still, war and suffering can change a person's demeanor, so, after a pause, he told the woman that he would be very grateful if she were to give him as much as even one egg. The woman, who in most people's eyes would be described as beautiful, smiled at him and told him to have a seat near the fire with her family of three children. The children, all younger than the age of ten, stared at him in his shabby uniform as he sat down on a log. He stared back at them, smiling, hoping that the ugliness of his eye was not too frightening.

The woman wafted the smoke from the fire away from them all as she finished cooking the breakfast. As the woman turned to speak to Nicholas, the oldest child pointed at Nicholas and said, "Mister, what's wrong with your eye?"

With a look of disbelief at her child's manners, she said, "John! You tell the soldier that you are sorry. **Right now!**"

The boy put his head down and said, "I'm sorry, mister. I was just..."

He was cut off by his mother. "I'm sorry about that. Do you

like children, Private?" There was a pause until he realized she was speaking to him.

"Oh, I'm sorry. Me? Uh, I don't know, I mean, I guess. I liked them when I was one, I guess." His words were coming out in random fashion, and Nicholas was now sorry he had accepted the invitation for breakfast. The woman's face did not change. Her smile returned as she passed around plates and eating utensils to the children and to him. After they all had their plates, she portioned out the scrambled eggs and bacon then sat on the log next to Nicholas with her plate.

"So, soldier, you never told me your name."

Nicholas suddenly became aware that he had never had a woman so beautiful this close to him. His insides felt so twisted that he could hardly even think about eating. He could barely speak, and when he finally did, he said, "Micholas Hass."

"Hmm," she replied with a short laugh. "**Micholas**...I've never heard that name before?"

His face turned red as he corrected himself. "I am sorry, Ma'am. My name is Nicholas. Nicholas Haff. May I ask your name?" he asked hesitantly. He was still awestruck by the beauty of the woman.

She raised her eyebrows and said, "Well, if we are going to sit and eat together, I guess you need to know it, right? My name is Beatrice Valentine. And I am glad to meet you. And these are my children, Esther, Ruth, and John. Say hello to Mister Haff."

The children, whose mouths were full of eggs and potatoes, all answered in unison, "Hello, Mr. Haff."

Nicholas tipped his hat to the children and greeted them with a soft-spoken, "Hello."

Beatrice seemed to be mesmerized by Nicholas and continued to stare at his face. Between the children staring at him as they chewed on their bacon strips and her staring at him, Nicholas became more and more uneasy. He began to rock back and forth in his nervousness as he attempted to eat his breakfast.

"So, Nicholas. May I call you Nicholas?"

"Yes, yes, ma'am. Everyone does, except my father. He just calls me son."

Beatrice shook her head up and down and smiled with her eyes, the most beautiful eyes he had ever seen. "So, Nicholas, why are you here today? Did you come to hear the President?"

Nicholas had never really had an adult conversation with an adult woman other than with women who might stop by their farm to visit his mother or Mrs. Samter, who came to chat with his mother for hours. The women in the church were not friendly to young boys, as they considered them to be bold, or to the young men who came to Pony Lake, seeing them often as being 'fresh.'

"Well, ma'am, to tell you..."

She gently touched his arm, "Beatrice. Please call me Beatrice."

"Yes, Ma'am. I mean, Beatrice. To tell you the truth, I didn't know that the President was even going to be here today. I am working my way home to Herronville, Pennsylvania, from Washington. That is where my unit got discharged. When I got here, I saw the crowds and couldn't imagine why so many people would want to come to this place. I tell you the truth when I say that I never wanted to see it again..." He looked down at the ground and then up at her, "I'm sorry, I'm babblin' like a brook. So, anyway, when I heard that Lincoln was going to be here today, I figured I would stay. I want him to see my eye. I want him to see my eye, and maybe then he'll know how much soldiers have suffered."

No longer able to contain her curiosity, Beatrice suddenly reached up near his eye and touched his face. "What happened to your eye? Does it hurt?"

She removed her apron and gently wiped the pus that oozed from his eye. "Someone told me that vinegar can help infections. I have vinegar with me. Let me dab some vinegar on the outside of your eye. I don't think it can hurt anything. It may sting a bit, but it might relieve the pain some. May I?"

Nicholas nodded his head, "It can't hurt nothin' at this point. I already see two of everything." He managed to laugh.

Beatrice reached into a woven basket and took out a small jar of vinegar. She dripped some onto the corner of her apron, then gently dabbed his eye. The sting of the vinegar caused him to jump a bit.

"Oh, I'm sorry!" she said apologetically. "But I think this will help you. I am going to put a little more on, okay?" He nodded his permission. This time she poured a bit more on her apron and wiped most of the pus away from his eye; however, this time, he did not react. So, she repeated the process several more times.

"Now," she said as she put the vinegar back into her basket, "I think we need to make a patch for your eye until it heals. That way, you will only see one of me!" She chuckled.

Nicholas liked her voice and her laughter. He had not heard a woman's voice in what seemed like months, and hers was very soothing. "I'll be right back," she said, touching his arm as she stood up and headed toward her wagon.

In the meantime, the children, after finishing their breakfast, began running about playing. Suddenly the crowd became silent, and someone yelled out, "He's coming! The train is coming! Our President is on the way!"

Nicholas listened intently, but he still could not hear the whistle of the locomotive. People began to cheer and shout, "Hip-Hip-Hooray! Hip-Hip-Hooray!"

Nicholas turned back to watch Beatrice as she rummaged through the chest that was attached to her wagon. He was still overtaken by her beauty and the softness of her touch. He felt guilty, thinking that it was even softer than Ella's, from what he could remember.

She finally found what she was looking for, removed something black from the chest, and walked back to Nicholas.

"What have you got there?" he asked curiously.

"It is just a piece of black fabric that I use to mend clothing. I am going to make a patch for your eye. I think you will be more comfortable and be able to see better." She took a pair of scissors from the woven basket and began to cut and snip, all the time staring at his head as if measuring it. Several times she placed the material on his eye and around his head. In a short period of time, she made a perfect eye patch and was able to place it over his eye and tie it in the back of his head. "How is that?" she asked, sounding satisfied with her work. "Does it feel okay? I can loosen or tighten it if you want.

Nicholas swiveled his head side to side. His double vision had disappeared, and he no longer felt the sharp pain in and around his eye. "Why," he stammered," it's like I've given birth to a new eye!" He stood up, and excitedly surveyed his surroundings. Then after a few moments, he looked down at Beatrice and, in a low voice, asked, "But what about the President seeing my eye? He won't be able to see it, and he won't know how us soldiers suffered. I need him to see my eye."

Beatrice looked up at him. "Nicholas, sit back down. I want to talk to you," she said as she patted the log next to her. Her voice reminded him of his mother's, causing his stomach to roll. Suddenly he could see his mother as she was surely waiting for him to come home. He walked to Beatrice and sat beside her.

Beatrice looked at him and then softly spoke. "Nicholas, the President is coming here today to honor the dead. He is very aware of the suffering of our soldiers fighting for our cause. I believe he is sympathetic to the soldiers fighting and suffering on both sides. Let us just stay and listen to the great man and to hear what he says to us and the others."

Nicholas would find it difficult to refuse this woman anything. He was smitten by her. She continued. "I have something I want to read to you, something that is very dear to my heart." She reached into her coat pocket and pulled out a folded paper and carefully unfolded it. "I want you to listen very closely."

Dear Mrs. Valentine:
It is with deep regret that I have learned of the death of your kind and brave husband and, especially, how it must be affecting your young heart. In this sad world of ours,

sorrow comes to all and comes with the bitterest agony. The older folks have learned to expect death. I am here to afford you some comfort for your present distress. While perfect relief is not possible, except with time, please do not feel that you will never feel better, as you are sure to be happy again. That happiness will certainly return to you is true, and if you believe that it will, it shall make you some less unhappy now. I have had experience enough to know what I say, and you need only to believe it and in yourself to feel better at this time. The memory of your husband and father to your children will always remain in your heart, however, it will be a sad, sweet feeling unlike the sadness you feel this day.

Please present my kind regards to your afflicted children and your entire family.

A. Lincoln

She stared at the letter for a short time before folding it back up, and then she addressed Nicholas.

"So, Nicholas, this is the letter I received from the President after my husband Ralph was killed on one of these battlefields that surround us. If you fought here, you know the misery that families have and will suffer. Please sit with me while the President speaks. Your eye will mend, and even if you never have sight in it again, you will have seen more with that eye than most people will ever see in a lifetime. The President knows of everyone's suffering. She reached out and touched his hand and with the other wiped the tears rolling down his cheek from beneath the patch she had made.

His voice was quivering as he spoke, "I will sit with you, Beatrice. I will stay until the President is finished speaking."

7.

The Haff Family

★★★★★★★

1823 - 1842

Conrad Haff and his wife Mary arrived in America in 1821 on the Amaranth. After landing in New York City, they made their way to Pennsylvania, finally settling in the newly formed area named Pike County. Their decision to stay there was mostly based on the landscape, which reminded them of their homeland. Although the population was sparse, most of the people residing in the village of Herronville spoke German, which made it a very comfortable place for them to live and to raise a family.

It was in a short period of time that Conrad and Mary were able to purchase a small piece of land close to Pony Lake and began to farm. They mostly raised chickens and turkeys, and in the spring tended to fruit trees that were on the property that they had bought. They planted vegetables and, in the fall and were able to make a profit by selling their small crops which, helped them sustain themselves through the autumn and winter. Also, during the winter, they subsidized their income with the sale of poultry and eggs. Mr. Haff also hunted and provided his family with venison, rabbit, and other meats.

In 1823, Mr. and Mrs. Haff gave birth to their first, and what would be their only child whom they would name Jake after Conrad's uncle in Germany. Jake was born with severe medical problems, and the parents were told by the midwife upon his birth that they should let the child pass on to his Maker. "He is not a healthy boy, and to let him live, will be a burden on you for your entire life."

As Mary heard the words from the midwife's lips, she exploded into tears and ordered the midwife to leave her home at once. She screamed through her sobs that she would care for the child and that the child would live to raise his own family one day. Her husband took the child from her as she passed out on her bed. When Conrad looked at the newborn, his stomach turned as he realized that the midwife was correct. Not only was the child's head a bit large and odd-looking, but also the two fingers were webbed. Also, to Conrad's eyes, the child's testicles were deformed as well. At least that is what Conrad perceived to be true. As he stared at the child, the thought of following the midwife's recommendation entered his head. But then he looked at his wife, and as he cradled the infant and wiped the woman's brow with a cool damp cloth, the thought vanished from his mind. He would keep the child as long as possible, and if the Lord wanted to take him, then that would be His wish.

The Haff family prospered on their land, and Jake, while never a completely healthy boy, was normal in most ways. He helped on the farm and learned his lessons at the feet of his mother. He read books, did arithmetic to the best of his ability, and had perfect penmanship since his webbed fingers were not on his dominant hand. Conrad and Mary coddled the child, and some would say they were overprotective of him. But Jake's parents were content knowing that they had saved the boy's life and that the Lord had blessed them with their son.

In the year 1842, Jake Haff met and began to court Margaret Olmstead. Margaret was a very short woman and several years older than Jake. By most standards, she was what a person would call 'crow's meat,' meaning that no one would really be interested in her as a spouse. However, Jake Haff was not in any position to find a woman of beauty or of any stature. When the opportunity arose to court her, Jake jumped at it.

It all began at Pony Lake, on the morning of a scorching hot day in August of 1842. Jake, as usual, went to the lake very early in the morning to bathe and to prepare for a day of working in his father's vegetable field. He undressed on the shore and slowly went naked into the cold morning water before taking the quick plunge into the deep clear water. When he surfaced and wiped the water from his face and eyes, through the morning mist, he could see a woman on the shore undressing. She, too, was preparing to enter the cold morning water naked. He immediately recognized Margaret Olmstead. Cautioning her, he yelled, "Margaret, I am here!" Acknowledging Jake with a grin, she continued to undress and was soon in the water swimming toward him.

"Good morning, Jake," she said nonchalantly. "Beautiful morning, but going to be hot!"

Jake, embarrassed and refusing to look in her eyes, replied, "It sure is!"

"You come here every day, don't you?" Margaret asked.

"Sometimes, well, yeah, but how do you know that?" he asked, staring across the pond, watching the mist from the water rise and small bass breaking the water, trying to catch their breakfast of flies.

"I see you. I come and watch you," she replied, again nonchalantly splashing water onto her face.

Jake swam underwater for several feet toward the shore to where he could stand on the rocky bottom of the lake but still have his private parts covered. "Why would you do that?" he asked, turning to face her, his face red with embarrassment. He knew he did not look like the other boys and was ashamed to have anyone else see him naked.

"Because I like to watch you swim. And I like to see you naked." She smiled.

Jake was shocked. She did not seem to be repulsed by how he looked underneath his clothes.

Jake was in a predicament. He did not know how to answer, and he could not swim to the shore to reach his clothes without her seeing him. Even though he was now aware that she had been spying on his morning ritual, he did not have the nerve to have her see him naked while he was watching. And worse yet, she was nearing him.

"Jake Haff," she said as she neared him. "have you never noticed how I look at you in church on Sunday?"

"Nope. No, I don't," he said as he tried to back away from the advancing woman.

"Well, I do look at you. Do you like me?"

Jake did not know what to say, "Well, yeah, I know you're a good Christian woman. And I also know that Jesus wouldn't like this situation that we are in right now," he said in an attempt to slow her advances.

"Have you ever kissed a girl," she cooed as her short legs kicked treading the water in place, "besides kissing your mother goodnight? That doesn't count." She laughed heartily.

"No, but I could have plenty of times," he lied. And before he could tell her when and where the kisses might have been possible, she lunged at him, her lips landing firmly on his. That was their first kiss. The magic of Pony Lake had happened again!

Three months later, Jake Haff and Margaret Olmstead were married. At first, they moved in with Jake's parents, who, much to his chagrin, continued to treat him as a child. Soon after, Margaret convinced Jake to move into a small house nearer to the town and the church. The young couple took up residence in the little house and began to plan a family. At the same time, Jake continued to work on the family farm and to raise chickens that his father gave them, from time to time.

Jake and Margaret attended services every Sunday at the church of preacher Kunstler. They prayed that the Lord would bless them with a child that they so desperately wanted. Nonetheless, their prayers were not answered.

The minister and his wife Marella comforted them by saying, "Seth and I also have not yet been blessed with a child, but if the good Lord wants to bestow the blessing of a child on us, that is

His doing and not anything that we can control. But I know that if we pray hard enough, the good Lord will provide us with what He feels is right for us to have."

Jake and Margaret believed the words of Marella, and they believed in the Lord. They would wait for the Lord to answer their prayers. Secretly, Jake prayed that Margaret would not have a child. He feared that the child might be born with the same deformities that had burdened him his entire life and that those same ailments that encompassed his private parts were the reason the Lord had not blessed them with a child.

Despite Jake's and Margaret's disappointment, Marella's prayers were answered, and in the fall of 1844, she and the minister were blessed by the Lord with a son, a son that they named Nicholas.

Jake and Margaret were excited for their best friends, the young minister and his wife. The good minister baptized the boy, and while Jake and Margaret believed that they both would be the Godparents, Marella announced that Alfred Samter and Margaret Olmstead Haff would have the honor of the child's spiritual upbringing in case tragedy struck the minister's family. And as such stories go, one month after the child was born, a fire on Christmas Eve took the lives of the minister and his wife, Marella. Jake happened to be nearby and saw the flaming house. He rushed into the burning home and was able to rescue baby Nicholas from perishing in the blaze that took the lives of his parents.

Because of the heroics of Jake, and the worst-kept secret in town that the Haff couple was barren, the child was given to Jake and Margaret. Shortly after the disastrous fire, the couple 'adopted' Nicholas Kunstler as their own and changed his name to Nicholas Haff. Margaret would often say, "The Lord works in mysterious ways."

8.
At the Telegraph Office
★★★★★★★
June 1863

I n the middle of April of 1863, Ella began to work as Jonathan Kuhn's clerk in the telegraph office. At first, Ella was uncomfortable working there, greeting all of the customers who came in. Most of them were men, and some were very nice, while others would ignore her and only speak their business with Jonathan. However, in time, she became accepted by most of the citizens of the town, and her duties became more comfortable and a bit mundane.

While the battle of Chancellorsville raged during the beginning of May, very few of the men and boys from Pike County and surrounding areas were killed. Personal notifications of any deaths to surviving families were not necessary as all were posted on what Jonathan called his 'Board of Mourning' in front of his shop. He and Ella sadly watched as the mothers, fathers, or widows walked away after reading of their loved ones' deaths. Their shoulders drooped and quivered as they returned to their horse or wagon to make the long trip home to tell the family that their loved one would not be coming home.

Jonathan would always put his hand on Ella's shoulder and say, "It is a shame what is happening to our country. I only pray to the Lord that none of our lads suffer as they lie dying on a battlefield." Then he would caress her shoulder, push himself tightly into her side, and while stroking her hair would finish by saying, "We need to thank the Lord that neither of us has a family member fighting in this horrific war." He would then remove his hand from her hair, let out a sigh and, return to his desk.

At first, Ella felt very uncomfortable with his intimate and unwanted advances, so she discussed it with her father. He told her that he thought it to be a gesture on Mr. Kuhn's part to calm her and to make her feel safe. He knew in his heart that Jonathan was more than calming her; he was indeed setting up a situation to court Ella. He also was sure in his heart that this might be Ella's only chance for love in her life. And with that, he assured her that Jonathan meant no harm to her but only good things. He prayed to the Lord that what he was allowing to happen was the good Lord's plan. But at night, before falling asleep in her bed, Ella wrote letters to Nicholas and put them in her little wooden box. She still hoped that one day, Nicholas would come home, and they would once again sit together on the big rock at Pony Lake and secretly hold hands.

As the summer drew near and battle after battle was fought in the South, everyone in the North feared that the rumors of the rebels moving northward were true. But Jonathan was aware from the telegraphs that he hid in his drawer that northward movement of the rebels was no rumor. Eventually, both sides would have to collide somewhere on northern soil.

He also feared that if the Union Army could not hold the rebel soldiers off, the tide of the war would change dramatically. The lackadaisical attitude of the citizens of the North would have to change drastically, as up until now, all of the bloodshed had been in the South. However, Jonathan had one other fear, and that fear came by way of his sporadic and revealing conversations with Ella. The small talk in which they did indulge was spattered with Ella's mentioning of Nicholas Haff. As much as he would try to sway the conversation away from Nicholas, she would always bring him back into it.: She hoped that he was okay, that they would one day sit on the big rock again and throw crumbs of bread to the small fish that lived under the rock. She couldn't help laughing when she told him, when just a child, she would wait for him to ride in front of her father's house on the big brown horse. She would run out and give him a glass of fresh-made lemonade.

Jonathan would swallow hard and nod his head affirmatively and assure her that the Haff boy would be fine. He would bring the talk back to how he, too, would love to have a boy as nice as Nicholas, how he remembered him as a child. And then he would ask Ella if she wanted to have a family, how many children would she like to have, and if she would like boys or girls. And when she replied to his questions, she always mentioned the name of Nicholas Haff. In time, Jonathan became extremely jealous of even the mention of Nicholas. His face would turn red, and he would take his leave and walk into the rear of the shop where the telegraph machine was located. His desire for Ella was becoming an obsession, but the danger signals were lost on Ella. She left the office each evening, bidding him a good night and wishing him a sound, restful sleep.

———————

As the month of June moved on, Jonathan's telegraph machine heated up with the news that there was a large battle brewing. It was also clear that it would be in either the southern part of Pennsylvania or the north of Maryland. Both sides were probing the mountains and fields of both areas, and a clash was inevitable. Also heating up were Jonathan's desires for Ella. Her presence every day was almost more than he could bear, and he was losing his self-control. His inappropriate touching and caressing were becoming more and more frequent.

Naively, Ella continued to do her work, posting telegraph messages on the board for the town folks to read. The occasional death notices were the only sobering moments for Jonathan as he would watch family members walk away mourning their relatives. A few times, he would have to go to the board and offer solace to the person and bring him or her into the office, offering a chair and a cool drink. Even during those moments, he would only glance at the person and turn toward Ella with lust in his eyes, all the while assuring the person that "Everything would be all right."

On the evening of June 30th, 1863, as Ella was cleaning her desk and preparing to leave for the night, the telegraph machine clattered out a message out that filled Jonathan with dread. His hands shook as he read it. He called Ella to the back room and told her to sit down. When she did, he read the telegram:

A large battle is about to take place in the small town of Gettysburg STOP
There are tens of thousands of troops on both sides poised to begin fighting STOP
There will be massive casualties STOP
The battle may last for days STOP
President Lincoln is assuring victory STOP
God Bless America END.

Jonathan ripped the telegraph from the machine as Ella sat stone-faced in her chair.

"I am sure that this battle will include our boys who avoided most casualties in Chancellorsville. However, I am afraid we will lose many during this engagement. I fear for your childhood friend Nicholas," he said.

The guilt he felt for wishing Nicholas's death in battle was overshadowed by his passion for Ella, and he stepped toward her, and as he stroked her hair said, "If anything does happen to Nicholas, I will be here for you." He knelt in front of her, holding and kissing her hand while at the same time, he reached down with his other hand, raised her dress and slid his hand up to her thigh. Ella's entire body froze, but her fear kept her from screaming out. As fast as he had placed his hand on her thigh, he removed it, stood up, lowered his head and mumbled, "I am so sorry. Please forgive me. I believe that the warning of the battle has done something to me. Please accept my apology. You are not obliged to come to work any longer. I just ask that you keep this between us. Two adults."

Ella rose from the chair, straightened her dress, and addressed him. "There is a terrible battle about to begin. You will need me here to assist you. You will have many homes to visit. I only pray that Nicholas Haff's is not one of them. And if he is, I shall deliver that message to his family myself. As to what happened here tonight, that will remain in this building between us. I will see you in the morning. Good Evening, Mr. Kuhn."

As she walked out of the small office, Jonathan Kuhn, picked up the telegraph, smiled and convinced himself that what had happened moments before was justified by the news of the telegraph he had received., The fire in his heart for Ella was still burning.

9.

Lincoln at Gettysburg

★★★★★★★

1863

Nicholas continued to chat with Beatrice before Lincoln arrived. Her mesmerizing beauty had all but removed Ella from his thoughts. She asked him questions about his family, his home, and his parents. She had the kindest eyes he had ever seen. As the morning drew to a close, the crowd began to move en masse toward the stage. Secretary of State Edward Everett was going to say a few words before President Lincoln would speak to the large crowd that had gathered.

Beatrice began picking up the breakfast plates and putting things away into the chest that sat in her wagon. Nicholas took a pail and headed for the small pond to bring back some water to wash the dishes. The children all tagged along with him, racing to see who could get to the pond first. Nicholas let them all beat him, much to their joy. On the way back to his family's camp spot, the young boy, John, asked Nicholas, "Did you know my father? He was a soldier too, but he got killed."

Nicholas was at a loss for words, but he felt compelled to answer the question. And though he had a lump the size of an apple in his throat, he put his arm around the boy's shoulder and said, "Nope, I didn't know your dad, but I'll bet you a dollar he was the best darn soldier that ever was. And the bravest!"

John leaned into Nicholas's leg as they moved toward Beatrice. "I'll bet you're right!" the little boy replied with a big smile. "I'll bet he killed a lot of rebels before they got him! I'll bet you a dollar too!" The four of them smiled, then Nicholas began to sing,

"*When Johnny comes marching home again...*" Soon they were all singing with smiles on their faces.

"Thank you, Nicholas," Beatrice said as he set his bucket down. "Now, you kids go and pick everything up and put it all away. The speech is about to start, and I don't want to miss one word of it," she said in a tone that meant business. "Nicholas, why don't you take a blanket from the wagon and go lay it on the ground as near to the President as you can, and we will find you. There is a red handkerchief in the back of the wagon. Tie it to a stick, hold it up, and we will be able to spot you. Go, go quickly," she urged him. "Go!" Nicholas did as she told him, going to the wagon and retrieving the handkerchief. He next broke a skinny branch from a small maple tree nearby and ran to find a spot for them to sit. Then he waited for them.

Beatrice, with the three children in tow, made it to a spot where they could see and hear clearly. Nicholas followed, and soon they were all seated on the blanket that he had placed on the ground under a small oak.

Edward Everett's oration began:

"Standing beneath this serene sky, overlooking these broad fields now reposing from the labors of the waning years, the mighty Alleghenies dimly towering before us, the graves of our brethren beneath our feet, it is with hesitation that I raise my poor voice to break the eloquent silence of God and nature. But the duty to which you have called me must be performed. Grant me, I pray you, your indulgence, and your sympathy.
"It was appointed by law in Athens, that the obsequies of the citizens who fell in battle should be performed at the public expense, and in the most honorable manner..."

Nicholas was confused. He wondered where Lincoln was and why he was not speaking. Finally, he whispered to Beatrice. "Where is Lincoln?" he asked. "Who is this guy?"

Beatrice smiled at him. "It's Edward Everett. He is one of the finest speakers in America. He was the Secretary of State for President Fillmore."

Nicholas, while impressed, was a bit embarrassed. And even though he would only have been six years old, he replied confidently, "Oh, I remember him." Beatrice nodded her head, not causing him any more humiliation. He sat up and, with his best efforts, attempted to listen to Everett's words.

"...Their bones were carefully gathered up from the funeral pyre where their bodies were consumed and brought home to the city. There, for three days before the internment, they lay in state, beneath tents of honor, to receive the votive offerings of friends and relatives..."

"Beatrice?" He whispered. "What does 'obsequies' mean?"
"Funeral," she said without hesitation.
"Oh. What is a 'pyre'?" Nicholas asked.
"A fire. Sometimes they burn corpses. That's a pyre."

Nicholas was confused by the words of the speaker. Nicholas thought that Beatrice must really be smart if she knew all those words. He asked no more questions, not understanding a lot of it, but sat listlessly during the long speech. He saw that the President was restlessly moving on and off the stage, also seemingly getting bored with Everett's fancy words. Finally, as the large crowd grew more restless, the speaker ended with words that Nicholas understood:

"...we bid farewell to the dust of these martyr-heroes, that wheresoever throughout the civilized world the accounts of this great warfare are read, in and down to the period of latest recorded time, in the glorious annals of our common country there will be no brighter page than that which relates the Battles of Gettysburg."

Everett received polite applause that perhaps, would have been greater, had he kept his speech to less than an hour, rather than the way too long, two hours.

The three children had fallen asleep a half-hour into the speech, and if truth be told, Nicholas would have joined them were it not for his infatuation with Beatrice. The speaker's words were lost on him and most of the crowd.

"That was quite a mouthful Mr. Everett presented, wasn't it, Nicholas?" she asked with a grin, knowing that he was bored to tears.

"It sure was," he replied. "It was a mouthful." And as he said it, he stood up, and Beatrice offered him her hand to help her stand.

"Well," she said, brushing her dress, "you did well not to nap with the children. I think you will do better in a few moments when our President speaks." And as the words came from her mouth, the tall, gangly man presented himself to the huge audience with much excitement. After taking a humble bow, he began to speak. Both Beatrice and Nicholas remained standing.

"Four score and seven years ago, our fathers brought forth on this continent, a new nation, conceived in Liberty, and dedicated to the proposition that all men are created equal.
"Now we are engaged in a great civil war, testing whether that nation, or any nation so conceived and so dedicated, can long endure. We are met on a great battlefield of that war. We have come to dedicate a portion of that field as a final resting place for those who here gave their lives that that nation might live. It is altogether fitting and proper that we should do this..."

At the words of "final resting place," Nicholas turned to Beatrice. "He's right. Lots of my friends are buried here. Why, a bunch of my friends were killed right past where he is speaking, right down by that tree that is all shot up! Josiah Pell died right by that tree—at least I think it was there." Then he turned away from Beatrice, and in a barely audible voice, he said, "He was my friend. I used to swim with him at Pony Lake."

Beatrice looked at the back of his head and took him softly by his arm. "It's okay, Nicholas. It's all going to be okay." Nicholas turned back to listen to the President, who, from where Nicholas and Beatrice stood, had a look of great sorrow on his face, one like that of a man with a great burden. Nicholas found comfort in the President's apparent grief. He felt a sameness with him. He had not thought too much about the tremendous battle until now. When he looked at the fields around him, he could see those three days of July. He saw his friends and comrades blown to pieces, and he saw himself lying on the ground and feigning death after killing the young southern soldier.

"...the world will little note, nor long remember what we say here, but it can never forget what they did here..."

"Beatrice, do you think people will ever forget what happened here? I know I won't. You won't." Beatrice again placed her soft hand on his arm as they listened to the conclusion of Lincoln's address.

"...that we here highly resolve that these dead shall not have died in vain—that this nation, under God, shall have a new birth of freedom—and that government of the people, by the people, for the people, shall not perish from the earth."

Beatrice took Nicholas by the hand and spoke softly. "I think you are right. I believe all those men that died here will never be forgotten, and I believe that the President's words will not fall on deaf ears. I believe that they will be remembered for a very long time. So, Nicholas, do you believe now that President Lincoln understands your grief? My grief? Everyone's grief who has lost someone here? You must always believe that what you have done here, no matter what the result of this tragic war, was not in vain. You and I must continue on our separate ways and help to nurture our families. Mine that is here," she said, nodding and looking down toward her three sleeping children, "and to your family and loved ones waiting at home for you. I will always remember you as a symbol of America and what this country is made of, which is strength, youth and the belief that our nation will become one again because boys—men– like you and my husband died and were willing to do so for the cause."

Nicholas's heart was broken. He felt as if his lungs could not get air. He managed to gaze into her eyes and to speak, "I will never see you again?"

She smiled and replied in an attempt to lighten the situation, "Well, Nicholas Haff, if you ever get to Emmitsburg, I live next to the only church in the town. You will know it when you are there. Look for the house that bears two flags, one of the North and one of the South. My husband died for the North, while his brother is still fighting for the South—brother against brother." She smiled as she leaned forward, kissed him on his cheek, woke her sleeping children, and whispered good-bye to him. He stood with a heavy heart and watched them all head toward their wagon while he gently rubbed his bad eye under the patch she had so aptly applied.

10.

The Final Letters

★★★★★★★

1863

Ella went to bed without her supper the night of the incident with Jonathan at the telegraph office. She did not tell her mother or her father what had happened. She was sure that her father would have killed him and even more convinced that her mother would have helped him do it. Other than holding hands with Nicholas at the lake, no man had ever touched her in such a way. She was upset and mystified by what had happened. Why would a man so much older than herself be so brazen as to make such an advance? She did not have any false views of her appearance. A look in her mirror confirmed that she was not as pretty as a lot of the other girls, and Nicholas was the only young man who had ever seemed to find her pleasing. But now that he was away in the war, with no certainty that he would even return, she became even more confused. What if he never returned? Would she ever be able to have a child, and who with?

She couldn't bear to imagine that he might not make it back alive, so she prayed with all her might that he would be safe and return to her. Then they could finally court and have a child together. She dreamt of the day that she would sit with him at the lake again, and together read the letters she had written him but had been too shy to mail.

She went to her wooden box and removed the most recent letter she had written and read it to herself. It was short, but she believed it to be everything she wanted to say, at least until Jonathan had aggressively pursued her that evening.

Dear Nicholas,
It seems like forever since I have seen you. It seems even
longer since we sat and talked, and you held my hand on
the rock at Pony Lake. I think of you every day and pray
that you are safe. I have things I want to tell you, and
I will write them here. However, you will not see them
until the day comes that you are home safely, and we are
together as a couple. I pray every night on my knees that
this thought is true and not a figment of my imagination.
Nicholas, I have loved you since we were children, and I
cannot stand the thought of not being with you, or even
worse that you are injured or killed in this war, in which
I know that you do not believe but have gone to do your
duty for our country.
I will love you forever. Please come home to me and make
me your wife.
Ella

She had never written the words 'I love you' to him before, and now as she reread the letter, it sounded foolish to her. She took the letter and placed it back into the little brown box with hopes that one day it would not sound so strange. She lay on her bed and began to write a new letter to Nicholas. She needed to tell someone about what had happened that evening with Jonathan. She knew she had not encouraged him, but that didn't stop the guilt from filling up her heart. Someone had to know, even if it was a letter that would never be seen by anyone but herself.

Dear Nicholas....
 She put her pen to the paper, believing that her thoughts were clear enough to explain what had happened to her at the telegraph office. However, after her salutation, she set the pen down, placed her elbows on her desk, and, while cradling her face in her hands, she wept. After a few moments, she wiped the tears from her face, dried her hands on her nightgown, and continued.

*I pray that you are well and being as safe as possible and
will be home soon. I miss our talks at the lake. Today was
a most unsettling day for me, and I have to tell someone.
I am currently working at Mr. Kuhn's telegraph office, as
he has been very busy with all of the death notifications
from the battles all over the country. My father thought it
a good idea for me to assist him with his duties. While I
was not overjoyed with the idea, at my father's insistence,
I took the task and have been there several months. Which
brings me to what happened today with Mr. Kuhn. As a
Christian woman, I should not describe what happened in
his office.*

Ella again placed the pen on her desk and considered whether
she should tear the letter to pieces or to confess to Nicholas the
incident with Mr. Kuhn. She believed that her life had been
changed forever. Having made her decision, she picked up the pen
with a trembling hand and moved forward with her letter.

*I will just tell you that Jonathan Kuhn is not a gentleman.
If I told my father what happened today, he would
probably shoot him dead, and the good Lord would not
find him guilty of any sin. In short, he tried to touch me
under my garments. I was so shocked that I didn't even
cry out. After a few awkward moments, he apologized,
and he and I came to an agreement that it would never
be discussed again between us. I am sorry that if you ever
read this that you will think less of me, but please believe
me, I did not give him any reason to think that he could
take advantage of me. I know I should tell someone, but I
know that I shall never tell a soul.*

As she began to sign the letter, she added words of hope even
though she believed those words would never be read by Nicholas.
I feel that I have destroyed your trust in me and that I am

not deserving of any love you could have given me. I will
always love you.
Ella

She took the letter, placed it under all of the others, tied them with a red ribbon, and put them back into the wooden box. As she lay in her bed, she thought of the events of the day. She made two decisions that night: She would quit working for Jonathan, and she would write no more letters to Nicholas. Her guilt would keep her from writing her beautiful, hopeful words to him. She would never feel the same. She felt that her innocence had been violated.

The next day she would tell Jonathan she could no longer work for him.

11.
The Safety of a Friend
★★★★★★★
1843

In the winter of 1843, February to be exact, Minister Kunstler was called away to New York City by the leaders of the church. They wanted to discuss new methods of preaching and how to recruit more members to his small congregation. It was his first opportunity to meet the leaders and to make his voice known so they might assist him with monies to furnish his relatively new building. While he was hesitant to leave his wife alone, he still needed to board the train in the morning and to ride into the city for the two-day meeting. He was sure he would return with the promise of money and new ideas that would enthrall his small congregation at the House of Purity. The night before his trip, he paid a visit to Alfred Samter, where they sat next to the cozy fire and chatted.

"Alfred, I will only be gone for a few days, two, weather permitting, and with any luck, I will return with some gifts for our church and maybe some money to do some nice things inside of the church itself."

Alfred rubbed his hands in front of the fire. "There is no reason to rush back. I will be sure that Marella is safe and well taken care of. I will check on her every day."

"I am sure you will. Alfred, can I confide in you? I have something on my chest that is so personal that I feel I cannot tell anyone. Yet, I feel that I have to tell someone because the guilt of it is killing me, and truthfully, possibly destroying my relationship with my wife."

Alfred swallowed hard, "Certainly, Seth, but I really don't know if I am the person that you should confide in. Maybe it would be better if you were to discuss this with a minister during your trip."

The minister waved him off, "No, no, Alfred. I have come to consider you as a brother. You and your wife have been so good to me and Marella, such good friends. And you have taken to my wife as if she were your own sister. No, it is with you that I need to share my problem." He smiled, attempting to make light of the confession he was about to make. "I assume that Eugenia is not in earshot?" he asked, looking around.

"No, she is in the bedroom, tucking Ella into bed. Our conversation will be private," Alfred assured him. Both men gazed directly into the other's eyes, seemingly knowing what was going to be said and heard.

"Alfred, I am weighed down with guilt. I want you to know that I have never lied to my wife. Never. But I have kept a terrible secret from her, one that is giving her much false hope. A kind of hope that runs so deep in one's soul that it is unfair, almost criminal, to allow someone to have such hope in one's life. I might actually destroy her mind while she waits in anticipation and trusts in the Lord to provide that answer to what..." Alfred stopped Seth in mid-sentence.

"Seth, you are on the verge of babbling, and I am unsure as to what you are trying to tell me. What hope? What anticipation? Please, I am willing to share your burden, but I need to know what it is that you are trying to tell me." He smiled and gave a short chuckle.

Seth forced a sad smile, folded his hands, and looked at the floor. "Alfred, I have been telling Marella, for many years, that she will bear a child. I tell her the Lord works in mysterious ways, and to know, when the time is right, it will happen. But the truth is, it will never happen for us. In my shame, I kept assuring her that it will. I told her to pray. What she doesn't know is that when I was a child, I was severely injured in an accident–no need to give you the details. There are no visible scars–but the injury was quite serious.

50

I overheard the doctor tell my parents as I lay in my sickbed, 'Seth will never be able to father a child.' I was only ten. Even as a child, I understood quite well the ramifications of what he said. And now that I am traveling, I wanted to lighten my conscience in case of an accident of any sort. I just wanted to tell someone."

Alfred reached out to Seth and held his hand, "Seth, do not give up hope. The Lord **does** work in mysterious ways, and if the Lord doesn't bless you with a child, there is no reason to tell Marella the reason. You will only destroy her faith in the Lord and in you for keeping such a deep secret from her. Your life will go on, and happiness will follow you and her with the good deeds you do for your congregation. I hope you will continue to try and have a child, as we both know, the Lord is kind and generous, and if it is His will, then you will have a child. And you and I will know that it was a miracle child!"

Seth looked up and nodded, "Yes, a miracle child."

Alfred reassured him again that he and Eugenie would be more than happy to check on Marella.

"Do you need any help with your baggage tomorrow morning?" Alfred asked.

"Thank you, but no, you don't need to rise at such an early hour. I don't have that much to carry," Seth replied. "But understand how appreciative I am that you listened to my concerns. My heart is lighter than it has been in a long time." They shook hands before he headed back home to pack his trunk and to confirm the final details of his trip with his wife.

In the morning, Minister Kunstler arose early and quietly moved to his wife's bedside and kissed her gently on her forehead. He stood over her for a moment and marveled at her beauty. How lucky he was that the Lord had blessed him with such a beautiful and pure woman. Maybe Alfred was right. The Lord would bless them one day with a child—a miracle child. With those uplifting thoughts, he walked down the stairs and placed his bible into his small trunk. He headed out the door, smiling as he took one last look up the steps to where his wife slept. He had never been away from her since they had married.

Marella heard Seth rise from his bed and felt the kiss on her forehead. Through her closed eyes, she saw the soft orange glow of candlelight, followed by darkness when Seth extinguished the flame. Marella also heard the sound of his footsteps going down the stairs and the heavy door opening and closing as he headed out into the cold morning and the lightly falling snow. She felt suddenly vulnerable that Seth's absence would be an opening for the devil to come into her house and her life. Her feelings for Alfred Samter had been growing every day. And now that her husband was not there to act as a barrier between them, she did not trust herself to resist the seduction of evil. There had been too many kisses behind closed doors, and physical feelings that should only come from her husband. She knew, if it didn't stop, she would bring sin and shame upon her house and her faithful husband.

The evening before, after Alfred walked Seth to the door and wished him well on his trip, he told Seth that he was optimistic about the trip. He would bring back great blessings for the growing church in the way of money and other, much-needed material items. Alfred, with a twinge of guilt, repeated his assurance that his wife would be safe. Then he closed the door and returned to the coziness of the fireplace. His animals were fed and safely secured in the barn for the night. A light flurry of snow was falling, coating the ground in soft clouds of white. Sitting in front of the fire, cracking nuts, and throwing the shells into the fire, he started thinking about Marella, all alone and what he would like to do to her. These lustful thoughts were suddenly interrupted by his wife.

"Alfred, what did the minister need?" she asked as she walked down the steps. "Is he going on his trip tomorrow, or do you think there will be a delay if a blizzard should come?" The thought of the trip being delayed set a spark off in Alfred.

"**What blizzard! There'll be no blizzard!**" he said in a raised voice more scolding than civil. "He didn't need anything. He just wants us to be sure Marella is safe while he is on his trip."

After a momentary silence, Eugenia replied in an accusatory

tone becoming all too familiar to him. "Yes, I am sure you will take care of **her** in **her** time of need."

Alfred continued to chew on the nuts that he was cracking, "And what might that mean? What are you suggesting?" he asked, staring into the fire.

"I am not suggesting anything, but it might be wise to remember that I am your wife and that you have pledged your love to me in the eyes of the Lord. So, I implore you, please ensure the safety of our good neighbor with a sense of dignity and respect for everyone. Good-night, Alfred," Eugenie said sadly.

Still lost in his thoughts about the lovely Marella and her being alone, he ignored her. Eugenia's words fell on deaf ears, and if he had paid attention to the words, they would have meant nothing to him. He selfishly thought only of himself and his love for Marella.

After Seth shut the door, Marella arose from the bed and went downstairs, started a fire, and brewed a cup of tea. She had much work to do in the church. The floors needed sweeping. The prayer books had been strewn about by the parishioners and needed to be picked up and filed in the pews. The walkway to the front door would need to be shoveled from the light snow that continued to fall.

While sipping her tea, she heard the whistle of the train leaving for the city. As the sound reached her ears, the fear that she felt as she lay in her bed returned. She was sure that evil would shortly enter her life. And as she gazed at the red embers of the fire, she feared that her desires for Alfred Samter, a married man, were far more than those for her husband.

Late in the afternoon, after all of Alfred's chores were done, he stated in a monotone voice from across the room. "I'm leaving now. I am going to the church to do some work that I promised Seth I would do while he is away and to check on Marella. It shouldn't take long, just a latch on a cabinet behind the altar that needs to be fixed." And with a bit of hesitation, added, "Do you want to come along?"

Without turning to face her husband, she replied in the same tone of voice as his, "No, and fixing the latch shouldn't take long. Give Marella my regards and tell her I will probably visit her later today. You go, supper will be ready shortly." She continued stirring the large pot over the fire.

Alfred packed some tools he would need and several that he would not, into his bag, and without saying good-bye, walked out into the cold air and began the short walk up the hill to the little church.

When Alfred arrived, he saw Marella on a ladder cleaning a window. As always, his heart skipped a beat at the sight of her. Afraid he would startle her, he walked slowly over to her, and then spoke softly, "Hello, Marella."

"Oh, Alfred, I didn't hear you come in. Why are you here?" she asked with a knowing smile.

As his heart continued to skip beats, he answered, "Seth asked me to fix the latch on the cabinet behind the altar."

"Oh, a latch, is it?" she asked, raising one eyebrow.

He looked up at her, and like every other time he saw her, he believed he had never seen such beauty. The kisses they had stolen in the past were magical. There was no longer any guilt in his heart. As she came down the ladder, she turned to him and asked him to show her the latch that needed to be fixed so that she could show him where it was.

Together they reached out and grasped each other's hand and moved toward the altar. She began to kiss him before they had taken more than a few steps. Moans and heavy breathing, and passionate words of desire, echoed throughout the church from behind the altar.

Slowly, the large wooden church door opened. The afternoon light pierced the dimness within, followed by the silhouette of Eugenia standing in the opening. She stopped moving when she heard the sounds that were like thorns pricking her ears. With a heavy heart, she turned and exited, quietly closing the heavy door behind her. Sadly she hurried home; her suspicions confirmed.

Finally, Marella tore herself from Alfred's embrace, stood up, and ran into the room behind the altar. Alfred turned and picked up his tools and walked slowly toward the door. He turned back one last time to catch a glimpse of his beautiful Marella, but she was nowhere in sight. At the entrance to the hall, he stopped and looked at the plaque on the wall honoring both him and Marella for their work in building the church. The words of praise seemed so undeserved now as he realized, briefly, what a hypocritical sinner he was.

Alfred left the church and headed home, not noticing the footprints left by his wife in the snow moments before. Once home, he sat down and ate supper with Eugenia and Ella, careful how he spoke about his day.

After Alfred left, Marella returned to the church hall and continued her cleaning. She shivered in ecstasy, replaying the passion of her encounter with Alfred, over and over in her mind. Neither Alfred nor Marella would ever know that Eugenia was privy to their secret. Because life on a farm can be very busy and filled with long and arduous tasks, Alfred and Marella would never meet alone or kiss again.

One month after the good minister had returned from his highly successful trip, his wife took him by the hand and asked him to walk to the church with her. They knelt at the altar, and after saying a prayer, she placed her hand on his arm, looked into his eyes and spoke softly. "Seth, I have something to say to you. Something that is going to change our lives." She stopped for a moment to calm the quiver in her voice, fearful that it would betray her. "Seth, the Lord has blessed us. He has chosen us to be the parents of a child. Our prayers are answered," she whispered into his ear. She leaned toward him and kissed him on the cheek and staring blankly at the window she had been cleaning the day she and Alfred walked behind the altar and conceived a "miracle child."

Seth stared at her in amazement, put his arms around her, and hugged her tightly. "The Lord is good. He has surely blessed us with the child we always knew he would!" he added with pride, hardly believing his good fortune. Not for one second did Seth think anything other than that a "miracle" had occurred.

Marella tried to return his strong embrace, but felt unusually weak and could only respond in a timid voice, "The child will be born near Christmas. It will be the greatest Christmas gift ever bestowed on us by the Lord," she said, filled with a new sense of guilt.

After a long pause and a prayer of thanks by both of them to Jesus and his Mother, Seth broke the silence. "Yes, yes," he added with a knowing smile, "it will certainly be our miracle child."

12.
Onward to Herronville
★★★★★★★
1863

Nicholas did not leave Gettysburg immediately after the President gave his short speech. No one will remember what he said. Mostly though, Nicholas was not even sure why Lincoln was saying what he did. He figured that Beatrice had understood, but to him, he hoped that it was not just more than the double talk that all politicians spouted to make the common people feel better about the bad situations that they had been forced to endure. Nicholas had never believed in the war, and now after fighting in it, he believed in it even less. He had seen young men on both sides of the line die. When he stopped to think about it, his mind filled with the horrors that he had endured. He could hear the anguished screams of terrified and wounded young soldiers. He could see the doctors cutting legs and arms off soldiers with rusty, dirty saws like ones he had used when working on his father's farm. He heard men cry out for their wives or mothers, and he heard men curse God when there was no answer to their pleas. All for nothing, he thought. "The Lord must be an evil God to allow this to happen," he mumbled as he put his bedroll on the ground. He sat and watched crowds of people traveling down the road, returning to their homes. He heard some praising the President's words while others walked in silence with their heads bowed and a blank stare in their eyes. Those, he thought, those are the ones who have lost sons and brothers and fathers in this war.

He was restless that night as his thoughts jumped from images of Beatrice, the beautiful woman who helped him understand some things about the war and made his eye feel better, to Ella, whose hand he longed to hold again. But as he lay looking into the sky, he fought back the conflicted feelings he had between Ella and Beatrice. Maybe it was the war; however, deep inside, he knew it was Beatrice. As he struggled to find the answer, he fell into a troubled sleep. He awakened with a scream. In this nightmare, he kept seeing the bloody face of the young rebel soldier that he had killed. He saw himself, again, lie on the ground covered in blood, determined to die or quit the war. This dream was becoming more frequent and terrifying. He stood up and shook off the chill of the morning and the fear that arose from this dream. Then he walked to the little pond that he had gone to with Beatrice's children the previous day, to wash his face and prepare for his journey back to Herronville.

Nicholas wondered if he would be home in time for the newly proclaimed holiday of Thanksgiving recently made official by the President. Unless there was a train to Herronville, though, that was not going to be possible. It did not really matter to him because he was going home, and the anticipation of seeing his mother and father, but even more so Ella, became more intense. With his eyes closed, he visualized himself walking with her around the path at Pony Lake, then stopping and kneeling in front of her to propose marriage. He was done dreaming about her; he was going to marry her and start a family.

He set out on foot, hoping to get a ride. If he could make it to Harrisburg, he could jump on a train, make it to New York City, and, from there, get a ride to Herronville on the train that ran to Elmira. It really did not matter to him how he got home. He only wanted to go home, far away from the war, and be with his family and Ella.

As he moved along the dirt road, many carriages passed him. The riders waved but did not offer a ride. He thought maybe it was because of his tattered uniform or perhaps the patch over his eye. As he felt the patch, he could feel the moistness from the seepage. He feared he would lose the eye but hoped that when he got home, Doctor Wilkins could save it. It was more than an hour before a man on a wagon stopped and offered him a ride, waving him aboard.

"Where you headed, soldier?" He asked, staring at him with suspicion.

"Home," Nicholas replied as he tried to cover his weeping eye inconspicuously. "I need to get to Harrisburg to get a train to New York City so I can catch a train to New Jersey and then to my home in Pennsylvania." He rattled off the schedule of cities as rapidly as if he were a conductor.

The man who was slight of stature stared at him and before moving the wagon, asked bluntly, "You ain't a deserter, are you? Cuz if you are, you need to get off my wagon."

Taken aback, a flush of anger surged through Nicholas's body. "I ain't no Goddamn deserter!" he snapped with ferocity, "I fought in Chancellorsville and Gettysburg with the 151st. I ain't no deserter!" he said as he almost pulled off the medal from his uniform to show him. "I saw many a man fall dead, and anyone who accuses me of deserting, I will kill with my bare hands!" He was startled at his response and immediately felt a surge of sorrow for his words. "I am sorry!" he apologized. "I didn't mean to disrespect you. I am truly sorry. I don't know what came over me. Please accept my apology," he said, extending his hand to the man.

The man raised his eyebrows, "No offense taken, son. My son was killed at Gettysburg, and you can understand my concern. There are a lot of men deserting, and while I hate them all, I understand that this damn war is causing them to do it. So, let's you and I get moving so you can get to a train. My name is Roberts, Nathan Roberts. Yours?"

"Nicholas, Nicholas Haff. And I'm sorry for being rude. I think I'm just tired." He smiled at Roberts, "So, let's go. I want to get home and see my future wife, Ella."

Roberts did not talk much, and Nicholas was satisfied to sit and look at the peaceful scenery. Cattle were grazing in the fields, and people were doing everyday things. There was no gunfire, no screaming, no signs of war—except in his head. Every so often, something came over him, a feeling of intense anxiety that surged throughout his entire body. And for a brief moment, he felt a rage. It came and went in a matter of moments. He was not a religious man, but he began to pray to the Lord that the feelings would stop, that the good Lord would give him peace.

After several hours of silence, Roberts turned to Nicholas, "You don't talk too much, do you," he said as a statement rather than a question. "What unit did you say you were with?"

Nicholas, who had been staring off into the fields, responded, "The 151st. We had some schoolteachers and farmers and guys like me who were just tryin' to survive," he said with a forced laugh.

Cautiously, Roberts spoke, "I heard of the 151st. You took a lot of casualties, didn't you," again stating rather than questioning.

"I guess. No more than the others. We fought as good as any of them," he replied, never directly addressing the man. "We fought damn hard."

"I'm sure you did. And I am sorry for all your losses."

Nicholas was uncomfortable talking about the battle. He was uncomfortable thinking about the war, and he was uncomfortable imagining what he would tell the people of Herronville when they asked about the war, especially if they began to ask about what happened to this one or that one. And he knew they would. Only a handful from the Pike County area survived, yet there would be many questions.

"Thank you, sir. And I am sure sorry about the loss of your son. I am sure he was a fine soldier and fought hard. I am truly sorry."

Both men were silent until the city of Harrisburg appeared in the distance.

"We will be there soon, Son," Roberts said, breaking the silence. Nicholas did not respond. His mind was occupied, trying to remember the names of those killed and answers to questions the hometown folks were sure to ask. And if the others who survived witnessed that he feigned death during the battle, would they tell the people of Herronville that he was a coward?

"I'm sorry, sir. I was in deep thought."

"I said, we will be there soon... in Harrisburg. You have any money to get to New York?"

"No, I figured I would just jump a train."

"Hmm," Roberts said, nodding his head. "I see. How about if I give you some money, and you can pay me back someday."

"How would I do that? I live in Herronville."

Roberts smiled at him. "Nicholas, let's just pretend that you were my son. I would have liked it if someone helped him get home. And I was only teasing about paying me back. It's a thank you for fighting for our country." And with that, he handed Nicholas enough money to travel home.

Momentarily, Nicholas had to fight back his urge to say no but then readily accepted the money from the stranger.

"Thank you. It's been a long journey since I left home last year. I have seen unimaginable things. And I think things have happened to me, but I have also met people that I will surely tell others about until the day I die. And I know I said it before, but I am truly sorry for your son's death." He reached out and took the offering, tightly gripping the man's hand and shaking it.

It was within an hour of Nicholas's receiving the money that the wagon pulled into the station where a locomotive sat huffing and appeared to be waiting for him. He jumped off the wagon with his bedroll, then walked in front of the exhausted horse, took the time to stroke the animal's face, and thanked him. As he approached Roberts, he thanked him again as well.

"Have a good life, Nicholas, and try to leave the demons behind. I will think of you and pray for you."

He stood, waving to the man and his horse as they plodded away.

13.
The Telegram
★★★★★★★
November 1863

True to her word to him, Ella stayed at the telegraph office after Jonathan's lewd advances. While he did not attempt it again, he thought constantly of her. He had convinced himself that he was in love with her, and worse, he was certain that Ella was in love with him. He based his assumption on the fact that she had not left her employment after his assault in June. Jonathan did not realize it, but his obsession had turned into a mental disorder of a major proportion. He dreamt about her, thought of her constantly, walked past her house late in the night, and longed to be in her room. And while their conversations were minimal, when there was communication between them, he misconstrued the words she would say. While describing his new horse to her, she replied that she would "love to see it," which he decidedly believed meant, "I want to come to your home." Jonathan's mind was in a downward spiral. Even so, he was comfortable with his fantastical thoughts. Ella, on the other hand, was unaware that she was in danger. She continued to work at the telegraph office, forgetting the promise she had made to herself, to quit her job the day after the incident.

It was on a Monday, the 23rd of November, that Jonathan's maniacal plan took place. No one had heard from Nicholas in many months. Since before the Battle of Gettysburg, none of the soldiers from the area, had yet returned home to bring any news. Jonathan took solace in believing that Nicholas Haff was probably dead, or a missing casualty, or else a deserter. He was also aware that any day Nicholas and the others could march into town and be hailed as heroes. In the wee hours of November 22 and into the early morning of November 23, Jonathan composed a cruel telegram addressed to the Haff family from the United States Department of War. The well-written document expressed that Nicholas was missing since the Battle of Gettysburg and considered to have deserted or was possibly missing in action, but it was unknown if he was alive. As he sat looking at the document that he would eventually read to Ella later in the day, he spoke to himself aloud as to how Ella would react:

"I will ask her to come into the back room and tell her to sit down as I have bad news for her. I will tell her that when I arrived in the morning, this telegram was waiting. I will reach out and hold her hand and gently tell her that Nicholas will probably not be coming home..." He sat mulling over the plan, hoping that when he reached out to hold her hand, she would not repel his touch. "...No, no she won't. She will want to ask me questions, 'What are you talking about?' or 'Oh my God! Why? What happened?' She will eventually ask to read the telegram, and when she does, she will become hysterical, and that is when I will take her into my arms and kiss her forehead, and she will put her arms around me and cry on my shoulder as I comfort her." Jonathan believed this was a perfect plan, and Ella would react exactly in the order he had imagined and how the events would occur. He sat rereading the telegraph for hours, believing this plan would surely send her into his arms.

A frost had come to Pike County. When Ella entered the telegraph office at 8:00 a.m., she was surprised to feel the warmth of the burning fire in the office. She was the one who usually lit a fire first thing in the morning to heat the building when necessary. She was also surprised to see Jonathan sitting at his desk at such an early hour. He sat motionless and spoke slowly.

"Good morning, Ella." He said stoically.

"Good Morning, Mister Kuhn. You are here bright and early today. There is quite a chill this morning, and the warmth of the fire is appreciated. My father did not light a fire this morning, and it was quite..."

"Ella," he interrupted, "I need you to come to the back room. I have something important to tell you. It's a personal, private matter."

Ella hesitated. She was still nervous about going into the room with him when there were no patrons in the office. "Ok," she replied, "but I need to leave the curtain open—in case a customer should come in and need assistance."

He had not thought of that possibility but now felt so confident in his plan that he did not think that anything could go wrong. "Surely," he said solemnly. "Certainly, leave it open, Ella. But please come here. What I have to tell you cannot wait." As Ella went into the backroom, Jonathan, without her noticing, pulled the shade, turned the key, and locked the front door.

His heart raced as he entered the room where Ella stood waiting for him, and for a moment, sanity nearly took hold of him. His mind told him that this was a foolish plan and to make up a story to tell her and to send her back to her desk. But as he looked at her, the obsession returned, and his mind clearly could see that the plan he was setting into motion was sure to work.

"Ella," he started, "please have a seat. I have something very unpleasant to tell you, and I surely am sad to be the one to have to tell you this frightful news." He tried to read her face, tried to figure out if she was more afraid of him or of the 'frightful' news she was anticipating to receive.

Her eyes showed fear as she spoke, "Mr. Kuhn, you are scaring me. What is this dreadful news you have?"

He sat across from her, slowly moving his chair into position to hold her hand as he had planned. "Ella, I fear that Nicholas will not be returning. I received a telegram this morning indicating that his whereabouts are unknown. He has been missing since after the Battle of Gettysburg." He reached out for her hand, but her reaction was not what he expected.

Standing up, she looked down at him and exclaimed, "That is

impossible! He will be home. He will return with the other men!"

Jonathan stood and approached her in an attempt to console her. "No, Ella, I'm afraid not." And reaching into his vest pocket, he retrieved the telegram he had falsified and handed it to her. "Here, Ella, have a seat and read this. I am so sad to have to be the one to share this with you."

He again moved forward, trying to situate himself to comfort her, to hold her as he had been dreaming of for months. Ella remained standing and read the words that he had written. "I am sorry, but I am afraid the words on that paper are true. He won't be coming home."

Ella read and reread the words, and as she looked at them, she suddenly felt Jonathan's arm on her shoulder, mumbling over and over that he was "So sorry." She pulled away from him and tried to ask him when the telegram had arrived, but he never responded. Instead, he now had a firm grip on her shoulder. Visions of Ella and him flooded his mind, and his desire for her became overwhelming. When Ella tried to scream, his hand covered her mouth.

After a brief struggle, he finally subdued the slight young woman. The sexual assault was swift and brutal, and when he finished, she lay on her side, pulling her knees against her chest and staring blindly away from him on the floor. He crawled away and collapsed, his head on his knees, repeatedly sobbing, "I'm so sorry."

14.
Welcome Home
★★★★★★★
November 30, 1863

It was on a very cold night, the last day of November, in 1863, when Nicholas Haff stepped off the train in Herronville. His only belongings were on his back and in his bedroll. The money which Nathan Roberts had given him had been spent on fares. He stood on the platform of the small depot and stared into the night as the train hissed and quickly moved away from the station. There were some lights glowing in the little town, and he wondered if his mother and father were still awake. He also wondered if Ella was sleeping. His yearnings for her had accelerated on the journey home. As he stood on the platform, he assured himself that he would find her in the morning. They would walk to Pony Lake holding hands, and he would tell her how much he missed her. He hoped that her feelings for him were mutual.

"I need to go home," he mumbled to himself, but he was hesitant to do so. He had not heard from anyone since before the Gettysburg battle, and he had never heard from Ella. He feared that he had been forgotten or maybe believed to be dead. Surely Jonathan Kuhn would have kept the town abreast of the daily battles of the 151st Infantry. With that thought in mind, the anger returned and raged momentarily throughout his body. He shook his head, attempting to rid the built-up fury and began the short walk to his father's farm. He wondered how many men from Herronville survived the slaughter of Gettysburg. The lingering guilt of his feigned death and the fear of anyone witnessing it pressed heavily on his mind.

When he reached the crossroad near home, he stopped and looked to the left and stared at Ella's house. A light was shining upstairs in Ella's room. He remained motionless, considering whether to knock on her door or to turn to the right and surprise his parents. As he thought about what to do, the front door of Ella's house opened. He saw her father speaking to someone on the porch. He approached nearer until he recognized the voice of Doctor Wilkins speaking with Mr. Samter. His visit with Ella would have to wait until tomorrow. He turned and walked toward his house, looking back wistfully at the light burning in the upstairs window of the Samters' house.

When he reached his house, he could see lanterns burning inside the front room. As he stood at the front gate, he stared solemnly at his home. His heart filled with fear and anxiety as he suddenly realized that he did not know how to approach his parents. He tried to think of what to say, words that would make everything that he had been through in the past year seem okay, words that would comfort his mother. And he wanted to say words that would prove to his father that he was truly a man and not the young boy who had left home to fight a war that he did not believe in, but one in which his father had.

He opened the gate, and as he walked toward the door, his mind wandered back to Ella, and he wondered why Doctor Wilkins was at her house.

He reached for the doorknob and then stopped, wondering if he needed to knock on the door of his own house or if he should walk directly into the parlor. His fears melted away when suddenly the door swung open with his father standing there, looking at him and extending his hand.

"Nicholas! I saw you standing out here. I didn't know who you were! Why didn't you come in? Come in! Come in!" he said, excitement welling up in his voice as he put his arm on his son's shoulder, escorting him into the house. "Margaret!" he yelled up the stairs, "Come here quickly! Nicholas is home! Our son is home!"

A scream of joy from upstairs was followed by Margaret rushing down the staircase. Seeing Nicholas standing next to his father in his war-torn uniform, tears began to flow down her cheeks. She stopped suddenly and then ran to him and hugged him intensely, kissing his cheeks over and over as she whispered his name. Nicholas was overcome with emotion as he wrapped his arms around his mother. "It's okay, Mother, I am home. Things will be good now. I am finally home."

The homecoming reunion lasted an hour before Jake suggested that they all sit down in the kitchen and have tea. As they sat at the table, Margaret, who had been staring at the worn patch on Nicholas's eye, reached over and gently touched his face. "Nicholas, what happened to your eye? Why is there a patch on it? Were you shot? Is your eye missing?"

With all the fuss over his arrival at home, he had completely forgotten about his eye. He reached up and gently removed his mother's hand from his face but continued to hold it on his lap, and with a tentative smile, he replied, "No, Mother, it is not missing. It is a bit infected from some contaminated water I used to wash my face. And a very kind woman helped me and used vinegar to reduce the infection." And as he said that, his mind returned to Gettysburg and to the beautiful Beatrice, who had helped him.

His mother removed her hand from his and returned it to his face. "Let me see the eye, Nicholas. Let me see what it looks like." At first, he hesitated, telling his mother that it was okay and that she need not worry.

After much bantering, his father stepped in and said, "Son, let your mother see your eye. You cannot keep that tattered thing on forever." Finally, he relented and slowly removed the patch, releasing a foul odor from the pus-covered eye. Margaret did not look away but quickly covered her nose with her handkerchief while Jake stood up and moved to the parlor.

"Your mother is much better at matters of medicine than I am," he said. One look at the expression on his mother's face told Nicholas all that he needed to know.

"How bad is it, Mother?"

"Well, I am not sure, but I am going to clean it up, and in the morning, we will go see Doctor Wilkins. He can treat it with a mixture of licorice root and garlic, which, hopefully, will cure it. Now, lay on the sofa, and I will clean it as well as I can." Jake kept his distance, lighting his pipe, hoping to cover the stench released into the room when the patch was removed.

As he lowered himself onto the sofa, his mother continued, "And tomorrow we will get you a bath and some nice clean clothes. You can throw away your uniform. It is tattered and filthy."

"Yes, yes it is, and that will be a good thing. I am tired of wearing it, tired of all the things I have seen while wearing it." As the words came out of his mouth, he regretted saying them. He did not want to startle his parents. "All I meant was that I have had these clothes on for a very long time. It is time to get rid of them."

Margaret smiled at him and propped his head onto the arm of the couch. She brought in a basin of cool water and a towel and slowly wiped the sticky substance from around his eye and cheekbone. Stroking his hair softly with the other hand, she quietly whispered under her breath partly to him and partly to herself, "My boy is home. My beautiful boy is home." As he lay listening to her, he closed both his eyes and smiled.

"Okay, Nicholas, that is as good as I can do. And, Jake, you can come back in here now," she said with a half-smile. "But tomorrow, we will be at Doc Wilkins bright and early."

At the mention of Doc Wilkins, Nicholas sat up. "I saw him coming from Ella's house tonight. Is someone ill there?" he asked.

Jake and Margaret looked at each other for support in answering the question, but neither one immediately answered him.

"Well," he repeated. "is someone ill at the Samters'?"

Jake nodded for Margaret to leave the room. She quickly agreed, picking up the basin of water and the towel on her way back to the kitchen. Jake took a seat next to Nicholas on the couch and took a deep breath, preparing to tell him the story.

"Is there an illness? Has someone been in an accident? Is Ella okay?" he asked without taking time to allow Jake to answer.

Jake took the pipe from his mouth, and attempting not to look at his eye, started to tell Nicholas why the doctor was at the Samters'. "Well, Son, there was an incident at the telegraph office. A terrible incident, and yes, it involved Ella..."

"What happened to Ella?" he interrupted as a surge of anger flow through his body.

"Let me finish. Ella, at the request of Jonathan Kuhn, took a job at the telegraph office. It seems that he took a liking to Ella, and from what we hear became obsessed with her. Well, recently, as I said, there was an incident at the office. No one knows for sure what happened, but the word around town is that Jonathan raped Ella. I am so sorry that I had to tell you this on your first day home." Jake tried to continue, but he was so filled with emotion that he had to stop.

Nicholas's face went blank but hidden behind his still face, an uncontrollable rage began building, just like what he had experience in his nightmares. He could feel it in every fiber of his body. His mind was reeling, and visions of the Gettysburg battle flashed through his mind. He saw men dying, and as always, the image of the young rebel he had killed appeared. He sat stone-like, staring into space with the images running through his mind.

"Son, are you okay?" his father asked, but Nicholas remained silent for several moments.

When he finally spoke, it was very measured. "Where is Kuhn now?"

"Why, he is in jail. The sheriff arrested him after Kuhn went to him and confessed what he had done."

Puzzled, Nicholas cocked his head, "He told the sheriff what he did? Why would he do that?"

"I guess he felt guilty."

He curled his lips and shook his head. "I will go and see Ella tomorrow."

"I don't know if the doctor or Alfred will allow you to see her. She is not well, at least in her head," he said, hoping that Nicholas would reconsider.

"No," he repeated. "I will go and see her tomorrow. And then I will go and see Kuhn at the jail. Now, where did Mother go? I want to see her before I go to my room. My room is still there, right?" he said, managing a fake laugh and smile which his father reciprocated.

"Of course, it is there! This is your home and always will be, and we are so happy to have you back! I think she is upstairs preparing your bed and laying out clean clothes for you for tomorrow. Why don't you go upstairs and see her and get yourself a good night's sleep." He stood up from his chair and patted Nicholas on his shoulder. "Good night, Son."

"Good night, Father. It's good to be home."

15.

The Visit

★★★★★★★

December 1863

Nicholas's sleep was erratic. His mind, which no longer shut down during times of rest, was more active than usual as his thoughts turned from the horrors of the war to Jonathan Kuhn. He tried to visualize what he had done to Ella and why he had done it. As his imagination brought up visions of the assault, he felt the anger and rage return, undulating throughout his body. He stared at the ceiling of his small bedroom. Even though he was grateful for the softness and comfort of his straw mattress, the coziness of his feather tick, and the joy of being home, his spirits were crushed by the news of Ella's attack.

Finally, an uneasy sleep descended on him, only to take him back into the recurring dream–the face of the young southern soldier he had killed. He woke with a jolt to the new day's dawn. He slowly got up from the warmth of his bed and quietly crept down the stairs. After lighting a fire in the kitchen, he went outside and headed for the hen house to gather eggs for breakfast. On his way, he stopped, looking at the farm that he had not seen in over a year. It was much the same. He had expected that, after being gone for a year, things would have changed, but they had not. His father's old horse was in the stable, and still in need of a good grooming. The barn and other outbuildings were still peeling paint, but from what he could tell, everything else looked the same. A sudden twinge of pain in his eye reminded him. He was most likely the only thing that had changed.

Nicholas opened the wooden door to the chicken coop, waking

the hens. Undeterred by their squawking displeasure, he picked up the basket and gently reached under their plump bodies sitting on the nests and scooped up enough eggs for his parents and himself. As he headed back to the house, he grabbed the pail sitting next to the well and filled it with water. He would heat it later to wash with before calling on the doctor and Ella. He did not care what Jonathan thought about him.

The kitchen was warm from the blazing fire when he returned to the house, so he began to prepare his breakfast. As he cracked the eggs, cut the ham, and put everything into a pan, his thoughts turned to Beatrice and her children. He touched his eye as he gazed into the fire, remembering her kindness and the happiness he had felt that day. Then as if someone, without his consent, quickly turned a page in a book he was reading, his joyful thoughts suddenly turned to the evil that Kuhn had done. The rage returned as he viciously stabbed at the ham and eggs he had moments before put on his plate. He forced himself to ease up and dipped some of his mother's fresh bread into the eggs and picked at the ham, no longer very hungry. He ate only a few bites as he waited for the water to warm enough to clean himself for his visit to the Samters' home.

His father was right. He felt much more presentable after he washed and dressed in the clean clothes that his mother had laid out for him the night before. It had been weeks since he had taken care of himself.

His movement around the house awakened his parents, who were not usually out of bed at the crack of dawn. However, as he prepared to leave, they both appeared in the doorway to their room.

"Good morning, Son!" Jake bellowed, cheerfully. "Did you sleep well? Where are you headed out to so early?"

His mother's voice followed Jake's. "Good morning, Nicholas. Where in the world are you going so early? Did you eat something?"

Nicholas froze. "Nowhere. I just thought I would take a walk around town. I would just like to see it again. I didn't want to wake you."

Jake stared at Nicholas for a moment. "Well, why don't you have a cup of coffee with us before you run off. No one will be in town yet. Come. Sit down," he said as he walked to the table and pulled out a chair. Nicholas, whose hand had been on the door handle, took a deep breath, removed his hand and moved back toward the table.

His mother wrapped her arm around his and walked with him to the table. "We are so happy you are home safe. Your father and I hardly slept. We talked about it all night. God has truly blessed us with your return. So many of our young boys died—and for what? Nothing will change. Slavery will continue no matter who wins the war..." Her words were interrupted by an exaggerated cough by Jake.

"So, Son, did you sleep well? Are you going to see the doctor today to have him look at your eye? Your mother and I are concerned about it."

He did not answer immediately, because he was distracted by thoughts of his upcoming visit to the jail.

"Nicholas," his father repeated a bit louder, "are you going to see the doctor today? Your mother and I are worried."

"Oh," he said, shaking thoughts of Jonathan from his mind. "Yes, yes, I am. I am going to stop by his house and have him look at me and also ask him if I can see Ella."

"Does your eye hurt?" his mother asked, looking at the discoloration of the eyeball, pus still forming around the rim. "Can you see okay out of it?"

"Yes, Mother. I can see just fine. A little double vision, but if I put a patch on it, it is better. It only hurts when I think about it. So please stop asking me about it, and then I won't think about it!" Realizing his tone of voice and seeing the shocked, stern look on his father's face, he faked a laugh. "I'm sorry, Mother. I didn't mean to snap at you. I am just tired of my eye." He laughed again. Still, Jake continued to stare at him, a bit confused by the abruptness of Nicholas's voice.

"I need to excuse myself. I have to go for a walk. Being home is a bit overwhelming right now. I'll be back later, and we can talk about what happened this past year. I'm curious as to what you two have been doing here since I left. It looks like nothing changed since then!" He chuckled.

"Okay, Nicholas, we are just so glad you are home!" his mother said as he walked toward the door. Jake said nothing, the frown still on his face.

The streets were empty, the early morning air calm and cold. The flurries had stopped, and the trace of snow from the previous night had blown off the streets. He looked to his left and right as he meandered about the small town. Nothing had changed, at least nothing to the naked eye. For him, though, the town would never be the same, not since Ella's rape.

He walked up the hill to the church he had attended ever since he could remember, where his biological father had been the pastor many years before. Once there, he stopped and stared at the still-vacant adjacent lot that remained, covered in old ash and burned timbers. This had been where a house once stood and where his parents burned to death in a Christmastime fire. It was the fire he had been rescued from by Jake Haff, the man he now called "Father" and who had raised him as his own. Most townspeople said this lot was cursed. No new home had replaced the former one.

"They are far better people than I will ever be," he said under his breath, thinking of his rudeness to his mother and father. "I must apologize to them both when I get home." And with those words propelling him, he walked to the church, the one his first father the pastor had built. He entered through the great wooden door and walked up the aisle. When he reached the altar, he knelt down to pray, asking for forgiveness for all the misdeeds he believed he had done in the war. He asked Jesus to forgive his sins, past, present, and future. His heart felt a little lighter as he stood and walked back toward the door. Pausing, he stopped and read the tarnished plaque in the rear of the church honoring his mother Marella, Alfred Samter, and the others of the town for their work

75

within the church. He smiled and walked out the door.

Nicholas stood on the steps of the church, debating his next stop when his anger suddenly raged up inside of him again, beyond his control. It was his thoughts of Jonathan and what he had done to Ella that seemed to trigger it. If he were to go to the jail to talk to Jonathan, he would surely act stupidly and do something that he would later regret. He cinched his coat tighter and turned toward Ella's house. He saw smoke coming from the chimney, assuring him that the Samters' were awake and that he would not be disturbing them.

As he walked down the hill to their house, Nicholas thought back to his childhood and the happy times he spent with Ella. He remembered riding on his father's buckboard past her house, sitting straight up, giving unnecessary commands to the large horse trying to impress Ella. She always heard him coming and would be standing in the yard, holding a glass of lemonade in her outstretched hand and offering it to him. It was the same horse and buckboard still used by his father to fetch supplies and to do whatever plowing there was to do on the farm. He smiled, thinking that maybe he would ride past her house again when summer returned.

Except for the mooing of a cow and an occasional bark of a dog, the small village was quiet and peaceful. As he approached the gated fence of the Samters' house, he took a deep breath and struggled to make his feet walk to the door. He raised his hand and lightly knocked on the door, a knock so soft that it could barely be heard inside. He stood motionless, wondering whether to turn and walk away or to knock again. His mind reeled, not sure if he wanted to see her. He feared what she might look like, or how she would act when she saw him. Giving up, he slowly turned and began to head for the gate, when a voice called from behind him.

"Who is that? What do you need, young man?" It was Mr. Samter.

Nicholas turned and faced him. "It's me, Mr. Samter. Nicholas. Nicholas Haff. I am back from the war and came to see you and

Ella." His voice quivered as he spoke, but much to his surprise, Mr. Samter rushed down the steps of his porch to Nicholas.

"Nicholas! Oh, praise the Lord, you are home safe!" he said with both hands on Nicholas's shoulders. "Come in! Come in!" He put his arm around Nicholas's waist and escorted him into the house. Mr. Samter took a step back, his head moving up and down. "Let me get a look at you, Nicholas! Aw, you look wonderful and are a welcome sight." His pleasure and excitement exceeded even that of his mother and father the night before. It was a greeting that he had not expected from the man. "Have a seat. Come sit by the fire and get warm. The weather has been deplorable. Oh, thank the Lord, you are home safely." As Nicholas sat, Alfred walked to the staircase and yelled to Eugenia, "Eugenia, come quickly. We have an honored guest! Hurry!"

He was a bit embarrassed by Samter's words as he sat, staring into the fire. He knew that Ella was above his head and wondered if he would get to see her. Alfred approached him and sat in the chair facing him. "So, Nicholas, when did you arrive? I am sure that you are very happy to be at home. We have all followed the war on the telegraphs and newspapers that arrive. It is truly sad that the Lord has seen fit to have taken so many of our young boys back to Him so early. But let's not talk of that now. We will have a lot of time to discuss that later. I see your mother and father almost daily. They have been very concerned for your safety. When you are settled in, you and I will have a long talk about the war, especially your time in Gettysburg! My, oh my, that must have been something to see!"

Alfred's eagerness to hear of Gettysburg was making Nicholas very uncomfortable. He and Alfred had never been very close, and now he wondered if Alfred was simply interested in him because of his participation in the war. "I would very much like to tell you about my experiences in the war, but be warned, it is not a happy story," Nicholas said. Behind him, he heard Mrs. Samter making her way down the steps. When she appeared, Nicholas respectfully stood up and turned to face her.

Nicholas had always found her to be a cold woman and not very friendly, not only toward him but toward most of the townspeople. On this day, however, she smiled, and when she reached Nicholas, she wrapped her arms around him and gave him what felt like an exaggerated hug. It made him strangely uncomfortable. As she stepped back from him, she spoke in a kind voice. "Oh, Nicholas, it is so wonderful to have you back home. I understand that the war was terrible, and I cannot imagine what you have endured. I have gone to church and prayed for you every chance I had."

And just as Alfred had done, she took a step back to inspect his appearance. "You look wonderful," she said. Then she stared at his face, took a step forward, reached out, and touched his face. "Oh Lord, your eye has been injured. You must go see Doctor Wilkins as soon as possible." She gently rubbed his cheek and turned her head to the side while looking at his neck. "Hmm," she said softly, "Did you know that you have the same birthmark on your neck as Alfred has on his leg? It looks like some sort of bird. They are almost identical. Isn't that a coincidence! Come look at this Alfred," she said as she raised her eyebrows.

Alfred's face flushed. "I have noticed it before. It is similar, but I wouldn't call it identical! Honestly, Eugenia, you say the strangest things sometimes." He managed to chuckle. "I am sure that Nicholas didn't come to visit us to hear about his birthmark—or mine!"

Eugenia smiled and then spoke to Nicholas, "We are all happy you are home. Please excuse me. I must go upstairs to tend to Ella. If you are not aware, there was an incident recently. I will leave you with Alfred to give you the details. Please give my regards to your parents." She hugged Nicholas again, touched his birthmark, looked at Alfred, and gave him a wry smile before walking to the steps without another word.

After a moment of silence, Alfred shook his head, smiled, and looking into the fire said, "Women, I will never understand them." He spat into the fire.

Nicholas tried to calm the tension in the room by asking. "Sir, can you tell me what happened to Ella. My parents have told me a story that I am having trouble believing."

Alfred nervously wiped his mouth with the back of his hand. "What did they tell you happened?"

Nicholas felt intensely awkward as he tried to tell him what he had been told. He feared if it was not the truth, he would upset him and cause friction between his parents and Alfred.

"Well, Nicholas, what did you hear. You can speak frankly. We are both men."

When he finally spoke, it was with hesitation, "…Uh… they said she was assaulted."

Alfred broke in, "She was raped. She was raped by Jonathan Kuhn, a man I trusted. I blame myself. He asked me if Ella could work with him at the telegraph office. I agreed. I even warned him to protect her from the filthy mouths of the men who sometimes gather there. It was my fault, Nicholas. I never should have allowed her to work there. And I know that the Lord will punish me one day. It was nowhere for a young girl to be. And now she lies in her bed staring at the ceiling. Dr. Wilkins says she will be okay but may never be right in the head again. He says that she may never trust men again—and who would blame her?"

Nicholas was stricken with embarrassment and sorrow and unable to reply.

As he watched him squirm, Alfred addressed him in a soft voice, "It's okay, Nicholas. The Lord will comfort her and punish Jonathan. He and I will both be punished."

The smoke from the fire was irritating his eye, and he found it to be a good excuse to end the conversation and excuse himself. Before leaving, he needed to ask one last question. "Mr. Samter, when do you think I will be able to visit with Ella? I have thought of her every day since I left for the war. I have great feelings for her."

Fear gripped Alfred when he heard Nicholas speak, yet he managed to maintain his composure. "Why, I think if you come here tomorrow, she may be able to see you. Remember, she is in a very delicate condition, and it would be best not to upset her with any talk of your feelings. Not at all."

Nicholas, content with his warning, stood up and extended his hand to Alfred, "I must leave now. I need to go to Dr. Wilkins' home and have him look at my eye. I fear I may lose it."

As Alfred escorted him to the door, he agreed with Nicholas, "Yes, your eye does look rather bad. I hope the doctor can cure it for you. I will give Ella your regards and tell her you may be here tomorrow to see her." Again, Nicholas shook his hand and assured him that he would be very gentle with his words to Ella the next day. "Good-bye, Nicholas. The entire town will celebrate your return and those of the men who have come back with you."

Nicholas cringed at his words, "How many have returned so far?" he asked with a quiver in his voice. "Have they talked much of the war?"

"No, only three others. And they don't seem eager to speak of their time fighting. God bless you, son. I will see you tomorrow. Now head over immediately to see the doctor."

16.
Truth Be Told
★★★★★★★
1863

The snow was falling thickly when Nicholas left Ella's house, and the temperature was dropping. He pulled his coat up around his neck and stuffed his hands in his pockets. He tucked his head down and turned and headed to Doctor Wilkin's office located in his home. It was a short walk past the church and the sheriff's office where Jonathan was in custody. Deeply disappointed that he was not allowed to visit Ella, the promise of seeing her the next day gave hope to his otherwise anguished mind.

When he got to the top of the hill, he turned and looked back at the Samters' home. "Maybe someday I will live there with Ella," he said to himself.

He turned and continued his way through the slowly falling snow. The jail loomed in front of him, and as he approached it, he felt his anger return. It was always the same feeling. It started with his having to take a deep breath, his arms feeling heavy, and his breathing becoming rapid. At the same time, thoughts ran through his mind like a locomotive leaving him angry, angry at everyone and everything he encountered. At this particular moment, his anger was focused on the sheriff's office and on its inhabitant. He tried to calm himself, believing that maybe after he talked to Ella, he would understand things better. Maybe she would profess her love to him, and then he would declare the same to her. Perhaps that would ease her pain as well as his. Right now, though, his entire body was raging with anger, and he stopped and faced the front door of the jail.

He grasped the door handle, and with no idea as to what would happen next, he walked into the jail. Much to his surprise, the sheriff was not there. The office was empty and starkly furnished. A small American flag hung from two nails on the wall behind an aging desk along with a badly painted portrait of President Lincoln not quite centered beneath it. "Lincoln," he whispered with anger, "He's responsible for all of this!" To his left, he spotted a locked wooden door that probably led to the cell of Jonathan Kuhn and maybe others. He had never been in the building before but was expecting that he would be able to talk to Kuhn, face to face.

Trying to figure out what he would do next, he stopped and leaned against the sheriff's desk. The anger had not left him, so he decided to say what he had thought about all night. He pushed himself off the desk, walked across the small room, and put his head against the door.

"Kuhn! Jonathan Kuhn!" he yelled. "It's me, Jonathan. Nicholas Haff."

Silence.

"Jonathan!" He yelled louder. "Can you hear me?"

More silence.

"Okay, Jonathan. I know you can hear me, so you don't have to talk. You just listen. I am home from the war, and I am preparing to propose to Ella, the beautiful woman you raped. If she is incapable of marrying me because of what you have done to her, I will kill you. I don't know, I might kill you anyway! I saw innocent men slaughtered in the war just because of what side they were on, so killing you will be easy. You ready to die, Jonathan?" Nicholas paused for a moment. He felt the anger subsiding as he lashed out at Jonathan. And now all of the thoughts that crowded his head the night before were evaporating. "Anyway," he continued, "I will be back. Maybe to kill you, maybe not. I think I will ask Ella what she would like me to do. Anything to say to her when I see her? Maybe... you're sorry?"

Silence.

"Okay, Mr. Kuhn," he spat out, "You have a nice day." He

turned and walked out the door and into the snow, which was now turning into a late autumn blizzard, the kind that stayed on the ground until April. He gathered his coat around him and continued the short distance toward Dr. Wilkins' office. His anger abated, and he was relieved of the pounding pain in his head that accompanied the surges.

Dr. Wilkins' house was quaint, not fancy by any stretch of the imagination. He had lived there ever since he arrived in Herronville when he was a young man and beginning to practice medicine. He was the only doctor for a fifty-mile radius, and his little office was often packed with folks from all over Pike and Wayne Counties as well as with people from New York State. Today, however, no one was waiting on the porch. Nicholas believed the heavy snowfall and early hour were keeping people away. He knocked on the door and then reached up and felt his eye. He had forgotten about it until Mrs. Samter had mentioned it. His thoughts were interrupted when Dr. Wilkins opened the door and looked at Nicholas, blankly. After a few seconds, he recognized him and exclaimed, "Oh Lord, Nicholas Haff! Oh my God! You are home!" He reached out and pumped Nicholas's hand. "Come in, come in! Oh, my Lord, let me get a good look at you!" Nicholas felt cheered and a bit embarrassed by the attention he was receiving from everyone who was welcoming him home.

"It is good to see you as well, Dr. Wilkins," he replied. "I just got home last night. It was a long journey, but I am very happy to be home. I am afraid this is not a social visit, but rather I need you to look at my eye."

"I can see that," the doctor replied as he squinted to look at Nicholas's eye. "Let's go into my office, and I'll have a better look at it."

Nicholas followed the doctor into his office, speaking as he walked. "I met a woman in Gettysburg who tended to my eye. She put vinegar on it and a patch over it. It got like this in Chancellorsville after I washed my face in some swamp water. She said that the vinegar would help the pain, and I think it did.

There were other guys that washed in the same water and didn't get anything wrong with their eyes. I guess I'm just lucky." He laughed nervously as the words spewed from his mouth.

Doctor Wilkins smiled. "Nicholas, slow down. You're tripping over your tongue! You're going to hurt it!" They both laughed as the doctor approached him. "Now, open your eyes as wide as you can." He examined the eye with what looked like a magnifying glass. "Does this hurt?" he asked as he gently touched the eye?"

"No, Sir... maybe a little."

A small amount of pus oozed from the eye when he touched it. He wiped the eye and then touched it again with the same results then stepped back from Nicholas. "Okay, Nicholas, cover your good eye. How many fingers do you see?" he asked as he raised one finger in the air.

Nicholas squinted and feeling uncomfortable, mumbled, "I see several."

The doctor shook his head and gave a comforting smile, "Okay, Nicholas, I don't know how much can be done for that eye. I am not an eye doctor, and the closest one is in New York City. So, unless you are going to go there, I can treat you here. I can give you something for pain if you need it, and you can come here to get the pus cleaned from your eye whenever you want to. I don't think you will be blind in the eye, but I am pretty sure that you will have vision problems for the rest of your life. But if you are careful with your good eye, you should be fine. I would suggest that you let me make you a nice patch for your eye. That will help by blocking the double vision that the bad eye is giving you."

Nicholas could feel the surge coming on him. He was not only angry at Jonathan, but he was also angry at the war, angry at Lincoln, even angry at Dr. Wilkins for his diagnosis.

"So," he said with a tone of voice he would never have used in talking to the doctor before the war, "you're telling me that I will have to wear a patch for the rest of my life? That I will have pus running down my face like a freak forever? There is nothing you can do? Is that what you're telling me?"

Dr. Wilkins was taken aback. This was not the Nicholas that he had known since he had delivered him. "Nicholas," he began in a stern but calm voice, "have a seat."

Nicholas, realizing the disrespect he had shown, immediately took a seat, "I am sorry, Dr. Wilkins. I didn't mean to show any disrespect. I am just so upset about my time in the war. And I just left Ella Samter's house without being allowed to see her."

The doctor nodded his head up and down, "The war memories will fade, Nicholas. And as for Ella, she is going to have a long recovery. What happened to her will affect her for the rest of her life. But her memories, too, will fade. In a way, you both will be fighting your own demons. So, let's you and I see each other once a week with that eye, and in the meantime, I will make you a patch, okay?"

Nicholas took a deep breath, "Yes," he answered, and then he added, "I stopped at the jail to see Jonathan Kuhn. I wanted..."

Dr. Wilkins interrupted him. "Why would you do that?" He asked with great concern.

Nicholas did not hesitate, "I wanted to ask him why he raped her. I want to be sure he gets what's coming to him. I will be glad to be the, uh, henchman."

The doctor allowed the silence to hang heavily in the room before speaking. "Nicholas, there will not be any need for a henchman...or anyone but the judge and jury to decide his fate. So, get those thoughts out of your head! I agree he is as evil as the devil, but if–and I am going to be very blunt–you have thoughts of harming him, please put them out of your head." Then with a warning in his voice, he added, "You are not in the war anymore. Murder and killing can no longer be a part of your life. Please, Nicholas, try and understand the situation. And you may want to know that Kuhn is no longer here. The sheriff put him in his wagon early this morning with his deputy and transported him to the county seat where he will stay until the trial."

Nicholas sat, stunned for a moment. "You mean he's not even in the jail? I was talking to the walls?" The anger welled up and raced through his body. He jumped up, and without thanking the doctor, walked out into the now raging blizzard, down the hill past the jail toward his house, talking to himself.

17.

Redemption

★★★★★★★

1863

Nicholas did not sleep that night before his visit to see Ella. He wondered aloud what he would say to her. For many nights on the battlefields, he had practiced what he might say when he saw her again. But now everything had changed, and he was unable to come to a decision on not only what to say but how to say it. At five a.m., he rose from his bed, where he had tossed and turned all night. The guilt of speaking to his mother so roughly the previous day was weighing on him as well as feeling remorse for talking to Dr. Wilkins in the manner that he did and for walking out of his office so abruptly. "I must stop by his office and apologize to him today! What is wrong with me?"

He walked down the steps, lit a lamp, and started a fire to warm the house, then opened the door to head out to gather some eggs. Outside, over two feet of snow had accumulated overnight. Thinking better of wading through the deep snow, he shut the door and made coffee for himself. If his parents wanted eggs, he would go gather them.

Drinking his coffee, he sat at the table, staring into the fire. Questions ran through his head, some about the war, others to the day in front of him. The smoke from the fire irritated his eye again, which reminded him of the kindness of the beautiful woman he had met at Gettysburg. And though he had never met him, he felt a tinge of sadness for her husband. He smiled, picturing her children and the happiness he felt when he raced them to the pond.

His mind wandered from her to the darkness of the war. He

saw men dying, crying for their mothers. *Men, men fifty years old calling out for their mothers as they lay dying.* He wondered if the horrible memories would ever leave him. He shoved himself away from the table, tossing the remainder of his coffee into the now blazing fire. He went to the door and pushed the snow away then headed to the shed through the heavy snow to get a shovel. "I will clean the snow from the path for Mother and then apologize to both my mother and father for my conduct," he thought.

The snow was wet and heavy. It took him several hours to finish shoveling a path to the chicken coop and the barn. By the time he finished, a bright sun, the kind that always seems to appear the day after a heavy snowfall, glistened on the virgin surface. It sparkled with a myriad of prism-colored specks. The brightness of the day seemed to invigorate him. "Maybe this is a good sign. Maybe today will be a new beginning in my life."

He stomped his boots on the front porch to clear off the snow and walked into the house. His parents sat drinking coffee. His mother looked at him with a forced smile as his father continued to glare at him, still annoyed from the night before when he had spoken to his mother so rudely. His heart skipped a beat as he walked over to his mother and knelt at her side, taking her hands into his. "Mother, I am so very sorry for how I behaved last night. I love you so, and you must know that I will never speak to you in that manner again. I don't know what has gotten into me. Please forgive me."

His mother rubbed his head. "You have had a very long journey through the war. I cannot imagine what you have gone through. I forgive you. You are the best son a mother could have."

He hugged her, stood up, and then walked over to his father. Standing directly in front of him, he looked down into his eyes. "Father, my conduct last night was intolerable. You have raised me to be a much better person than what I showed to you last night. Please forgive me. I promise to be the man of dignity that you have raised."

His father went silent for a moment before he spoke. "Nicholas,

I forgive you. However, please know that such conduct will never happen again in this house. You are my son, but you are also a man. Please act like one."

Deeply ashamed, Nicholas said, "I promise you father, I will never treat you or mother with disrespect again."

Nicholas, eager to change the conversation, announced, "I am going clean up, and then go visit the Samters'. I was not permitted to see Ella yesterday, but Mr. Samter assured me that I would be able to visit her today for a short time."

"Oh, dear, how is she?" Margaret asked with great concern.

"Mr. Samter said that she was okay, but the doctor indicated that she may never be right in the head. I will just be glad to see her. I don't care what her condition is. She has been my friend since childhood, and I thought of her every day during the war."

"He should be hanged," Mr. Haff chimed in. "Young men are dying by the thousands for nothing in this goddamn war, and he is sitting in a cell, a nice warm cell, eating food that should be given to our soldiers. I hope they hang him, the sooner, the better." After taking his last gulp of coffee, he put down his cup, put on his coat, and looked at Nicholas. "Tell the Samters hello and don't stay all day. I am going to need you to help me with the chores today. Too much snow for me to do much by myself." He gave a short wave to his wife and Nicholas, then headed out the back door toward the barn.

When Nicholas turned the corner to head down the hill to the Samters, he looked at the church and spoke aloud, "Please, Lord, please let her be okay. I love her. Please make her well."

He suddenly remembered all the men that he had seen die on the battlefield, and it scared him. "If God let all of them die and suffer, why would he help Ella? He doesn't care about anyone. He is not a kind God." Shocked at himself, he said a quick prayer and apologized to God for his evil thoughts. He started walking again until he stood on the stoop of Ella's house.

Eugenia answered the door at his knock and greeted him warmly. "Come in, come in, Nicholas. Are you frozen? My, that was some storm! I swear it gets worse every year."

"It sure does, Mrs. Samter, but last night when I was in my bed, I thought about all the nights that I slept on the hard ground in the snow and the rain. So I would say that the good Lord blessed me with a fine feather tick and a roof over my head last night!"

Eugenia smiled, ushered him into the parlor, and offered him a seat on the sofa. "I appreciate your hospitality, Mrs. Samter, but I cannot stay long. I promised my father I would help him with chores. It seems like since I've been gone, his health has declined somewhat and with the storm and all..."

Eugenia interrupted. "So, I am assuming you would like to visit with Ella. Well, she knows you're coming, but she is very apprehensive about seeing you. I think your visit will perk her up. But please don't stay too long. She is still very nervous about seeing anyone. In fact, you will be the first outsider that she has seen since the attack." At the word 'attack,' Nicholas fought back the feeling of anxiety that usually led to a flourish of anger.

"Yes, Ma'am, I will keep my visit short. And I hope to God that Jonathan gets his due."

Mrs. Samter did not respond, but instead, motioned for him to follow her up the stairs. On the landing, she called out. "Ella? Ella dear. Nicholas is here to visit. Are you proper?" she asked as she knocked lightly on the door. It was several minutes and another knock before Ella answered.

"Yes, Mother. Please have him come in." There was hesitation in her voice as Eugenia opened the door and allowed Nicholas to enter.

"Remember, Nicholas, not too long. Have a nice visit." She walked back down the stairs but left the door open.

Nicholas slowly approached her bed, gazing at her lying propped up on her pillows. *She has blossomed into such a beautiful woman since I left.*

"Ella, I am so sorry for what has happened to you. I had no idea until..."

"Nicholas, please. My misfortune is nothing compared to what you have been through in the war. Since my mother told me you were home yesterday, my spirit has risen. I feel alive again."

Nicholas swallowed hard. All of his dreams and wishes for the past year had not been in vain. A strange calmness came over him. It was the first time since he left for the war that he felt he could breathe freely. There was no anger moving through his body, and his smile was genuine.

"Come, pull a chair up next to me. I want you to talk to me. I want to remember things that we did as children, happy things. The times we spent at Pony Lake," she said, smiling as he pulled a chair next to her bed.

Nicholas was speechless. All of the things he had planned on saying, wanted to say, were now overtaken by the warmth he felt from the sound of her voice.

"Do you remember when I would trick you into stopping at my house for lemonade? Did you know that I made that especially for you?"

He swallowed hard and tried to reply. Instead, a tear formed in his eye. He wanted to breakdown and sob. He forced himself to contain his emotions, emotions that were like none he had ever before experienced.

"Why, of course, I remember!" he managed to blurt out, and then more smoothly added, "And did you know that I planned my trips past your house on those hot days, knowing that you would wave me down?"

She smiled softly and reached out to hold his hand, "I don't think my parents will care if I hold your hand," she said as her eyes twinkled.

The time passed quickly, and Nicholas realized that he had overstayed his time. He rubbed her hand softly, and as he began to say his good-byes to her with a promise to return, Mr. Samter appeared in the doorway. "Okay, you two, I think it is time to say good-bye for now. Nicholas may come back tomorrow, but you need your rest."

Nicholas rose from his seat and assured Ella that he would

return the next day. The kiss that he wanted to place on her lips was impossible with her father standing in the doorway. Walking out the door, he turned and threw her a wave and a kiss.

Downstairs, as Nicholas was putting his jacket on and wrapping his scarf around his neck, Alfred spoke. "Nicholas, I didn't want to speak in front of Ella, and you mustn't tell her what I am going to tell you as it will surely upset her. I just came from talking to the sheriff. He has just returned from attempting to deliver Kuhn to the county jail."

"Attempting?" Nicholas interrupted.

"Yes, he had Kuhn shackled for the journey on his wagon. They were just outside of town when the blizzard struck. The wagon turned over, and Kuhn was thrown. He was killed when his head hit a boulder, and the wagon landed on top of him. The sheriff said that because he was shackled, he couldn't protect himself. So, there will be no trial. The Lord works in mysterious ways."

Nicholas went silent for a moment, then smiled. "Funny how he couldn't protect himself. I guess the Lord does work in mysterious ways. I only regret that I couldn't have..."

"No, Nicholas, don't say what you are thinking. He is dead, and the Lord will judge him."

"Yes, yes, He will. I only wish that he had suffered. Have a nice day, Mr. Samter. I will see you tomorrow morning."

18.

Back to Pony Lake

★★★★★★★

1863

The winter of 1863-64 in Herronville was long and dreary, and the snow was relentless. Nicholas tended to all the chores on the farm, as Jake Haff had become ill in January with what Doctor Wilkins diagnosed as meningitis. He told Nicholas and his mother that there was little chance that Jake would survive. He tried various remedies to stave off the debilitating disease. First, he had Margaret boil Hemlock wood into a tea and giving it to Jake to drink twice a day. Then the doctor tried administering a concoction of mercury and honey in water. Neither worked, and Jake died on February 12, 1864. He was kept in a makeshift receiving vault until April when the ground became soft enough to finally dig a grave. A funeral was held, and Jake was laid to rest on April 20, 1864. Several of the citizens spoke of his greatness and the love he had for his family. His tombstone was simple. On it was inscribed:

Jake Haff
Loving Husband of Margaret
and
Proud Father of Nicholas

Nicholas was deeply saddened by his father's passing. Still, he continued to visit Ella every day. It wasn't until around March that she felt psychologically prepared and able to return to her routine of helping her father on the farm and aiding neighbors who needed her assistance.

The day of Mr. Haff's funeral, much to the surprise of many townspeople, she stood shoulder to shoulder, holding hands with Nicholas as the coffin was lowered into the ground.

The stories of Nicholas visiting Ella regularly were becoming fodder among the town folks, and now, with their show of affection at the cemetery, many of the rumors being spread were on the edge of scandalous. Some went so far as to suggest that maybe Ella was not raped but rather was romantically involved with Jonathan Kuhn, and that the entire episode was made up by her to cover the pregnancy that was now slowly being revealed. However, Ella knew the truth, that she was raped, and now she was with child. Both she and Nicholas knew the baby could not be his. It was with these matters in hand that Alfred Samter, on the day of Jake Haff's burial, asked Nicholas to meet him the next day behind the altar of the church. It was the first time that he had spoken to Nicholas since the discovery of his daughter's being with child. In fact, he had not even given Nicholas his condolences at the gravesite. Nicholas only nodded his head, knowing what the conversation the next day would concern and would be sure to incite his anger.

The next day Nicholas sat in the front pew waiting for Mr. Samter. He was not kneeling or praying. He had only been in the little church one other time since before the war, and if not for his father's funeral and this meeting, he would not have ever been there again. His faith was lost on the battlefields of Gettysburg. He could not understand why a kind and loving God would allow men to do the things to each other that he had witnessed. He questioned why God left women, such as Beatrice, to live out their lives with only memories of a husband she loved. He looked at the altar and said, "You, Jesus Christ, you are the greatest hypocrite of all time. You teach kindness and send young boys off to be mutilated while you cover your intentions by saying, Free Will! I say you don't even exist!" His voice had elevated to the level of a Sunday sermon. As he finished his tirade against the Lord, Alfred Samter, carrying a handful of tools in one hand, walked past him, motioning with his empty hand to follow. He stood up from his seat, anger rushing through him. His entire body was tense. With his fists clenched and his jaw taut, he followed Alfred, trying to bring his emotions under control.

When both men were behind the altar, Nicholas blurted out the first words as he surveyed the back of the church. "**Why** are we meeting here? Why in the church? I know what this conversation is going to be about, and I find it unsettling that we are having it here."

Mr. Samter replied with great authority in a tone more meant for the scolding of a child than one used for speaking to an adult. "Why we are meeting here is not relevant, but if it is important for you to know, I have promised the minister to do some chores here. I also find it to be a private place, a place of peace. It is a place where sins can be forgiven by the Lord. But while I listened to your vile words against the Lord as I stood in the back of the church, I may have chosen the wrong place to meet. And the words I had planned on telling you would probably be best kept to myself." He stopped for a moment looking to see if Nicholas was reacting to his words and then continued. "But that is not why I asked you here, Nicholas. I want to first say that I have always liked you and that I have the utmost respect for you and your family. And I am very saddened by your father's passing. He was a great man; however, my respect for you has diminished. I have not spoken to you in quite a while because of the part you have played in Ella's condition. You have broken my heart and my wife's heart. I thought that you would have come forward to me, as a man, and asked for Ella's hand. You may have passed your test for bravery on the battlefields, but you have failed miserably here as a man. I need to know if you are going to do the right thing for my daughter. I am assuming that you **do** love her."

Nicholas glared at him. He had learned over time how to control himself, but he was on the verge of doing something that would send him to prison. He proceeded slowly with his words. "Mr. Samter, first of all, I am unsure as to why this conversation is taking place in the church. It is most unsettling to me as I find religion to be nothing more than a place people go to escape the reality of life. Secondly, your disgusting suggestion that I am the father of the child in Ella's womb is absurd, and I find that your belief that Ella and I have had relations also disturbs me so greatly that it places me on the verge of doing harm to you. You are typical of a phony religious zealot. Your mind has been rotted by the words you read in your bible. You think you are so righteous! You are nothing more than a filthy-minded pig! How dare you speak so disgustingly of your daughter? You, you who stand behind the altar that you kneel and pray in front of every Sunday, and now speak with such vile suggestions of your most prized possession, **your** daughter who was so violently attacked. And now you are suggesting here and now that she is not pure?! You, Mr. Samter, it is **yourself** who you should have no respect for!"

Nicholas turned and began to walk toward the large wooden door, but then abruptly turned back to face Alfred and continued. "But we are here, and here are the answers you are seeking the truth to. I am **not** the father of the baby though I wish I were. It was conceived by Jonathan Kuhn at the time of the vicious rape, but I **will** claim it as mine. That is what men do who love a woman. And I do love Ella! I have loved her forever and, with or without your consent, I will marry her. And personally, I hope it is without your consent because I want nothing from you—EVER! We will marry soon, and we will leave this town, if for no other reason but to raise our child without the accusing eyes of Herronville staring at us every day."

Nicholas opened the door to leave, but when he looked back, the light shone through, showing Alfred Samter standing beside the altar repeatedly mumbling words heard only to himself, "Nicholas, I am your father...I am your father..."

The first week of May was filled with sunshine. In fact, plants were beginning to break the wet ground, much earlier than usual.

However, the brightness of the days was darkened in the town by the shocking news that Alfred Samter was found on the shore of Pony Lake with a bullet hole in his head. It looked to be self-inflicted.

At the funeral, the minister spoke of Mr. Samter's love of the church and of his family. Eugenia asked the minister to read from Psalm 127: 3-5:

Behold, children are a heritage from the Lord, offspring a reward from him.
Like arrows in the hand of a warrior are the children of one's youth.
Blessed is the man who fills his quiver with them! He shall not be put to shame when he speaks with his enemies at the gate.

The minister went on to eulogize Alfred as a great family man and citizen of Herronville. He never spoke of his suicide or the reasons that people thought caused him to commit it. The congregation, led by Eugenia, Ella, and Nicholas, went to the cemetery. Eugenia stepped forward as the casket was lowered into the ground, and in a tone fit for a prayer, whispered, "You should have told him."

19.

Revelation

★★★★★★★

1864

Shortly after the shock of Alfred Samter's death, the rumors and gossip of Nicholas and Ella's courtship subsided as they were seen about town and working in the families' gardens together. It was quite apparent to all that the two were in love and that an engagement was sure to be coming soon. Still, the rumors continued as to who was the baby's father. Some were adamant that the pregnancy resulted from a love relationship between Ella and Jonathan, and that the attack occurred in a fit of rage after she told him that she was pregnant, while others who were in Ella's camp insisted that Ella would never carry on without being married. It was surely a rape, adding that Jonathan got what he deserved. A small group of folks claimed that Nicholas had gotten home just about the time that she would have conceived the child.

This gossip did not fall on deaf ears. In June, one month to the day that her father killed himself, Nicholas, while sitting on the rock at Pony Lake where they held hands when they were children, proposed to Ella. "Ella, I have loved you since we were children, and now I want to be with you for the rest of our lives. I have thought of you every day that I have been on this earth. Please marry me." There was no ring, but he did promise to be a loving husband and supportive father to the child that was yet to be born.

The two kissed passionately. Ella sighed deeply, and as she squeezed his hand tightly whispered to him, "How a man could love me as much as you do is more than enough reason to live and bear this child, but your love for me pales to my love for you."

Two days after the proposal, Ella received a visitor at her house from the telegraph office. The man, Robert Thompson, was the current telegraph operator, having been sent to Herronville shortly after Jonathan's demise. Ella had met him briefly at her father's funeral when he offered his condolences. She welcomed him into the house, and he spoke hesitantly.

"Miss Samter, I am sorry to come at your time of mourning, but it was necessary to talk to you, actually to ask a favor of you. As you know, I am sure, that since the tragedy of Mr. Kuhn's death, I have been working tirelessly at the telegraph office. I am in need of help, and I was wondering..." He paused for a moment as Ella's mother entered the room then continued. "I was hoping that you might consider coming to my aide, so to speak." He smiled at Eugenia and added, "Good morning, Mrs. Samter."

Before Ella could respond, Eugenia spoke. "She will not. As it is plain to see, she is with child, and why you would think even for a moment that she would return to the place where she was attacked is beyond me. As for Mr. Kuhn's death, it was not a tragedy. It was the hand of the Lord striking him dead. So, Mr. Thompson, the answer is no! So please take your offer to someone else in the town! I am sure there are many men who are capable of learning your skills. Have a good day." She turned and walked back into the kitchen, leaving Ella and Mr. Thompson standing at the door, both feeling a bit.

He fumbled with his derby and began to apologize. "Oh my, what was I thinking! I am such a..." Ella, not wanting him to embarrass himself even further, stopped him.

"No, no, please, it is fine. You have to know that my mother is not herself. The attack, the death of my father, and my recent engagement to Mr. Haff seem to have put her out of sorts. However, I must tell you though that her answer would have been very similar to mine, but not as gruff," she said with an apologetic smile. "But I do have a suggestion for you. Mr. Roman, who works at the general store, is capable of operating the telegraph. And while he is not an expert, he would work in a pinch for you. Kuhn had him come in to help on occasion. He is a nice man and reliable in showing up when he is needed." She then reached over and unlatched the front door. Mr. Thompson put on his derby and gave Ella a polite nod of his head.

"Thank you, Miss Samter. I shall look for Mr. Roman–I believe his name is Benjamin–at the general store. Again, my condolences to you on your father's passing, and my congratulations to you on your engagement to Mr. Haff. He is a fine young man and a patriot. Please tell your mother that I apologize for my insensitivity. Have a nice day. Good-bye."

"Good-bye, Mr. Thompson, and have a nice day." She smiled after shutting the door and thought what a peculiar man he was.

Two days after Mr. Thompson's visit, Eugenia and Ella sat at the table having an early dinner. Ella watched as her mother picked at her food.

"Mother," she said cautiously, as her mother had been extremely irritable since her engagement. "You are very pensive tonight. You are picking at your peas like you are afraid of them." She offered a smile and light laugh as she spoke.

Eugenia pushed her chair away from the table and, with a voice filled with stress, replied, "I don't have much of an appetite lately." And then her words began to quiver, "I need you to go to Nicholas tonight and bring him here. I want to talk to you both about this engagement." Eugenia then stood and walked out the back door into the late afternoon sun.

A cold chill ran down Ella's spine. She had never heard this tone in her mother's voice before. Something was wrong. Unable to finish her dinner, she cleaned the dishes and put the food away. Then, she did as her mother asked and walked the short distance to Nicholas's house. After a brief visit with Margaret, the two walked hand in hand back to Ella's, both questioning each other as to the purpose of the meeting. Ella's hopeful guess was that her mother was going to present them with some sort of sentimental object, perhaps something of hers, or maybe an item of her father's that she wished them to have. Nicholas was not as optimistic. Eugenia had, at least in his estimation, turned a bit cold toward him since they had become engaged. "Maybe she is going to tell us that she doesn't approve of our engagement," he said, and then realizing that his tone was too serious added, "Well, she could be right. I am a bit of a nuisance, especially when I come to your house for dinner and overdo it by eating too much!"

His chuckle was returned by a squeeze of his hand from Ella and a smile. "You do tend to eat a lot of food!"

When they entered the house, Eugenia was sitting in the chair in the living room and barely stirred when they arrived. Without turning, she said, "Come here and sit down by me." Both Ella and Nicholas looked at each other, then took a seat on the nearby sofa.

As they took their seats, and without as much as a greeting to Nicholas, Eugenia began speaking. "I have something to tell you, something that should have been told to you by your father whose death, by the way, was a cowardly act, leaving me to have this conversation on my own." She spoke as she stared straight ahead into the fireplace still filled with ashes from the last fire Alfred had burned. She spoke from the same chair that Alfred had sat in and prayed with his family telling them of his love for her, Ella, and the Lord.

She continued, "Many years ago, I witnessed something happen, at least I am assuming it happened." Eugenia sat, not looking at either of them as she delved into a long soliloquy. She told them about Alfred's infatuation with the minister's wife and the flirtations that went on between the two of them. "The minister was oblivious to it all. He was a very naive man, but I wasn't, and I could see what was happening between the two of them. They were acting like school children. I felt like a fool every time we would visit the minister's home, and they would disappear into the kitchen to make snacks. I could hear the giggles and laughter, only to have the minister say, 'They sure do enjoy making snacks. Isn't it wonderful that the Lord has blessed us all with such great friendship?' If I hadn't been there, only God knows what would have happened right in front of the minister's eyes. The minister was such a fool."

Ella and Nicholas sat stunned, wanting to speak, and to ask questions. However, each time they tried to interrupt, Eugenia acted as if she did not hear them and continued with her story, a story she had wanted to tell them for many years.

"So, the particular day I am speaking of was a day that changed my life. And now, unfortunately, it is changing everyone's including the lives of you, who are sitting here listening to my ramblings." Her face was taut and pale. She rose from her chair and walked to the sofa sitting next to Nicholas. Then she took his hand. "Nicholas, I love you like a son. I need to tell you something, both of you," she said, looking toward Ella. "Nicholas, I have... I don't know how to say this... and Alfred should have told you. I tried to tell you the day I mentioned the birthmarks that are so much alike on you and him. You are Alfred's son. I had so hoped that he would one day tell you. The only ones who ever knew were Marella, your father and me, but he was never aware that I was privy to the day you were conceived. I will not tell you where I was or where it happened. But I was there. I am so sorry. So very, very sorry." Tears rolled down Eugenia's face as she stood up from the sofa and walked to the steps. She turned to the couple and said, "I am afraid you have some very difficult decisions to make in a short amount of time." She wiped the tears from her face as she walked up the steps leaving Nicholas and Ella sitting on the sofa staring into the ashes of the fire.

20.

End of the Line

★★★★★★★

1864

Mr. Thompson, having taken Ella's advice, hired Benjamin to be a part-time telegraph operator, and after several weeks of training, he gave him the key to the office. His duties included working weekends. What Ella did not know was that Mr. Roman, while a respected citizen of Herronville and a faithful member of the church, was at times prone to overindulge in whiskey. With this condition being unknown to Mr. Thompson and at the recommendation of Ella, he hired him and entrusted him with all the duties of the office. Most of the folks in the village thought it was an error to trust him. They feared that many of their important communications, along with the news of the war and events of the outside world, would be missed if it was his responsibility to deliver them. However, Mr. Thompson dismissed their gossip, and on Friday, July 8, 1864, Benjamin accepted the key and the duties of the telegraph office. Robert had nothing but kind words about Benjamin's work. "He is doing a fine job! I am very happy with his performance. He is an asset to my office." Robert Thompson was now free to travel to visit his family in New York City with hopes of convincing his wife to move to Pennsylvania with their children.

Ella and Nicholas, still in a state of shock and confusion, continued their daily activities around town and working in their gardens together. They kept their secret very close. In fact, Nicholas and Ella had made the decision not even to tell his mother. "What purpose would it serve?" Ella said to Nicholas. "There have been enough hearts broken. One more will not bring any changes to what has been done."

But, a decision had to be made. While both fully realized the scandalous situation they were in, they were still very much in love. Unfortunately, an incestuous marriage would be wrong. Yet their love for each other was so strong that it was not out of the question for either of them to seriously consider going ahead with it. In mid-July, at Nicholas's suggestion, the couple met at their rock on the shore of Pony Lake, where he had proposed to her. They needed to make a decision about their current situation. Nicholas arrived early and sat on top of the rock, watching the small bluegills and sunfish chase each other in the shallow water near the shoreline. He looked up at the wispy boughs of the white pines swaying lazily in the wind when he saw Ella approach, carrying a wooden box.

"Hello!" he yelled as he waved to her. "Have you brought us a lunch?" He laughed.

She grinned. "No, something much better. And maybe the answer to our problem." She handed him the box as she climbed onto the rock and sat next to him.

"Have you been here long? You are here early."

"Long enough to learn that sunfish and bluegills don't seem to like each other, and I think bluegills are bullies." He looked quizzically at the wooden box. "So, what is in the magic box? Whatever could be in here that could fix the mess we are in?" he asked hopefully. "Ella, I am so sad," he added, his eyes moving from the box to her.

"Well," she said, reaching for his hand, "in the magic box are my insides. Everything that has ever been important to me. All of my dreams that have never been revealed to anyone, not even you. There are dreams in there that I believed would never come true. It is my magic box, and I want you to take it home. I want you to look inside of me. It is true that our lives are now in turmoil, but my dreams are not going to be destroyed by a turn of fate."

His smile slowly disappeared as his face turned ashen. "Ella, I am not sure what you are saying. Dreams in a box? Your insides?

I am confused." Ella heard the fear and uncertainty in his voice.

"Once you read what is in the box, I am praying that you will come to the same decision that I have come to."

Still staring at the box, he mumbled, "And what is that?"

"That regardless of the situation, I love you, and we should be together. How we conduct ourselves during our lives will be up to us. Have you changed your mind about me?" she asked in a determined voice, her eyes filling with tears. "If you have, tell me now, and I will take my dreams and leave, no matter how much I love you."

Nicholas was filled with anxiety. The feelings that used to be anger took on a new form. "Ella, I will always love you. We will somehow make this work. I know your mother hopes that we will not continue on, but if she does not accept us, then we will move away. I love you, Ella." He set the box on the rock, pulled her close to him, and kissed her. After sitting and gazing into each other's eyes for what they felt to be the best moment of their lives, they climbed off the rock. Ella was content with her decision to be married one day, and Nicholas filled with anxiety as he carried all of Ella's dreams in his hands.

Benjamin Roman loved to drink and dance, and during one warm night in late July, he attended a Polka dance in the nearby town of Lackawaxen. By all accounts, the dance started in the afternoon and lasted into the wee hours of the next morning. He had arrived early and had been drinking heavily before arriving. He drank more than his share of corn liquor that night and, as usual, made a fool of himself trying to kiss women on their cheeks. On unsteady legs, he would ask woman after woman to dance with him. However, after being turned down by one after the other, he would make a spectacle of himself as he danced across the dance floor alone.

At 4:30 in the morning, after falling asleep against the wall of the dance hall, he was awakened by Jacob Hansel, who was on his way to his blacksmith shop to begin his workday. Jacob walked up to the sprawled figure of Benjamin and nudged him with the toe of his boot. "Benjamin, get up! Time to go home," he said loudly.

"Thank you for waking me," he muttered to Jacob, not really meaning it. Slowly Benjamin stood up, braced himself against the wall, then staggered to his wagon and began his way back home to prepare for his day's work.

When he arrived home, he tried to sober up in the two hours left before he had to be at the telegraph office. Still not in his right mind, he staggered to work and tried to open the door several times by stabbing his key into the padlock. Finally, he succeeded and entered the building, collapsed on the comfortable chair in front of the telegraph machine, and readied himself to work for the remainder of the beautiful sunny day. Regardless of his best efforts and the click-clack of the telegraph machine, he was unable to stay awake.

At 1 p.m., the Erie Railroad locomotive number 171 left Port Jervis, New York, heading west to the newly built prison in Elmira, New York. The train was carrying 833 Confederate prisoners, mostly captured at the battle of Cold Harbor, VA, 128 Union soldiers responsible for guarding them, and the engineer and crew of the train. Unfortunately, also traveling on the same track was Erie coal train number 237 loaded with coal and heading east to Hawley, PA. The responsibility to warn the train of any danger that might lie ahead was telegrapher Benjamin Roman's.

Still incapacitated from last night's revelries and in a mental haze, he mistakenly gave the 'all clear' signal to both trains. At approximately 2:30 p.m., the trains collided on a blind curve known as King & Fuller's Cut. Sixty-Five Union guards and Confederate soldiers were killed, while several hundred others were injured. The dead and wounded would be cared for by citizens from all the surrounding communities. The following day, after learning of his tragic negligence, Benjamin Roman left his residence and was never seen again.

On the day of the great train wreck, Ella and Nicholas were weeding Mrs. Haff's garden. Word of the crash quickly reached Herronville and the surrounding towns, asking anyone who could, to come and help with the dead and the injured. Nicholas and Ella rushed to Nicholas's wagon and quickly headed off to the site of the horrendous scene, giving rides to others who were on foot. Neither one spoke as Nicholas encouraged his horse to move quickly to the horrific scene. The only words spoken were prayers being mumbled by the passengers in the back of the wagon. When they arrived, hysteria already filled the air, with the screams and cries of the victims of the wreck and those attending the injured. Stepping off the wagon, Ella and Nicholas stood in shock as they surveyed the scene. Then, they moved forward to offer assistance where they could.

Nicholas was called to help at a boxcar that had overturned and contained a hundred or more Confederate prisoners. Ella, in spite of her condition, looked to offer whatever aid she could. She was drawn forward toward the engine of the train, which lay on its side, creaking and smoking. The engineer was pinned against the boilerplate of the train and slowly being scalded to death by the escaping steam. He screamed in agony but somehow, saw her approaching him through the crowd of people staring at him.

"Go back, go back, it's going to explode," he groaned.

Ignoring the engineer's warning, she stumbled through the people who tried to hold her back. She had to try to save him. When she reached him, she knelt next to him and took his hand to comfort him as he mumbled in final moments for her to move away. Seconds after he took his last breath, Ella rose, and the boiler exploded, sending her hurtling into the air and onto the ground. When the danger appeared to have passed, other rescuers moved in and gently picked up her lifeless body and moved it to the site where the other victims of the wreckage were lined up, side by side.

21.

Herronville

★★★★★★★

1865

Ella's death, accompanied by Eugenia's revelation of Alfred being his father, hit Nicholas hard. Any progress he had made mentally from his time in the war was lost. There was nothing that he did during the course of his daily life that did not remind him of her. He read her letters in the wooden box over and over.

He and Eugenia drifted apart. She blamed him for taking Ella to the crash site. "What were you thinking, Nicholas? You are directly responsible for her death!" she had told him the day they buried Ella next to her father. However, she did admit to herself that, though Ella's death was horrific, the thought of trying to love a child conceived during a rape would have been as difficult as coming to grips with the possibility of Ella and Nicholas ever being married.

On sunny days, he took walks on the path to the rock at Pony Lake and sit where she had asked him to read the letters in her magic box, to look at 'her insides,' to decide if he loved her. It was clear to him that he loved her. He never really got the chance to tell her the answer to the question that she wanted to know. He wanted to tell her how much he loved her, how he had loved her since the days when she made him lemonade. He wanted to share with her how he showed off by doing an exaggerated tug on the reins and brought his father's horse to a stop as he loudly barked out, "Whoa!" and chatted with her. He loved her from the times they sat on the rock as teenagers and secretly held hands and how he had thought of her every day during the war, or how he had dreamt of her every night at that time. Sadly though, He never had the chance to tell her that they would not be wed. And that decision caused him to feel enormous guilt. He kept the secret from his mother, and her sorrow for him only added to his guilt. There was no one to talk to, no one who would understand. He finally decided that he had to leave Herronville; too many ghosts now inhabited it. He would have to leave his mother with hopes of returning one day, with hopes that she would never know the truth.

———————

On April 10, 1865, word was received at the telegraph office that the war had ended the day before. It affected Nicholas in a very strange way. He felt a freedom knowing that the war he did not believe in but had regardless fought in was over. It had been almost a year since Ella's death, and his urge to leave Herronville grew stronger with the war's end. He had hinted of his desire to leave to his mother, explaining that he "had to get away." A week after the South's surrender, as he and Margaret ate dinner, he spoke to her about his intentions.

"Mother, if I were to leave here, would you come with me?" he asked.

His mother sat up straight, "Where would we go? I am an old woman. I don't believe I could leave here. Where in the world would we go?" she repeated.

He did not have the nerve to look at her but rather stared at his half-empty plate, "I don't know. Somewhere," he mumbled.

She laughed, "Well, Nicholas, where in the world is somewhere?"

"I don't know, but would you go?"

"Oh, Nicholas, I am too old. But I know you are not happy. You have not been happy since before Ella's death."

"Why would you say that? I loved Ella. She made me happy!

110

And living here without her is not good for me. I need to leave." His voice was quivering. "Why would you think I was unhappy before? We were in love."

His mother peered at him, "Nicholas, I know your secret. Eugenia told me the truth before Marella knew she was even going to have you. She was aware of Alfred being unfaithful. She knew you were his son. Neither of us thought in a million years that you two would fall in love." She pushed her chair back, stood up, went to Nicholas, and pressed his head gently against her side while he stared into the hearth with tears falling from his eyes.

In September, on a warm, late summer day, Nicholas packed his father's wagon while his mother watched. Turning to her, he repeated, "I promise I'll be back for you."

Margaret smiled softly and repeated, "I'm an old woman, Son. I will stay in Herronville. This is my home."

Saddened by her decision, he put his arm around her shoulder, "Okay, Mother, I understand."

Then he asked her to walk with him to Pony Lake. They sat on the rock and talked about his father, Ella, and of all the picnics and great times they had enjoyed at the lake. Unfortunately, Alfred's death on the shore of the lake had dampened much of the good times. They sat staring into the water and at the bluegills chasing the sunfish.

"So, tell me again about this town you are going to, Nicholas."

Nicholas turned to her and spoke slowly, "As I told you, I only walked past it on the way home after I was discharged from the army. It's called Emmitsburg."

Part Two
EMMITSBURG

Prologue

Nicholas Haff sat on the side of the dirt road two miles south of Harrisburg, staring at his dead horse. Actually, it was his mother's horse, but he had taken it when he left home in Herronville, Pennsylvania. His journey to Emmitsburg, Maryland, would have to be curtailed until he removed the animal from the side of the road and buried her.

"Poor old thing. I never should have taken you," he muttered while kneeling next to her and caressing her mane. It was the same horse he had ridden when trying to impress his young girlfriend, Ella, when he was a child.

The horse was pulling the buckboard carrying Nicholas and his belongings when she slowed to a crawl, then collapsed. Nicholas had anticipated that the old horse would probably have to be put down after they arrived in Maryland. He had started this trip to get away from the pain of the deaths of dear ones so close to him, but after a while, it became more of an excuse to travel and find the woman who had cared for him when he was suffering from the fatigue of war. He met her when he stopped to hear Lincoln speak at Gettysburg. She had treated him with kindness and nursed the infection in his eye. The eye never totally healed and still oozed pus and caused double vision. Now he wondered if what the North had fought for was worth it as the country seemed more divided than ever. The Negroes seemed as lost as puppies that had wandered from their mothers. He stood up beside the horse's corpse. "I'm sorry, old lady. It's my fault," he said with a quiver in his voice.

The horse's eyes were wide open, and he could see himself mirrored in them. As he looked at the animal wondering how he would be able to dispose of her, he realized that other than his mother and father, he had known the family horse longer than any other living creature on earth. In his mind, he could not justify leaving the animal to lie on the road allowing the vultures and other predators to rip and tear at her hide. He looked around and saw several farms in the distance. Without much thought, he started walking toward the one that appeared to be closest, leaving the wagon and his belongings behind, hoping a vagabond would not pilfer any of it.

The war had ended several months before he began his trip to Emmitsburg; however, the battles continued to be fought in his head where images of places and people sometimes appeared. One vision, in particular, occurred along the route as he imagined confederate soldiers passing by his buckboard and begging for food. En route, at times, he encountered a vagrant sleeping against a wall which he mistook for a corpse. He felt that his life was unraveling before him. He hoped his anxiety and episodes of rage would be changed by this trek to Emmitsburg to reunite with the woman who had befriended him in Gettysburg. He wanted very much to kindle a relationship with her.

Shaking his head, he came out of his daze when he neared the farm. Right now, he needed a shovel to dig a hole and bury his horse.

When he approached the farm, a dog began to bark and howl as it ran toward him. His blood turned cold as he got into a defensive position, sure he was going to be attacked. As the black and white long-haired mutt approached him, he stomped his foot and yelled, "git!" and the dog lay down, his head on his paws looking up at Nicholas. Nicholas laughed as he realized how ridiculous he must have looked to the woman as he stood in his defensive position, hands in front of his face with his fist clenched as she stood on the porch staring at him with her head cocked.

He gazed back at her, deciding whether to ask to borrow the shovel. He was not too far from Gettysburg, and people there were still wary of former confederate soldiers looking to come north and start over in life. Personally, he had no animosity toward them, as most of them had lost everything. He pitied them and felt sorry for their families, and in his dreams, he attempted to reach out and touch the faces of those who he had watched die.

Both the woman and Nicholas stood in place and continued to stare at each other. The black and white dog was now creeping closer to him, tail swishing.

"Mister, you are on my property! What do you want?" the woman yelled, a slight quiver in her voice. "You'd be wise to turn around and move on. There is nothing here for you."

Nicholas turned quickly to look down at the dog, who was no longer a threat. In fact, he was tugging on his pant leg, hoping for a treat. Without breaking his stare at the woman, he reached down and patted the dog's head.

"I need a shovel!" he yelled to the woman. "My horse has died, and I need to bury her. She is lying on the side of the road."

The woman peered at him. "You ain't a deserter, are you? Cuz if you are, I will shoot you dead!"

Nicholas continued to scratch the dog's head. Her threat did not scare or deter him. He had faced many enemy bullets and was not afraid of her threat.

"I just need a shovel," he repeated. "If you could help out, I would appreciate it and would surely be grateful. And I am certainly no deserter. I fought in the army at Gettysburg and lost many friends there."

It was several minutes before either of them spoke. And with what Nicholas decided would be his final plea, he yelled, "Please, ma'am, I need a shovel to bury my horse!"

As she turned away, she spoke loud enough that he could hear her, "I have tools. I will get them. Come and help me carry them and I will help you. I can't leave a horse on the road." Nicholas trudged toward her house, followed by the friendly dog.

22.

Harriet

It took Nicholas and Harriet, the woman whom he met the day he stopped and asked her for a shovel, two full days to complete the burial. By the time the enormous task was complete, the odor had begun to fill the air, and blowflies were landing on the hide. As he tamped the dirt down on top of the grave, tears welled up and said he was sorry out loud, turned and stood staring south toward Emmitsburg.

The first evening Harriet had offered him the loft in her barn to pass the night. He thanked her after eating her offering of lima beans and salted ham, then climbed the rickety ladder to the loft, nestled into the hay, and lay looking through the slats of the roof as the moonlight passed through. Recent memories flooded his mind; Beatrice, the woman he hoped would love him as much as he believed he loved her; his elderly mother, whom he feared and fretted would be dead before ever seeing her again; and Ella, the woman he had loved from the time they were children, the same woman he watched as she attempted to rescue a train engineer in a horrific accident. She was the true love of his life, yet even before her untimely death, he was unable to marry her due to circumstances beyond his control. He closed his eyes and slept, but dreams of war and death permeated the solace that usually came with sleep.

He awoke to find Harriet pitching hay to several animals in the barn below the hayloft where he nestled. She was a muscular woman he had realized, when she had helped him dig the grave for his horse the previous two days. *She's not a particularly pretty woman*, he thought as he stared at her pitching the hay with ease.

Nowhere close to the beauty of Beatrice.

"Good morning," he called to her. "How are you this morning?"

"That it is. Are you going to sleep the day away?"

He no longer had a timepiece since the day he lost his pocket watch on the battlefield at Chancellorsville and had never really missed it until now. He could tell the time within a few minutes by looking at the sun's position. However, as he stood now in the dark barn, he was without a clue of the time.

"Almost noon," she said without emotion. It was how she appeared to Nicholas, emotionless, except for when he first encountered her and threatened his life, thinking he was a deserter. She stopped pitching hay and leaned on the pitchfork. "Can I get you some breakfast? You'll be needing something in your belly for your journey."

"That isn't..." he began.

Interrupting him, "Yes, it is. That's what decent people do, feed their guests, wanted, or unwanted." Still emotionless, she continued, "And it ain't gonna be anything that good. Some eggs and a piece or two of bacon. Not much bacon here anymore. The Union boys took most of my pork months ago, and I am waiting for my last hog to get a bit larger before I butcher him." She turned and grasped her fork and threw one last pile of hay toward a cow. "Get down off of the loft and get cleaned up and come into the house. Wipe your boots before coming in, and I'll make you something."

Nicholas moved to the loft ladder, and as he descended, he turned to thank her, but she had disappeared. Approaching the open barn doors, he watched her as she entered the house and considered that it might be best if he washed his face and just moved on with his journey to Emmitsburg. *I feel I am being a nuisance here.* However, as he washed his face at the pump and began to wipe it on the sleeve of his shirt, she stood in the doorway and motioned to him, announcing that his breakfast was getting cold. It was then that the aroma of the bacon flowed from the house to his nose, and any idea of him heading south was forgotten for the moment. "Wipe your feet!" she yelled, pivoted, and returned into the house, the screen door slamming behind her.

Nicholas wiped his feet on the straw mat; in fact, he wiped them until he heard Harriet mumble, "Don't wear the darn thing out." As Nicholas walked into the kitchen, the enticing smell of the food caused him to drool a bit. He had nothing to eat in the past two days, with the exception of jerky that he had brought from home. This was the first time that Harriet offered him anything to eat other than a place to sleep since his arrival for assistance.

"Sit down, eat," she said. "The house is a mess. I'm not much of a housekeeper." She was right. As Nicholas looked around the cabin, it wasn't like the comfortable home his mother and late father had provided him in Herronville.

"I think it's just fine, and your cooking is real good!" he exclaimed, biting into a piece of bacon. "Real good. It may be the best I've ever had!"

"It's bacon and eggs, how good can it be?" she said and shook her head.

"Well, it's good." He laughed. "I was starving, but that doesn't mean it wouldn't be good even if I wasn't starving. It's really good. Thank you, ma'am. It's really good."

"Okay! Stop! I am sure it is good. Nicholas, eat!" she said, her lip curling into a half smile.

Nicholas cleaned his plate and wiped it clean with a hunk of bread. Harriet had disappeared into the parlor, which was the only other room of the house and served as a bedroom and parlor. There was dead silence, and Nicholas was unsure as to what to do. Should I just leave? He sat and waited. He then stood up and yelled into the other room. "Ma'am! Harriet, are you here? I think I'm going to leave now! Thank you for your hospitality and help with my horse. I have a few coins I will leave on the table. Thank you again. I'm leaving now!" he barked.

Suddenly from behind him at the door, she yelled, "Okay, and you don't have to leave coins."

Her response startled him, and he turned violently. In a flash he lashed out. "Don't ever sneak up on me! I could have killed you! Don't ever..." and he stopped in mid-sentence. Bowing his head, he continued, "I am sorry. I am so sorry. I did not mean to say those things to you. I sometimes have, I don't know, I guess anger problems. My doctor said it's from the war. I'm sorry. I will leave now. I didn't mean to scare you."

Harriet never flinched. She stood firmly in the doorway staring him down.

"Okay, Nicholas. If you haven't noticed, this farm is run down. I can't keep it up since my husband left. I have no one to help me. Would you like to stay on for a while and help me put it back in order? I don't have much money to pay you, but I will feed you, and we can fix a place for you to sleep in the barn. Please?"

"I don't know. I'm supposed to be going to Emmitsburg. Where is your husband gone?"

"It don't matter where he is, he's gone. Emmitsburg can wait. It'll be there. If this farm isn't repaired, it won't be here much longer, and I will be bankrupt."

"If it's okay, I will stay here tonight and sleep on it. If that is okay, I will need to take your horse and retrieve my wagon from the road. If that's okay with you," he stammered.

"That'll be fine with me, but I will go with you to get your wagon. It's the only horse I have." And with that, she walked to the corner, picked up her rifle, and said, "Let's go get it."

23.

Dillsburg

☆☆☆☆☆☆☆

As he lay in the loft the night Harriet asked him to continue living at her farm, he wondered what to do. He had very little money and really, no promise that he would find Beatrice in Emmitsburg. Even worse, she might be aghast when he showed up at her house without warning. I don't even know if she is still there. His thoughts jumped to Ella, his childhood love, in fact, the love of his life. It was an episode of his life that he hated to hang on to, but he knew that he would never forget her.

And to make matters worse, disturbing images of the war continued to haunt him. As time passed, he focused more on the friends who had died next to him on the battlefield. He hated it when people called him a hero because he went to war. The heroes are all dead. I'm no hero.

After thinking it over, he decided to stay and help Harriet for a while, and to move on to Emmitsburg in a week or two. He nodded off and dreamt of Rebels attacking and men dying next to him and of a train wreck. He awoke with a short yelp, covered in sweat.

He stood up, stretched, removed his sweat-soaked shirt, and wiped his skin with it. Brushing the hay from his pants, he climbed down the ladder, slapped the old horse on the rump and walked to the water trough, soaked his shirt in it, and splashed water on his face. He spied Harriet digging in the dirt alongside the house. Not wanting to startle her by walking up behind her, called out her name.

"Harriet! Good morning!"

She turned and looked at Nicholas, "Good morning. I see you've slept in again!"

121

He was taken aback, "What time is it? The sun is barely up!"

"It's past time to be out of bed. And don't expect any breakfast, I'm busy now." And without taking a breath, "Are you staying or not?"

Nicholas, the statement about not having breakfast foremost in his mind, without hesitation, answered her, "If you make me breakfast, I'll stay."

Without hesitation, she dropped her hoe and walked toward the door, "Okay, but don't take all day eating it. Wipe your feet before you come in."

Within three days, Nicholas realized that his best friend was going to be the shaggy dog that greeted him when he arrived. He began to call the dog Grant, named after the great general.

Nicholas sat, staring at the woman's back as she fried eggs and a small amount of sausage. "She has the oddest demeanor I've ever encountered. No wonder her husband left." He smiled as the thought ran through his mind. He thanked her as she slid the wonderful smelling eggs and sausage from the skillet to his plate.

Harriet sat at the far end of the table, finishing her coffee. She looked up and, with a tone of authority, said, "You can start digging some post-holes behind the house. We will need to eventually get a small herd of cows in here, and I don't have time to dig all the holes myself. I can do it, but as long as you are here, you can do it." She paused long enough to look at Nicholas to see if he had any reaction, negative or otherwise.

"I can do that. Do you know where you want the fence?"

"Far away from the house that I don't smell cow shit. I'd say at least several hundred yards, probably, farther the better."

"Okay, I'll get at it right now, I think it's going to be a hot one. Sun is warm already."

Without a word, she moved from the kitchen into the rear of the house. He had never been invited into the other room and figured he never would be. He walked toward the door with Grant at his heels and headed to the barn to grab some tools.

"She is without a doubt the strangest woman I ever met," he

said, half to himself and half to Grant. The dog looked up at Nicholas with an expression of agreement. Nicholas petted his scraggy head and smiled as he walked into the barn to gather tools to begin the chore of digging post holes in the hard soil. As he looked about the barn, he realized that Harriet had made no more mention of fixing the barn up into a livable situation for him. *Maybe it's just as well because if she doesn't start to be friendlier to me, I may just soon leave.* He thought before throwing several shovels and hoes over his shoulder. Ready to earn his keep, he headed toward the weed-strewn field with Grant still tagging along.

About a quarter-mile past the back of the house, he tossed the tools to the ground, startling Grant and causing him to bark, which in turn made Nicholas laugh. "It's okay, boy. You can help me dig if you want to." He smiled at the dog, who was still showing signs of uneasiness. He picked up a hoe and scraped at the dirt, exploring for a soft spot of soil. After several attempts, he found a place that looked as if it had been dug at one time, possibly for another post. He looked up at the autumn sun; he couldn't remember a fall day as warm as this one.

As he cracked the soil, thoughts of digging at Gettysburg flashed through his mind. Some were in digging ditches to give his platoon protection from the Rebels, and some were for the graves to help bury his comrades who had fallen from the bullets of the Rebels. Those same thoughts turned to anger as he remembered again, friends who had died, and the faces of the young southern boys he had killed, who fell at the pull of his trigger, boys no older than fifteen.

He leaned on the handle of his hoe daydreaming of the war, while Grant sought shelter from the heat under a nearby briar patch. He relived his day with Beatrice, the woman he hoped to find in Emmitsburg. She, who had been so kind to him and had bandaged his eye. She very possibly saved him from complete blindness even though his vision was still distorted from the polluted water he had washed in near Chancellorsville.

The heat bore down on him and causing his daydream to come

to an end. Pulling off his shirt, he began to dig the first of many holes. While he dug, he began to hum a tune, and then slowly began to sing:

Oh where, oh where ish meine dog gone?
Oh where, oh where can he be?
Mit his ears cut long und his tail cut short...
No, that's not right, it's the other way around.
Mit his ears cut short and his tail cut long,
Oh where, oh where oh where ish he.

Not knowing the rest of the lyrics, he began to hum. He looked at Grant napping in the shade of the bushes. "I guess that's where he be, under a bush!" he laughed and continued to hum.

Again, without warning, "Don't you know the rest of the words?" Harriet quizzed.

Startled, he turned quickly, lifting the hoe above his head in a defensive position. "I told you, don't ever sneak up on me!" he hollered at her. Quickly gaining control of his anger, he lowered the tool and said, "Sorry. You startled me again. I don't like to be scared." Harriet didn't react, but instead sang:

I loves mein lager, tish very goot beer
Oh where, Oh where can he be?
But mit no money I cannot drink here.
Oh where, Oh where ish he?
Un sausage is goot, baloney of course
Oh where, Oh where can he be?
Dey makes um mit dog and dey makes Um mit horse
I guess they makes um mit he.

Nicholas leaned on his hoe and scratched his head. "I never heard the rest of that song, other than that first verse."

Harriet laughed, and when she did, Nicholas was surprised. He had never seen that side of her. The only side he had seen so far was the one giving him thoughts of leaving and traveling to Emmitsburg.

"Well, I don't think my new friend would appreciate the words," he said with a smile as he looked over at his new best friend snoozing in the shade of the bush.

"I won't tell him if you don't," she said with a grin. "Do you think you're digging too far away from the house? I know I told you I don't like the smell of cow manure, but I don't expect you'll be around to tend to the new herd when I get it, so maybe move it in another hundred yards. I don't want to have to drag hay too far out," she added nervously. Nicholas stared down at the hole he had begun to dig, aware of her apprehension.

"Sure," he said. "I can dig anywhere you want me too. I'll just finish up here and move closer to the house."

"That'll be fine, Nicholas. That will be fine." She turned and quickly headed back to the house.

"Thanks for the song," he murmured when she was out of earshot. He tossed his hoe on the ground and walked over to the sleeping Grant. Disturbing his sleep, he sat next to him. "Grant, I swear that woman is crazy. Something is not right with her. One minute she's singing and nice, and the next minute she is nuttier than a hoot owl." Grant picked his head up, stared at him, then dropped it down onto his two paws. Almost immediately, he closed his eyes again and was soon sleeping with a slight snore. Nicholas scratched him behind his ear, got up and retrieved his hoe. He began filling the small hole he had started earlier.

As he began to undo his work, he noticed something white and dirty, standing out from the dark brown soil. He scraped at it with his hoe, then dropping the hoe, he picked up the shovel, put his weight on it and scooped a large amount of dirt out of the hole and tossed it to the side. Exposed pieces of a broken white material stared up at him. Bending down, he scraped through the packed dirt with his fingers, and as he uncovered more of the fragments, he stared at them and mumbled, "Bones. These are bones." He picked up the shovel and began to dig at the hole until he found more and more bones. With a sudden clunk, he exposed what appeared to be a rounded white stone. Digging more, he saw that it was the top of a human skull. Startled, Nicholas jumped to his feet and quietly said, "What the hell!" He knelt back down and dug with his hands, removing a skull that looked like it had been crushed. Quickly he tossed it back into the hole, chards of it falling into the dirt. As fast as he could, he began to scoop the dirt back over it with his bare hands. When he stood up, he looked toward the house and saw Harriet peering in his direction. He stared back and whistled for Grant, then picked up his tools and moved closer to the house to dig the holes, wondering what to do. *I'm thinking it might be time to leave Dillsburg.*

It was later than usual when Harriet called him to dinner. He was hesitant to reply to her, trying to decide whether it was better to tell her he had changed his mind and was going to leave, or to sneak out in the middle of the night. The problem was, he had not earned enough money to buy a new horse or mule to hook his wagon to for his journey to Emmitsburg, and the truth was that he had been so occupied working on Harriet's ranch that he had, more or less, forgotten about Beatrice. He was very unsettled since finding the skull and didn't know if he should tell Harriet. Maybe she already knew about it. He walked to the pump, washed his face and hands, and went to the door. "I am here. Should I come in?" He always announced his arrival, not feeling comfortable entering her house without asking permission.

"Yes, dinner is ready. Come in, but wipe your feet first."

Upon entering the house, Nicholas sensed something different. There was a tablecloth, much nicer dishes, and shiny silverware. There was an aroma in the air that he had not noticed since leaving his home. It was the smell of a woman's perfume. It was comforting. Harriet was not in the kitchen, but he heard her milling around in the room next to the kitchen.

"I'll be out in a moment," she yelled from the other room. Within moments she opened the door and stepped into the kitchen. Nicholas stared at her. The person he had come to know, the lady who wore men's clothing and had skin as hard as worn leather, had transformed into a beautiful woman. She wore a blue dress and a beautiful necklace made of shiny stones. Her brown hair was no longer in a bun but now hung to her shoulders, neatly brushed and shiny. Nicholas stared in awe at the transformation, standing motionless. Harriet smiled. "Have you never seen a woman before?"

At first, Nicholas was speechless. Then he quietly responded, "Yes, but I have never seen a caterpillar turn into a butterfly that is so beautiful." As the words left his lips, he was embarrassed, almost ashamed. He had never spoken words like that to any woman, even to Ella, or Beatrice, the woman he wanted to know better and, in his mind, had married a thousand times. "I am sorry," he said quickly. "That was out of line. I apologize," he said as he bowed his head.

"Nicholas," she said, stopping him before he could add any further apologies. "I am flattered. Please, there is no reason to apologize. I just thought it would be nice for a change. I haven't dressed up, well, in years. So, I am very flattered by your compliments. Now, shall we have a seat and enjoy our meal? I made a rabbit stew. I hope you like it," she said with a smile he had never seen on her.

"Yes," he stammered, still staring at her beautiful transformation. "Yes, I do. My mother made it often."

"Well, I hope I can match your mother's. I am sure hers was wonderful," she said with the same soft smile. "Well, are you going to sit down. If the stew cooks any longer, it will be ruined. So, have a seat, and I will dish it out. Sit!" Laughing softly, she took his plate and ladled the stew into his bowl. She then took a freshly baked loaf from the counter, cut a large chunk, and placed it on the edge of his bowl. "The butter is nice and fresh." She filled her bowl with the stew and sat down at the table across from him.

"So, Nicholas, tell me a little about your life. I feel that I have not been quite as civil with you as I should have been. I am sorry for my behavior. That damn war has made me into quite a different person. It's changed me," she said, looking down at her stew.

Nicholas never looked up. "It's changed everyone," he snarled. "No one is the same. It's made everyone different."

Harriet's face turned pink as she hesitantly asked. "How did it change you, Nicholas?"

Nicholas continued to stare into his food. "Everyone seems to have changed. They change when I talk to them. They look at me differently than they did before I killed; before I saw men die. I think they think I'm a killer or evil. I had a girlfriend; her name was Ella. She died. My father died. Ella's father died—he deserved to die, but he died. It seems that everyone that I knew died. Now even my horse died!" He choked out the words and tried to swallow, as tears rolled down his cheeks.

Harriet rose from her chair and said softly, "Nicholas, none of that is your fault." She edged toward the back of his chair, stood behind him and started massaging his neck. He took a deep breath, composing himself.

"I'm fine, I..."

Putting her finger to her lips, she whispered, "Shh," and took him by both hands, helped him to his feet and led him slowly into the room where he had never been.

24.
Dreaming

✰✰✰✰✰✰✰✰

When he woke in the morning, she was gone. The night had been one of confusion. He had only kissed Ella, but what happened last night in the bedroom was unexpected. He felt guilt, guilt that enveloped and squeezed him so hard that he had to stop and breathe deeply. After Ella's death, he had promised himself that he would save himself for Beatrice, if it were to happen, if she would have him. As he lay in Harriet's bed, he closed his eyes and unwillingly fell into a deep and troubled slumber. He was having the same old dream that he had over and over since the war. First, the boy's face appeared, blood splattering onto him when he pulled the trigger. Then, another face appeared, a face that he had never seen in his dreams before. It was Alfred Samter, Ella's father, the man who had died on the shore of Pony Lake after shooting himself in the head. He was a man whom Nicholas had come to despise, a man that, at least to Nicholas, was a hypocrite, hiding behind the robes of Jesus Christ, another man that Nicholas considered to be a hypocrite. Jesus was a man who preached peace and was supposed to have some sort of control over his followers. Why would he allow such cruelty as wars? His dream became entangled with Ella's father and Jesus. Both were walking on the shore of Pony Lake. He could hear them talking about him. Alfred was telling Jesus that Nicholas was a non-believer. He told him that Nicholas had blasphemed the church and God the Father. Jesus was shaking his head. He faintly heard Jesus speak, telling Alfred that Nicholas would burn in the fires of hell for eternity unless Alfred could make him repent. The dream ended abruptly when he saw himself step out of the laurel bushes that covered the coastline of the lake, pistol in his hand, put the gun point-blank at Alfred's head, and pull the trigger. He looked Jesus in the eyes and said, "Hell don't scare me. I've already seen it." Jesus smiled and slowly disappeared. Nicholas, soaked in sweat, awoke, screaming and repeating the words, "I'd do it again! I'd kill him again!" He grabbed his chest, bit his lip, and slowly pulled himself together enough to dress and leave the room where he had forsaken a promise he had made to himself.

25.

Those Bones

☆☆☆☆☆☆☆

The note on the table said she was taking the wagon and going to town to get supplies and that he should make his own breakfast if he knew how to cook. She ended it with, "I hope you enjoyed last night!"

Nicholas put the note on the table and walked outside to the water pump. He stood staring off into the distance. His thoughts of what had happened the night before were bouncing around in his head; however, he replaced Harriet's warm body with what he imagined Beatrice's body would feel like. He had often thought of kissing her lips. He had kissed Ella's lips on the big rock they sat on at Pony Lake, but his fantasy of Beatrice was better than the actual kisses he and Ella had shared. He looked to the south, wondering how far Emmitsburg was. He had passed by it twice, once after the Battle of Gettysburg on his unit's march to Washington to be discharged, and then on the way back home. That was when he met Beatrice. They sat together at Gettysburg and listened to the President give his speech. He still did not understand the words Lincoln had said that day, but it was on that day he fell in love with Beatrice. *She is the most beautiful woman I ever saw. I need to go to Emmitsburg. I know I love her; I need to know if she loves me.*

He shook the daydreams out of his head and pushed the pump handle. As he splashed water on his face, he gave one last quick thought to last night and then headed to the barn to get tools to finish digging the holes he had started the day before. Grant, who was sleeping next to the barn, perked up his ears and headed toward Nicholas for attention. "Hey, Grant, how was your night? I'll bet not as good as mine!" he said with a chuckle. And as soon as he said it, he felt a surge of guilt overcome him. Grant's nudging brought him back to the present. "Okay, boy, let's get to work," he said, rubbing Grant's back.

It was not as hot as the day before. He hoped to finish digging all of the holes and to ask Harriet for his pay so he could continue his journey. He knew he had told her he would stay, but the more he thought of Beatrice, the more he wanted to go to her. The episode with Harriet, while being exciting, confused him. He had never expected that to happen. But now that it did, he hoped it would not become an issue with him leaving. "If I have to, I'll sneak out at night!" He began to poke his shovel into the hard soil, hoping he could dig all the holes needed before dinner. But as he dug, the bones he discovered yesterday began to prey on his mind. He stopped every few minutes and stared at the location. Regardless of his attempts to dig fresh holes, he was drawn to the hole with the skull. Finally, he grabbed his shovel and pickaxe and walked over to the location where he had been the day before. Grant, who had been lying next to him, stood up, stretched, shook his head, visibly disturbed by having to get up and move with Nicholas.

He stood above the place where he had piled back over the skull. "Who are you?" he asked. "How did you get here?" He began to dig. He wanted to find the bones before Harriet returned home. The soil was soft, and he was able to dig quickly. When he got close to where he thought the skull would be, he put his shovel down and began to dig with his hands, not wanting to damage the bones any more than they had already been. Grant sat next to him, watching curiously. The top of the tarnished skull was revealed as Nicholas carefully scraped the dirt away from around the fractured bones. Gently picking it up, he stared into the sockets. The dirty face stared back blankly into Nicholas's eyes. He had seen many dead men. He even saw exposed skulls of soldiers who were shot by canons and rifle shells but never an entire head stripped of its hair and skin. "Were you a soldier?" he asked the fractured head. He set the skull on the ground and shooed Grant away from the head that he was curiously sniffing. "Git, lay down," he ordered the dog. He considered whether he should look for the rest of the body, or to return to his job of digging holes for the fence. "Well, I've come this far, I might as well see all of you." He gingerly picked up the head. "I shall call you Alfred, because just as you are, so is he. Dead." He smirked as he said the words, then set 'Alfred' next to the pile of dirt, picked up his shovel, and returned to his digging.

The shovel began to scrape what sounded like either bone or rock. He stopped and tossed it aside, almost hitting Grant, who had edged closer to him, always eager for a bone. He got down on his knees and slowly digging into the soil with his hands, partially uncovered what looked like a shoulder bone or rib. After digging even deeper, he found was another skull, this one was not all bone, but had hair and pieces of skin attached to it. As the realization of what he had discovered became clear to him, he jumped to his feet and stepped back, staring into the hole. How long have they been here? How did they get here, and are there more? His mind raced with possibilities, and he feared he might have come upon something that would be best left well enough alone. Without voicing what he was really thinking, he thought he should move away from Harriet's farm as soon as possible.

Just as quickly as the thought crossed his mind, he grabbed his shovel, covered the bones, and moved as fast as he could back to the area where he had been digging the fence post holes. As he dug, his mind filled with thoughts, evil thoughts of how the bones were put in the shallow grave, and who put them there. He also knew that Harriet might have put them there or, at the very least, knew who had buried them. *Maybe it was a lover? Maybe two lovers? Will I be the next lover to end up in the ground? I should have resisted last night! I will leave tonight. I will wait until she falls asleep, hook her horse to my wagon, and move on toward Emmitsburg.*

As Harriet cooked dinner that evening, Nicholas tried to act as if everything was normal, but he was unusually nervous. He could feel her staring at him as if she suspected he had committed or was going to commit a crime. He tried to start a conversation with her, but his words sounded shallow, and her replies even more so. After much vacillation, he finally asked her if she had ever married. This question was far removed from the mindless conversation that had been taking place. Harriet did not reply immediately, but instead stared at the table and pushed her meal about on her plate.

"Why, have you not asked me that before? Is it because I had you in my bed? Or is it because you have never been in a woman's bed before? Or is it that you have fallen in love with me?" She paused. "Which is it? Or is it something else, Nicholas? Tell me. Why are you asking me now?"

Her answer to his question and her questions to him made him sit up straight. He had never heard a woman speak in such an unseemly and forward manner. He wanted to ask her why she was speaking in such a vulgar way, but in fact, he really wanted to ask her if she had killed the men that he had found buried in her yard. *Had she bludgeoned those men to death?* Instead, he calmly rose from his seat, "I was merely trying to know you better. I apologize if I have offended you. Thank you for the dinner and company, I am going to my bed. I will see you in the morning. And I will continue to dig the fence post holes. Good-night, Harriet." He walked toward the door when he was abruptly stopped by her voice. A voice as stern as any schoolmarm.

"Yes, I was married. I was married to a man who was a drunkard and a horse thief. He was hanged for stealing a horse near Gettysburg. And I was glad. I went to the hanging and never shed a tear as I watched him dangle from the rope and kick his feet," she said proudly. "I yelled to him during his last breath, 'You'll never hit me again, you son of a bitch!'"

"I am sorry to hear that story," Nicholas said softly. "No woman deserves to be treated like that. He surely deserved to swing at the end of a rope."

"Well, he's gone now. And I don't care a bit about him. And if he hadn't stolen a horse, he might still be alive and beating me."

"Again, I am sorry," he repeated. "Good night." He pushed the door open and walked to the barn, followed by Grant.

She knows! She knows that I am taking the horse!

He continued quickly into the barn, his stomach churning with a feeling of paranoia.

26.
Into the Night

☆☆☆☆☆☆☆

Nicholas sat on the edge of the loft, scared. Grant, too seemed aware that something was not right as he kept turning in circles trying to nest in the hay. Nicholas's thoughts rambled through his mind. It was like an endless loop of gunfire and screams. It reminded him of his time on the battlefield after he feigned death to try and end the visions of the carnage that he was encountering every day. He thought being home and away from the horrific scenes of violence that he would be able to return to who he had been before the war. Instead, as time passed, his stress had only gotten worse. He couldn't go a day without these visions filling his head. And now he had discovered more death. His thoughts went from asking Harriet if she knew about the men, to reporting to the sheriff what he had discovered on Harriet's property, to hooking his wagon to her horse and fleeing into the night. Her words that evening of her husband dangling on the end of a rope for horse stealing resounded in his head. However, the thought that he did not allow himself to dwell on, and was kept in the back of his mind, was that she was a killer. He refused to give it the attention he believed it deserved. *In my heart, I believe that woman killed those men, and I don't want to be buried next to them.*

Not knowing if his life was in danger, he decided he would take a chance on borrowing the horse and continuing on to Emmitsburg. *I will release the horse when I get close to the town, then stash the wagon in the woods, and set up camp until I can make a plan.* Grant still seemed uneasy and kept rubbing against his leg. Nicholas smiled. "You're goin' with me. If I'm gonna hang,

136

I'll need a friend there to comfort me!" he said with a forced laugh.

He couldn't figure out why he thought Harriet was directing her words about her husband's hanging at him. *One thing is for sure, I'm not going to hang around here and end up in a hole meant for a fence pole!* He stared down at the old horse standing in his stall, sleeping. "Yeah, you get some rest, we have a long day ahead of us." Grant barked at Nicholas as if in agreement. "You might just be smarter than the man I named you after," Nicholas said, addressing the hound. "Which wouldn't be too hard to do."

He decided to wait until the candles in the house were extinguished, then wait an hour or more before he hooked the horse to the wagon, and tried to slowly walk the animal out of the barn with as little noise as possible. There would be no reasonable alibi he could give to Harriet if she were to come out and find him during his escape. The more he thought about Harriet taking him into her bedroom, he realized it was her way of keeping him at her house. *She probably figures that I would want to do that every night. That I wouldn't want to leave! Maybe if I hadn't found those heads, maybe then I would have. Maybe those heads belonged to men who also were in her bedroom and tried to leave!*

It was a chilly night, but Nicholas was beginning to sweat, and his heart started to beat hard and fast. His anxiety became such that he was having trouble breathing. He climbed down the ladder from the loft and walked outside for air. Grant, who was still not situated in the hay, followed him out. As he looked into the sky, he remembered during the war how he would stare at the moon, wondering and hoping that Ella was doing the same. It was a bond he believed to be between them.

The final night of the Battle of Gettysburg was wet, and the moon was hidden. Lee had retreated, and the 151st Pennsylvania Volunteers–what was left of them–111 out of the 467 who started, rested uneasily. Nicholas had feigned death on the last day of

137

the battle. He had seen enough. As he looked into the sky, he remembered lying in the mud. Scared. Scared for many reasons. The other men knew he had pretended to be dead, and he feared they would return to Herronville and disclose his cowardice to his neighbors. He was scared that there would be another battle like Gettysburg, and that night he wrote a poem in his head for a letter that would never be sent. He looked down at Grant and began to recite the words he thought he had long forgotten:

"If I die, if I die
You will be my last thought,
If I die, I will bring the image of your face to my grave
If I die, if I die
Do not believe I am a hero, but honor those who died with
me
If I die, I will take my last breath saying 'Ella, I love you'
You are what..."

"Who in the world are you talking to?" A shock went through his body, as his long-forgotten letter was interrupted by Harriet's voice.

"Oh, Harriet, I was just reciting a poem from my childhood," he lied.

"Oh," she replied coyly. "Ella must have been your true love if you carried her in your heart throughout the war. I'm sorry, but I was standing here listening. I'm sorry. Forgive me."

He shifted his weight nervously, wondering if she suspected that he was going to attempt to leave in the middle of the night. *Why else would she come out here? She has never done that before.*

Trying to deflect the conversation, he said, "It's okay. Sometimes I think of the war, and when I do, I think of her. I **did** carry her in my heart. But she is gone now, and I must teach myself to move on." And then without a moment of hesitation, or with any thought, he asked, "Do you ever think of your husband, or miss him? I know you said he was no good, but surely there must have been a time..."

"I came out here to apologize for the conversation at dinner. It is no concern of yours of my past life, and none of mine, yours. I hope you will stay here for awhile. I need your help to finish up with the work you started. I like you, Nicholas. I hope you'll stay for a period. And just in case you are wondering about my morals, I do not offer my bed to just any man, but I find you special. Please do not think less of me for our encounter."

Nicholas was feeling vulnerable and thought it would be a good time to ask her about the bodies he had discovered. Still, he could not help thinking that the bodies he had uncovered were others she had taken into her bed. It preyed on his mind every waking moment. *Had their heads been bashed in while they slept?* But, instead of posing the question, he took a deep breath and said, "There is nothing to forgive. We are two of a kind, both suffering in our heads from romances gone bad, or separated by death, or maybe both. "Now, if you'll excuse me, I think I will take Grant with me to the loft tonight. Have a good evening, Harriet. I shall see you in the morning."

She nodded, her lips forming a smile of sadness, she turned and walked toward the house. "Have a good sleep, Nicholas."

He knew he couldn't sleep but would spend his time peeking through the spaces of the barn's siding, waiting for the house to go dark. "When it does, I will pack the wagon and hitch the horse," he said more to himself than to Grant, who was fast asleep in the hay, twitching every so often from a dream.

Several hours later, the lanterns inside the house were extinguished. He pictured her in the bed, remembering how she had touched him, and how he did not respond. Instead of pleasure, he felt guilt flowing through him and feeling that he was being unfaithful to Ella and Beatrice at the same time. One was dead, and one probably had no recollection of him. What should have been a memory of happiness became one of shame. That, combined with his fear of her killing him, was forcing him to leave. He walked the big horse to the front of the wagon and began to hitch her to it. When he was done, he called to Grant in a whisper. Grant lumbered toward him, stopping to stretch his legs and shook himself to get the loose straw off his matted fur. Nicholas reached down, picked him up, and set him on the seat of the buckboard. Then he pulled himself up next to Grant and slowly walked the horse out of the barn and down the trail toward the main road that would take him to Emmitsburg.

27.

Franklin Town

☆☆☆☆☆☆☆☆

Nicholas made the decision to travel at night during his escape from Harriet's farm and to travel in the forest during the daylight hours. After three hours, and what he estimated to be approximately three or four miles, he coaxed the old horse a half-mile off the road into a heavily wooded thicket. He was tired and looked around for an area where the horse could graze on grass and weeds while he attempted to rest. When he arrived at an area appearing suitable, he brought the animal to a halt, jumped off the buckboard, and helped Grant, who had been standing on the seat staring down at him, to do the same. "Dog, you are one lazy animal, and if I may add, not very good company. You slept all the way here!" Nicholas laughed as he picked Grant up and placed him on the ground then moved forward to unhitch the horse. Patting the horse on the nose, he said, "And you, I have no idea what your name is, so I am going to call you 'General' because you always will be leading me. In fact, I am going to call you 'Abner,' just like my general in the war, Abner Doubleday."

He walked to the back of his wagon and searched through his sacks. The only food he had brought was jerky and very little of it. Grant gazed up at him expecting his breakfast. "Well, Grant, I think we have a problem. One of us is going to have to forage for food. And seeing as how you don't have any skills in that area, at least none that I can see, I will have to go out on my own. Maybe I will find a chicken or a farmer that would be willing to share some grub." Nicholas took Abner's reins and tied him to a sapling and instructed Grant to stay with the horse. However, as he set out, Grant was right behind him.

He did his best to keep his bearings in the early morning light. The last thing he wanted was to lose track of where he had left his wagon and Abner. *Why didn't I think of food before I left? Maybe I should have stayed where I was? I am sure by now, Harriet has somehow contacted the sheriff. I am sure to be found and hung.* He walked for over an hour before he saw a house in the distance, smoke coming from its chimney. Grant nudged him and looked up at him quizzically, making Nicholas smile. Although his mind was filled with anxiety, he spoke to the dog in a comforting tone. "Don't worry, boy, we'll be okay." He stopped and peered at the house, hoping to see an outbuilding where he could possibly steal a chicken or gather some eggs. He had only several dollars to offer for food, but he hoped that the people living there would offer something for free.

As he approached the house, he spotted children playing in the yard and several chickens pecking at the ground. At first, Nicholas considered walking toward the children and offering them a dollar for a chicken and a couple of eggs. On further consideration, he feared they would run into the house and cause a parent to overreact, possibly confronting him with a gun. At the thought of someone pointing a weapon at him, he realized that he was helpless. He had no gun, only a knife. *Not much of a fair fight, a knife against a gun!* "Need to get a gun somewhere," he muttered. By now, the children had seen him standing near the thicket at the edge of the woods. One of them waved and yelled to him, "Hey, mister! Whatcha doin' in the huckleberry patch?"

He froze as he tried to come up with an answer. Suddenly it came upon him. He figured he was miles away from Harriet's ranch. There certainly would not have been time for anyone to know of the theft of a horse and dog yet. *I will concoct a story and certainly be able to gather food for a day.*

Giving them a big wave, he began to walk steadily toward the children. "Hello!" he yelled out. Suddenly timid, Grant stayed several feet behind him. "My name is Nicholas, and I have a dog with me. His name is Grant!"

The children stood their ground, not sure if he was telling them the truth.

The tallest one, a boy, hollered back, "I don't see no dog!" Nicholas turned back. The boy was right. Grant had lain down to rest in the tall grass and was not visible to the boy.

Nicholas quickly walked back to Grant, picked him up, and showed him off to the children as he approached them. "His name is Grant! Like General Grant! But he's smarter than him though!" he said, faking a laugh as the dog struggled to be put on the ground.

Nearing them, he counted three children, the tall boy, a shorter one, and a little girl. None of them showed any sign of being afraid of him. The girl squealed, "Grant? Here, Grant!"

The oldest boy came forward toward Nicholas in a defensive posture. With a tone to match, he said hesitantly, "My name is Jacob. What is your name, and why are you on this property, and why were you in the huckleberry patch? There ain't no berries this time of year!"

Nicholas smiled, reached down, and scratched Grant behind the ear, and looked up at the boy. "Jacob? That's a good biblical name. My father's name was Jacob," he lied. "My name is Nicholas. Already told you his name," he smiled as he looked and pointed at the dog. "To tell you the truth, Jacob, I got lost. We were camped about two miles or more from here, and me and Grant, well, we got turned around..."

Jacob interrupted, staring at the dog, "Well, what were you doing in those woods? How did you get turned around? Why were you in the woods?" Then he looked up at Nicholas and continued, "There's nothing in the woods, except snakes and a deer or two. You weren't hunting, you ain't got no gun."

He hadn't expected the young boy to be so inciteful, so he decided to tell him the truth.

"Well, Jacob, the truth is, we were looking to find some food. We ran out about a day or so ago, and we are really hungry. So, if you could spare some bread or an egg, anything really, we'd be very grateful."

Grant had worked his way around Nicholas and was happily being petted by the girl. "My name is Sarah!" she announced loudly.

Under the direct stare of Jacob, Nicholas responded in a kind voice, "Why that's a beautiful name, for a beautiful little girl, and also a very biblical name!"

He hadn't noticed that the smaller boy had slipped away and was not in view, which was now making him nervous. "Where'd your little brother go, Jacob?" he asked unsteadily.

Jacob didn't reply to the question. Instead, "Did you fight in the war? If so, what side?"

Nicholas was beginning to feel very uncomfortable now, and his anger was flushing over him. He whistled for Grant. "I think we will just be moving on. I wish you could have been a bit more hospitable, but we will be going now. C'mon, Grant, let's see if we can't find us a rabbit or squirrel to fix for dinner." Grant, who was enjoying his massage by Sarah as if he had been used to such regular pampering, barely responded to Nicholas's call. Jacob and Nicholas exchanged stares, and as Nicholas turned to walk off toward the berry patch with Grant finally tailing behind, Jacob hollered and stopped him.

"Come into the house. My mother made cornbread last night; it is a bit hard, but with butter on it, it's good." Nicholas turned to thank him, but Jacob had already started toward the house. Nicholas and Grant quickly followed him and Sarah. *Maybe I can persuade him to give us some food for our trip to Emmitsburg.*

As he trailed the tall boy and his little sister through the door and into the kitchen, the small boy appeared from behind the door, slamming it behind him and Grant. Sitting directly in front of him at a large wooden table was an old man, rifle on his lap. He gazed at Nicholas for a time, then said, "I bet you were one of those goddamn Yankees that killed our boys. Now eat some of that cornbread, then we'll talk about the judgment of the Lord."

28.
Return to Gettysburg

☆☆☆☆☆☆☆

Rather than return the gaze of the man, Nicholas looked down at Grant, who was cowering at his feet, looking up at him. The poor dog was scared from the noise of the door being slammed. "It's okay, boy." Then turning his attention back to the old man who was clad in a mix of Confederate uniform and tattered civilian clothing. "I did," he said unemotionally. "And I believe you may have been on the other side, killing those of us dressed in blue."

"I was," came the man's reply. "Did you fight down the road?"

"I did."

"Did you kill anyone?"

"I did."

"How many?"

"More than I wanted to. You?"

"Not enough."

He was in Chancellorsville, but he didn't fight there. At least he didn't fight in a battle, but it was where Nicholas affirmed to himself that he didn't believe in the war. He didn't care if anyone owned a slave; he didn't care about states' rights. He wanted to go home. He was a farmer, not a killer. He swore he was not going to kill anyone, at least that is what he was thinking at the time. He had heard of an upcoming campaign in which the rebels were heading north, and a significant battle was set to begin. But before that battle, he would encounter one of his own, one that would haunt him for the rest of his life.

A soldier who was not from Herronville had joined his unit as they were en route from Fredericksburg; in fact, he wasn't from the Northeast, but rather from the Michigan 19th Volunteers. Up until that time, Nicholas had been sleeping in a dog tent by himself. When Private Thompkins arrived, he was assigned to Nicholas's tent. It was two nights into the march when it first happened. Awakened by Thompkins' hand touching his leg, Nicholas removed the soldier's hand and returned back to sleep. He believed Thompkins had been dreaming. Two nights later, Thompkins lay in the tent on his pallet, drinking from a bottle of whiskey. Nicholas refused the offer of a drink, thanked him, closed his eyes, and pretended to be asleep. All the while, Private Thompkins continued to drink, babble nonsensically to Nicholas, and sing songs that sounded like they had been made up by the soldier. Two things happened that night. First, the drunken soldier reached over and attempted to kiss Nicholas on the mouth at the same time he placed his hand on Nicholas's groin. Startled, Nicholas scurried out of the tent, breathing deeply, his heart skipping several beats. Without re-entering the tent, he reached in and pulled his bedroll out onto the ground, where he crawled under his blanket and tried to go back to sleep. The second thing that happened was gunfire coming from the wood line. A small skirmish ensued. It was by no measure considered a battle; however, it was the first time Nicholas had fired his rifle toward the enemy. Thompkins never appeared from inside the tent to return fire.

The roll call at the morning reveille found Thompkins to be AWOL. However, upon returning to his tent, Nicholas discovered Thompkins dead in his bedroll. Two bullet wounds, apparently from stray bullets fired by the Rebels, one in his chest and one in his head, had found their marks. Later that day, after a prayer was said, Nicholas and several others buried him in a shallow grave. Over it, they placed a cross made of two sticks that they had lashed together with some leather laces. Nicholas walked away from the grave with a smile that was more of disdain than of sadness.

He went back to his tent and removed Thompkins' belongings. Then, he sat on his bedroll and cleaned his pistol, and prepared for the trek north where they would bivouac at a small town in Pennsylvania called Gettysburg. He was getting closer to home.

———————

Nicholas was seated at the opposite end of the table from the old man while Grant leaned against his leg, seeking safety. A half-smile came across the man's face as Nicholas stared at the cornbread placed in front of him by the older boy, deciding whether to eat it or not. Finally, he put a piece in his mouth, broke a piece off, and reached down to share it with Grant.

"Got a name?"

"Nicholas, Nicholas Haff."

"German?"

"Yep. On my father's side. French on my mother's side. You have a name?"

"Andrew, Andrew Jones. Welsh," he added. "Born in Charleston, now a resident of nowhere. Thank you, Mr. Lincoln."

An uncomfortable silence enveloped the room as both men sat staring into each other's eyes.

"Well, Nicholas, you can start by telling me what you are doing on this property?" The man was still cradling and patting his gun as if it were a child.

"I told the kids. I got lost looking for food. So, I am just guessing, because you are sitting looking across from me with a rifle cradled in your arms, and by the way you introduced yourself to me, that I am not going to get much more than this cornbread, which by the way is delicious. My dog would also appreciate a bite of scraps if you could spare anything." Nicholas stared at the man's hands to ensure he wasn't going to make a move on him.

"I like dogs. I like them a whole lot more than people. I especially like them more than people like you—northern boys." He paused and looked at the children who had all settled nervously on the floor. Sarah played with Grant, who was enjoying a scratch behind one of his ears. "You see these three kids?" he asked, and without waiting for a response continued. "They ain't mine. I been raisin' them since I found them hiding after the final battle. I was walkin' in circles, my boys had scattered, and I was tired of fighting and was going home. I was done. I thought I could work my way back to the south, but that was futile. The Yanks were everywhere. So, I headed to the north and east and was able to hide in the woods, just like you been doing, and I ain't stupid. I know you're hiding from something, but I really don't care. Everyone is hiding from something, and that's how I ended up with these kids. They were hiding in the woods too, hiding from their daddy who beat them every day." Andrew looked down at Grant, "Jacob, get that dog a bone, or some smoked meat. And don't call him Grant. We will call him Lee for now. If that's okay with you, Nick," he said sardonically.

Looking up from Grant, Nicholas responded, "Nicholas."

Andrew chuckled, "I prefer Nick, and as long as I have the gun, I will do and say as I please, Nick."

There was an uncomfortable feeling in the room, and Nicholas knew he had met his match, for now.

"So," Andrew said, stretching his legs, "as I was saying before I was rudely interrupted, "I was in the woods and come upon these children, half-starved and dirty as an opossum. At first, I thought I would just leave them to make it on their own, but then I got to thinking, if I were to pretend to be their daddy, I might be able to stay here above the line. I knew the war would end soon, and from everything I had heard, there wasn't much left in the South. So, I 'adopted' them, found this old shack, and set up housekeeping," he laughed almost maniacally while staring at Nicholas.

In the meantime, Jacob tossed the dog a meaty bone, "Here, Grant," he said as the treat landed at Nicholas's feet.

Andrew's head snapped toward Jacob. "Boy, come here!" he ordered. Jacob looked at Nicholas with fear in his eyes. It was the same fear Nicholas had seen in other boys' eyes during earlier times. "I said, come here!" The boy moved cautiously toward the man, and as he approached him, the words, "Assume the position!" blared out of Andrew's mouth. Jacob immediately knelt next to him.

"What did I say the dog's name was to be?"

"Lee, sir."

"So, you disobeyed me, didn't you!"

"Yes, sir."

As Jacob answered the question, Andrew swung the stock of the rifle and crashed it into the boy's face. Blood spattered about the room. Grant began to howl in terror. Nicholas's move toward Andrew was thwarted by the rifle pointed at his face. In a strangely calming voice, Andrew said, "Sit back down, Nick. Don't let's have a problem. The war is over, but I am the commander of this field we are now engaged on." He then addressed the boy, "You pick yourself up, go outside and lay in the dirt, and you pray for forgiveness. You tell the Lord how you have disrespected me. Don't make it two, where there used to be four. Now go."

29.

Billy

☆☆☆☆☆☆☆

His bitterness after the battle of Gettysburg had ended was heightened when his captain, a man whose name he had forgotten, or more likely, had forcefully put out of his mind, called him from his tent. His unit had been all but wiped out except for a small percentage of men who would travel with him to Washington to muster out in a couple of months. As he crawled from his tent, the captain stood stoically, his right arm wrapped around the neck of a young soldier.

"Private Haff, this is a soldier of the South, The Confederacy," he said, spitting the words out as if they had burnt his tongue. "This young man has been interrogated and has decided to stay loyal to his President, Jefferson Davis. I have given him the opportunity to help us in our fight. He has, however, decided not to do so. Inasmuch as he has made that decision, I want you to take him and dispose of him off of the battleground, away from the other men who died for their cause. Do not bother to bury him. Let the animals and birds of prey do what they will with him."

Nicholas had given up any urge to pull the trigger on anyone. He had seen too much death, and had the battle not ended; he was considering deserting. Now he was facing a direct order to kill a man. A boy. A young boy, maybe fifteen.

"Sir, with all due respect, do you believe it is necessary to kill him? He's only a kid. Can't we just take him prisoner?"

The captain glared at Nicholas, "Look around you. What do you see? That's right, dead bodies. Bodies put there by people like this piece of shit." Releasing the man, he shoved him toward Nicholas. "Now, Heff, or whatever the hell your name is, take this traitor of America off into that field over there and do as I ordered you to, and that, son, is a direct order. If I don't hear a gunshot in that field in the next five minutes, the next one you hear will be your last. Now take him and go dispose of him."

———————————

Nicholas sat back down on his chair at the table, facing Andrew. Grant was crouched in a corner, cowering. Jacob, holding his face, went outside, and through the open door, Nicholas could see him lie down in the dirt, his hands folded in prayer. Terrified, Sarah was sitting on the floor next to Grant, trying to comfort him. The younger brother, the one who had slammed the door, stood over Jacob, and yelled down at him. "You pray! You pray harder, you son of a bitch!" And as he screamed the words louder and louder, Jacob bawled out to the Lord for his forgiveness. Nicholas, with his head cocked, knew that this was a scenario that had been repeated many times.

Who was number four? What was number four? Where was number four? Nicholas thought.

Andrew bent over to tie his bootlaces. "Don't even think about attacking me, Nick. I don't want to hurt you or your dog, at least not yet anyway. So, tell me again about your time in the war, the war that set all them darkies free."

Nicholas looked over at Grant. He was shaking with fear, Sarah as well. *I wonder what he's done to her.* His mind raced, trying to figure a way to escape and to take the children with him. The gun he had taken from home was in his bag at the campsite with the horse. He was sure if he could reach Andrew, he could easily overpower him. After some thought, he began.

"Okay, Andrew, if you want to know, I killed a lot of you devils. Too many to count, and I loved every time I pulled the trigger and watched one of you drop to the ground. And I am glad that every Negro in America is free. And you, Andrew, are not even half the man any of those former slaves are. If I had the chance, I'd put a bullet in your head too. But you are a big man, you're holding the rifle, and here I sit, at your mercy. Me and three little kids. And I think there were once four. Did you kill the other one? Did you rape her? Or maybe him? Did you rape him? That's what I heard you rebel boys did. I heard you liked to bugger each other."

Andrew was silent. In fact, both were silent. There was not a sound in the entire room.

"What's your name?" Nicholas asked the boy. They stood a good distance from the battlefield behind a large oak tree riddled with bullet holes. It had seen better days.

"Don't much matter. You're gonna put a bullet in my head anyway. But for what it's worth, it's Billy. Billy Southworth. So, go ahead and kill me, I ain't scared of dyin'. I believe in the Lord, and I know I'm gonna go see him as soon as you pull that trigger, him and all of my friends who died out there," he said, nodding his head toward the fields of Gettysburg.

Nicholas wanted to smile. He had long given up on Jesus Christ. He wasn't sure about him before the war, but after he saw his first man blown apart by a cannon shot, he was sure that no loving God would allow that to happen.

"Well, Billy Southworth, tell me this. First of all, before I even ask you, tell me, how old are you?"

The boy tightened his jaw. "I'm fourteen, but my birthday is next month. At least I think it is, I lost track of time. But I know I'm gonna be fifteen," he said almost proudly.

Nicholas stood two arm lengths from him, "So, Billy Southworth, if I were to let you run off into those woods, would you think that the Lord did it, or would I become your savior."

Billy's eyes lit up. He bowed his head and forced the words,

"I don't know. But I sure would be grateful. I need to go home. No one is left to take care of my mother. But, if you kill me, I'd appreciate it if you would say a prayer over my body and send me to heaven properly. The Lord's prayer would be nice." He raised his eyes and looked at Nicholas. "I'd sure appreciate it."

Nicholas smiled. "Okay, Billy Southworth, you're free to go home. Now you turn and run. You run south as fast as you can to your momma. And don't join up with any more armies. Go home! Git!"

The boy mumbled a 'thank you' and began to run as fast as he could. Suddenly, from behind Nicholas, a shot rang out. Nicholas ducked and fell to the ground covering his head. When his eyes opened, he was staring at his captain's boots. Looking up, the captain stared down at him. "Get up. I knew you didn't have the guts to do it. Get up!"

Nicholas pushed himself from the ground. The captain staring past him, gave what would be his last order, "Get a shovel; bury him." As Nicholas looked behind him, he saw Billy Southworth lying dead, a bullet shot through his head.

"When you are done, place yourself under arrest and come to my tent. Understand?"

Nicholas continued to stare at Billy. Billy would never be fifteen. "Why did you do that? He was just a kid. This war is almost over! Why did you do that, you son of a bitch?"

"Just bury him," the captain repeated and began to walk away, his rifle at his side. Nicholas pulled his .44 caliber from his holster and shot the captain one time in the head. He looked back and forth at the bodies, walked to the battlefield, and returned with a shovel. He dug two separate graves, Billy's deeper than the captain's. *At least an animal will have a tough time getting at the boy.* He patted the dirt down on both graves, satisfied in knowing no one would ever wonder what happened to either. "Could've been killed in the battle, could've deserted," he mumbled to himself.

He stood over Billy's grave and said the Lord's Prayer. He then looked to the sky and said," I will never believe in a God that allows us to do what we have done and what I have witnessed here."

30.
And Then There Were Four

☆☆☆☆☆☆☆

Andrew pushed himself away from the table and stood to address Nicholas. "Your blasphemy of all that is sacred to me has probably just cost you your life," he mumbled. His eyes wide open, he moved toward Nicholas grasping the stock and forearm of his rifle. Other than the sound of Andrew's heavy breathing from his nose, there was silence. The two boys had disappeared from his view. Sarah and Grant huddled in the corner, Sarah's head resting on top of the dog's.

Nicholas peered into his eyes as he approached him.

"Gonna kill me, Andrew? Gonna shoot me as I sit here? Gonna do it in front of that little girl? It wouldn't surprise me one bit. That's what you Rebel cowards do. So, go ahead, go ahead, shoot me!" he screamed at him. "Your Lord is going to punish you, Andrew. You're going to burn in hell with the rest of your yellow-belly southern boys."

Andrew was seething. He raised his rifle, and his hands trembled; however, he was still out of the reach of Nicholas.

"You need to settle up with the Lord," the crazed man said as if he were a preacher. "You need to get on your knees now and ask him forgiveness for your blasphemy. **DO IT NOW! GET ON YOUR KNEES AND TELL THE LORD YOU ARE SORRY FOR YOUR SINS!**"

Continuing to stare into his eyes, Nicholas slid the chair back. As he began to kneel, he suddenly rolled toward Andrew. Surprised, Andrew shouted out to the Lord, and the weapon fired into the ceiling as Nicholas crashed into his legs. The rifle was knocked out of the reach of both men. Andrew was the stronger of

155

the two men, and it soon became apparent to Nicholas that he had underestimated him. However, he refused to give in, and with one last effort, he attached his teeth to the forearm of Andrew and bit down hard. Andrew screamed in pain, which was not as loud as the gunshot from the rifle, now in the hands of Jacob. Andrew's grip on Nicholas released, as Nicholas stared wide-eyed up at the boy.

Jacob stood above the dead man, rifle in his hand. "I had to do it. He would have killed you just like he did our big sister after she said 'no' for the last time." Jacob set the rifle on the table and looked at Nicholas. "So, can we come with you, mister?" he asked without concern for the situation that surrounded them. "We can bury him in the back. He weren't no good anyway."

Stunned, Nicholas pushed himself up from the floor and put his arm around the boy, "Sure, the three of you come with me. You gather all the food you can while I take him to the woods and bury him. And thank you, Jacob," he said as he looked down at the lifeless body.

As Nicholas dragged Andrew to the field in the rear of the house, he was surprised at how light he was, but even more surprised at the strength he had possessed. The ground, unlike that at Harriet's house, was not hard, and as Grant lay off to the side, panting heavily, he dug a shallow grave. As he pulled the body to the hole, he spoke to him. "Andrew, I dug this hole, especially for you, just deep enough to allow us all to get back to my horse and carriage before an animal comes and digs you up and eats you for dinner. My regrets to the animals that it won't be much of a meal, as there ain't really much to you, you no good son of a bitch!" And with those last words, he pushed Andrew into the pit, covered him, and patted the dirt softly. He threw the shovel on top of the dirt, looked toward the sky, and spoke, "Here ya go, Lord, another of your good followers!"

31.
Edward

☆☆☆☆☆☆☆

The life Beatrice was living in Emmitsburg was not as idyllic as Nicholas imagined it to be. After the war had ended in 1865, the dreams everyone had of peace were not realized, especially in border states such as Maryland. It was in these states that brothers and other family members had taken opposite sides during the war. Her husband had fought for the Union and died at Gettysburg, and her children had not recovered yet from their father dying in that battle. Her brother-in-law, Edward Valentine, who had joined to fight for the Confederate cause, was now living with her. In July 1864, his leg had been shot during the Battle of Peachtree Creek in Georgia during the Atlanta Campaign. Without an invitation, Edward journeyed to Emmitsburg and took up residence with Beatrice and her family. It wasn't long before he became physically and mentally abusive to her and the children, often striking her in a rage as he disparaged his dead brother for his participation in the Union Army. Her unwelcome hospitality to him had come at a steep price.

During dusk one evening in September 1864, as he sat on the stoop of Beatrice's house bemoaning his hatred of the north and all who had fought for them, a rider approached. In the dim light, Edward eyed him suspiciously. The man pulled back on the reins of the horse, halting right in front of Edward.

"I am looking for Edward Valentine."

"Who might be askin'?" he replied crossly.

The man dismounted and approached him. "Are you Edward Valentine?" and putting his hand on his sidearm advised, "I won't ask again. Are you Private Edward Valentine?"

Edward stood up from his seat on the steps. "And if I don't answer you, what might you do? I bet that you're just another Blue Belly lookin' for a reb to kill. Well, you got one here, and I swear if you pull that pistol, it will be the last thing you ever do before you rot in hell with the rest of your Yankee rubble."

The man removed his hand from his revolver. "Actually, I'm Corporal Sidney Pell. I am from the 8th Kentucky Cavalry. I was sent to find you by Lieutenant Bennett Young. I believe you were imprisoned with him for a time before he escaped."

"I might be. The Bennett Young I know, was a private."

Pell smiled, "Well, he's a Lieutenant now. He got commissioned."

Edward stared into Pell's eyes and mumbled, "Uh-huh." Then after a moment continued, "Never pictured him as no officer. Who you say you are?"

Pell began to answer and then stopped, walked up the steps, and entered into the house.

"Hey, you son of a bitch," he screamed as he limped up the steps in an attempt to stop him.

Pell, already in the house, reached back and held the door open. "I can't talk outside. It is too dangerous, but we need to talk."

He glared at the intruder. "We need to talk? Talk 'bout what? I ain't got nothin' much to talk 'bout. The war is all but over. We ain't gonna win it. Fuckin' Lee couldn't get out of his own way at Gettysburg! If he'd a listened to Longstreet, we'd all be celebratin' in Philadelphia now! But instead, we're just waitin' to be told when and where to surrender." Edward's eyes never blinked as he took a breath and continued his tirade. "And to answer your question, yeah, I knew Young. I heard he was killed after he escaped. And if he is alive, why would he send you to find me? That don't make no sense. No sense at all!"

Pell chuckled. "The lieutenant made it to Canada, and for some strange reason, seems to think that you would be a good recruit to take part in a plan he has to help get the Confederacy back on its feet. I can't believe that you are the same man that he knew in prison and helped him escape," he said, shaking his head in disbelief. "But I've come a long way to get you, so let's talk."

Edward bit his lip, "I already don't much like you, but as long as Young sent ya, go ahead and say your piece, and then move on."

There was a long pause. Pell, without an invitation to do so, proceeded into the living room and sat down on a hard-backed chair. A young boy came from nowhere and scooted out the door, followed by a small girl. Their mother was right behind them and stopped in the hallway when she spotted the two men in the next room.

"I'm sorry, Edward, those two have been at each other all day!" she said. "Hello, sir. I am sorry for disturbing you."

Edward glared at Beatrice, "Ya need to get control of them Goddamn kids, or they'll end up just like their daddy, too ignorant to know right from wrong! Now, move on out of here. I need to talk to this man." Beatrice nodded her head toward Pell, who had stood up and tipped his cap as she left the room.

Pell furled his eyebrows, "That's a very pretty woman that you are disrespecting. If she isn't your wife, who might she be?"

"Ah, it don't matter. She's my dead brother's wife. He died up the road on the second day. I told him not to join with Lincoln, and now he's dead. Never much liked him anyways," he muttered. "So, go ahead and talk. I don't really remember your name, but that don't matter. Say what you need to say and then git outta here."

Pell chuckled again, "Okay, Valentine. Here's the plan. It's very simple. The Lieutenant is putting together a band of raiders. We are going to enter Vermont through Canada and proceed to a small town called St. Albans. There, we're going to enter the town, rob the banks, go back into Canada, and put the money into the Rebel treasury. Hopefully, the money will help extend the war for us. I'd like to say the Lieutenant ordered me to ask you to join us, but he didn't."

"Then why the hell are ya here?" he snapped.

"Well, Valentine, this isn't a volunteer thing. His orders were to bring you back with me. And if you refused, I am to kill you. There are very few people who know of this plan, and unfortunately for you, you're now one of them. So, you need to pack a bag and be ready to leave tonight. We cannot travel during daylight hours. Too dangerous."

As darkness fell, Beatrice sat in the high grass with her three children, John, Esther, and Ruth. The grass was higher than usual after a troop of Union soldiers had recently passed through and stolen their animals. She pulled gently on the grass and chewed on the end of a long strand as John and his brother rolled a hoop, and their little sister jumped rope, causing small poofs of dust as her feet hit the dirt after each turn of the rope. Daydreaming of a better life, she was oblivious to the young corporal who quietly approached her and sat next to her. He, too, sat and stared off into the distance and then back at her face. He had never seen such a beautiful woman. His first attempt to speak to her caused his mouth to dry up, and his speech to stutter in embarrassment. After several tries, he gained control of his voice, but his words came out with a hint of insecurity.

"Beautiful evening!" he said much too loudly. "Your children are good looking kids. Do you like Emmitsburg?" The words felt rambling as he spoke, and much to his dismay sounded incoherent."

Beatrice jumped slightly. "I'm sorry. You startled me!" she said, surprised. "And I didn't catch your question, sir."

"I am sorry, ma'am, I didn't mean to scare you," he said apologetically with a tip of his hat. "I was trying to compliment you on your children."

Beatrice smiled softly. "My children are very good children, thank you."

Pell blushed and introduced himself, "Sidney Pell, ma'am, I'm glad to make your acquaintance."

Beatrice's eyes sparkled and, along with a slightly friendlier smile, responded, "I'm Beatrice, Beatrice Valentine. And I am likewise happy to make your acquaintance," she answered as she extended her hand to Pell. "And what brings you to Emmitsburg?" she asked as Pell softly held her hand then slowly pulled it away.

"I came to borrow Edward from you," he said too quickly. Her smile suddenly disappeared.

Her body stiffened and shifted into a defensive posture as she began a tirade. "Borrow him? Please do. Please take him and do not return him. Why anyone would want him in their possession is beyond me! He is a brutal, woman and child-abusing, drunken, ingrate of a man, and if he wasn't my dead husband's brother, I would have killed him long ago. So, please, Corporal Pell, do me a favor and take him away and do not bring him back here! Furthermore..." Pell stopped her mid-rant.

"Ma'am! Calm down!" he said loudly, grasping her arms. "You're shaking. What is wrong?" She stared at him coldly but did not say another word. "Tell me," he pleaded, "what is wrong. What has happened here? You are trembling!"

Pushing herself away and standing, she looked down at Sidney, "Good evening, Corporal Pell. As she was walking toward her house, calling the children to go inside, she turned back. "I **beg** you, if you take him, **please** see that he doesn't return here. Good evening!" She turned and walked up the porch steps, her dress flowing with each step she took as the children moved to her side.

Pell remained seated, watching the children head toward the house. Eventually, he called out, "Mrs. Valentine, may I see your children for a moment? I have something for them."

She looked at him and then to the children. Nodding her head, she said, "Yes, but don't have them long. They have chores to do!"

"Okay, thank you! Come on over here, kids." And as they approached, he asked, "How about a piece of stick candy?" He invited them to sit with him. It didn't take much coaxing as the word candy drew them close quickly. Sidney pulled out several pieces of candy, handing one stick to each child. Without hesitation, he began to ask the three children questions concerning Edward Valentine. At first, the children were reluctant to answer; however, shortly into his prodding, which was, in fact, an interrogation, he saw a bruise on Esther's face. Reaching out and touching the spot, he asked her, "What happened here, honey?" The silence was uncomfortable as the three children looked to each other for an answer. Pell smiled, "Another candy stick for whoever answers first!" he exclaimed. It took mere seconds until John piped out. "Uncle Edward hit her. Now give me the stick!" Pell reached into his leather pack.

"He did? Were you doing something bad?" he asked her.

She bowed her head and mumbled, "No, I said I hoped that President Lincoln would win the war soon."

Pell shook his head in agreement. "And does he do that to your mom?"

Again, John asked, "Another stick?"

"Sure," Pell answered, "but first, the answer."

"He does it to all of us, especially when he's drunk. Knocked my tooth out once," he said, displaying a broken canine.

Pell handed them all another stick. "Thank you, and let's keep this talk a secret. Don't tell your mother or your uncle." Nodding in agreement, the children ran through the high grass back to their house.

It was dark when Edward reappeared from inside the house.

"Let's go, Valentine. We've got a lot of miles to go," Pell barked as an order.

Edward packed his horse, mounted, and yanked on the reins yelling back at Pell, "Let's go. Let's get this done!"

Pell let Edward move ahead of him and then quickly turned his steed and returned to the house where Beatrice and the children stood on the porch returning his wave.

He motioned to the mother to approach his horse, "Beatrice, what you asked me today, I promise you that will happen." With a slip of the tongue, he added, "Edward will not return from Vermont. I, however, **will** be back." Realizing that he had divulged secret information, he quickly tipped his hat. Reaching into his pouch, he tossed several candy sticks to the children, spurred his horse, and caught up to Edward.

32.
Walking in Circles

☆☆☆☆☆☆☆

It was dusk when Nicholas was able to round up the kids, pack sacks of food and begin the trek back to where he had left his horse, Abner. He wondered what he would do with them. *I can't just show up at Beatrice's house with three children, one of them a killer.* He grimaced at the thought. Night fell quickly, and he began to have misgivings that he was heading in the right direction.

I should have marked this trail. He was afraid he had been gone too long while considering the possibility that someone could have absconded with Abner and his wagon. If that occurred, he would have more problems than he already had, that and his dilemma of 'inheriting' the children. None of them had said a word since their departure from the house.

It was Jacob, the oldest one who spoke first, "Mister Nicholas, are we lost?"

Nicholas gulped, "I don't think we're lost, but I'm a little bit confused."

Sarah piped in, "I'm tired, and I'm hungry. Grant is, too!" she whined.

"If we walk to the south a bit, we will come out on the road to Emmitsburg and Gettysburg," Jacob offered.

Surprised, Nicholas asked, "Are you sure?"

"Yes, sir, I've been through these woods many times hunting. I know where we are, and to tell you the truth, I'm a bit tired of tramping around in the dark. I'd like to get settled in for the night and let the boy and Sarah get some sleep," Jacob answered, showing his concern for the other two children.

Nicholas was embarrassed. "So, how far are we from the road, Jacob?"

Jacob looked around at his surroundings and then up at the sky. "About two miles. We would have been a mile, but you walked us around like Moses in the desert. Come, follow me." Nicholas burst out laughing as the children looked at him blankly, wondering why he was amused.

Jacob walked to the front of the line, "C'mon," he said, "and try to be quiet. We don't want to attract any large cats, that is if there are any left after the war. I think they might have all been killed. But let's don't take no chances."

It was less than an hour before they broke out of the woods and came upon the main road. Nicholas, relieved, thanked Jacob and quipped, "Good thing we had you, we'd have been walking for a week!"

"Probably," he responded. "So, do you have any idea where your horse might be?" The three children looked at Nicholas with hopes he would say 'yes.' Grant stood next to Sarah, also hopeful, his tongue hanging out.

Nicholas looked around at his surroundings, "North," is all he said and began to walk on the road. He knew the spot where he had turned into the woods, near a large oak tree, that for some unknown reason, had been stripped of its bark. When he looked back, Sarah was on Jacob's shoulders, and the little boy, who spoke very little, was tagging along with Grant. He wondered what he would do with them.

"So," he said as he slowed the walk down, "do you have any parents?"

The children looked at each other with fear in their eyes. Nicholas eyed them all with suspicion. "Well, do you, or don't you?"

After a few moments, Sarah spoke. "Our dad is dead. Momma killed him. Killed him and my..."

She was quickly interrupted by Jacob. "Ain't none of your business, Mr. Nicholas."

At any other time, Nicholas would have reprimanded the boy, but, under the circumstances, he simply stated, "Yep, you're right, it's not. Let's keep moving. My horse and wagon ain't far from here."

The night got even darker as clouds began to cover the moon. Nicholas peered into the darkness and whistled, hoping to stir the horse to whinny. The children followed in silence, except for Sarah, who several times complained of being hungry, only to be told to "Hush" by Jacob. Focusing his vision to keep from stumbling in the dark, he saw in the distance the silhouette of the horse and his wagon in front of the glow of a small campfire. Startled, he stopped the children and told them to stay put and quiet until he investigated the situation. Then he patted Sarah on her head and whispered. "Shush little girl; we will soon eat."

Someone is trying to steal my wagon! Well, they're in for a big surprise! He pulled out the rifle he had taken from the old man and began to slowly approach the campfire. Veering off to the left, he formulated a plan to ambush the would-be horse thief, hoping he wouldn't have to shoot him, but knowing he would if necessary. He was a hundred yards from the dying fire. His intuition told him not to go any closer, but his anger at the thought of someone stealing his horse and worldly belongings overrode that thought. So, he proceeded cautiously.

When he reached the outside of the camp, he scrutinized everything he had left behind. Abner was still in the same place he had left him, but it appeared in the dim light of the fire that someone had put a pile of weeds or grass in front of him as well as a bucket of water. *Someone has cared for Abner; they can't be all bad.* He slowly approached the animal. Speaking softly to him, "Hey, boy. Hey, old Abner. I'm back. Sorry, I was gone so long. Who fed you? Don't worry, old boy, I'll get you some nice grass tomorrow when we move out of here!" Nicholas patted the horse's head and turned to yell to the children when a voice behind him spoke loud and clear:

"I fed him, you son of a bitch! And now I'm gonna kill you. Put your hands on your head! Didn't I tell you that's what happens to horse thieves?"

He didn't have to turn around. He knew who it was. He placed his hands on his head without turning around. "Harriet. So, you found me. How?" he asked.

"You don't tie a horse up with a short rope and leave him for long periods of time. They will whinny loudly. I knew where you were going, and this is the only way there. I was on my way to find you, and, well, I guess you could say that your horse, my horse, gave you up," she said with a scowl, then a chuckle. "So, here is what we're gonna do. We're gonna go back to my farm, and you're gonna dig a hole, up by where you found those other bodies that you didn't think I knew you found, and you are gonna join them."

Nicholas turned slowly, not knowing if she would shoot. "Okay," he said softly, "but I have a problem. In those woods are three children that I have found and are relying on me to care for them. I need to have them come here and be fed and to be given advice on what to do next. I can give them directions along with a note and tell them to go to Beatrice. She is a kind person and will care for them. They can tell her I sent them. She'll take them."

Harriet's rifle, still pointed at Nicholas, lowered a bit. "Children? What children? Where are they?" she asked, with a bit of fear in her voice. "Where are they?"

"In the wood line. Can I call for them? And if you're not going to shoot me now, you can put the rifle down. I'm not going anywhere while the children are with me."

Harriet hesitated. "Whatcha gonna do with them?" she stammered, her rifle still pointing at him.

"I don't know, but a least let me call them here. The little girl is hungry," he pleaded.

She looked at Nicholas and then into the dark sky.

"Well, can I call them?"

"Yeah, call them. But don't get no ideas that they are coming with us. I ain't taking any kids with us, cuz you ain't gonna be around to help with them."

"Okay, let me feed them, and then you and I can leave. Jacob! Come here! All of you come here! I found the horse and the food. Hurry."

Harriet sat down on a rock, her rifle still in her hands. "I don't want to meet them, so don't bring them near me. I'm not big on kids. They annoy me," she said, her voice dripping with sarcasm.

He snickered. "Did you hate those men you buried too?" She didn't reply. The three children broke through the thicket and approached Nicholas.

The little girl stared at him. "Feed me! I'm starving!"

He smiled, "Okay, let's get everyone some food. I'm not much of a cook, but I'll make something."

"Jacob is a good cook," Sarah announced. "He'll make us all something."

Jacob wasn't listening to her. Instead, he had wandered over to Abner, and as he lifted the horse's leg to check his hoof, he spotted Harriet sitting on the rock at the edge of the woods. He stopped and peered through the darkness at her. Then he spoke. He spoke one word which turned Nicholas's head toward the rock that she sat on, the word from Jacob's mouth was loud and clear:

"MOTHER!"

33.

Reunion Minus One

☆☆☆☆☆☆☆

Harriet was the first woman he had sex with. On several occasions, he had touched his fiancée Ella's breast while sneaking a kiss as they sat on the big rock at Pony Lake. But he had never been touched in the way that Harriet touched him when he had slept in her bed. If he had not found the bodies of those men, he might have stayed with her longer. *Who knows, maybe I would have stayed and not moved on toward Emmitsburg.* But now, as he sat in the darkness, her shadow loomed as large as that of his horse, rather her horse that he had stolen. He recalled the words she had spoken about her late husband being hanged for horse stealing. He wondered if she had notified the sheriff of his thievery. However, as these thoughts raced through his mind, his mouth opened, and words spilled out.

"So, are you going to have me hung like you did your husband?" he blurted out. The only sound came from the crickets and a snort from Abner. Grant, tired from the long trek, slept alongside his friend Sarah. Nicholas continued, "Well, are you? I need to know, because as far as I can tell, Jacob is your boy, and I need to figure out what to tell you to do with the other two kids. I can tell you where to take them. It'll be a good home for them in Emmitsburg. I know a woman there who will be happy to take them, that is if you'll make arrangements to take them there. She'll even take in Jacob if you don't care to take him back home."

Harriet never moved and never took her hand from her rifle. Her legs were crossed, and her head was cocked to the side while she chewed on the inside of her cheek. Straightening her head, she uncrossed her legs and sat up, slowly addressing Nicholas.

"You ain't the smartest person I've ever met; of course, you ain't the dumbest either. But please, before I kill you, tell me how you thought you were gonna get away with stealing my horse and supplies. I mean, you don't even know where the hell you are! Did you think I couldn't track you down? Why did you leave like you did? If you had asked me for the horse, I might have even given him to you. He's old, and I really don't want to dig a hole that big again. So, before I kill you, at least try to give me a reason not to pull the trigger on this gun!" She crossed her legs again and assumed her previous position.

Nicholas was at first at a loss for words. Jacob stood next to Abner, and the other boy sat off near the wood line, occasionally swatting at the flies that Abner was attracting. Nicholas looked over at Sarah, and without much thought, said, "I found the two bodies when I was digging fence post holes for you. I just figured that I was next. So, I ran. So, go ahead and pull the trigger, but let me tell you what I would like to ask you to do with the two extra kids. The little one, her name is Sarah, and to tell you the truth, I have no idea what the other boy's name is." Then in a more casual voice somewhat closer to how they spoke before he left her, he whispered, "Anyway, he's a bit odd, and kind of, well, different. He don't talk too much and seems to like to be alone." Then continuing, he added proudly, "Nothing like your boy Jacob who had no problem killing the old man back in the woods to save us." Harriet's head snapped toward Jacob. Silence again overtook the forest. The fire was turning to embers before she spoke.

"Okay, Nicholas, I'm gonna make a deal with you. Kinda like making a deal with the devil. I ain't gonna kill you. But I do want you to know that I did kill those men you found on my ranch. Both of them abused me, and well, so did my daddy, my brothers, and my uncles, and I swore that one day, well, I promised myself that I wouldn't be abused again. But they continued, and well, you got to see the results. Yep, I killed them." She sat up, pulling her knees to her chest. "Jacob saw me kill the second one, got scared, and took his sisters Minnie and little Martha. Her name is Martha, not Sarah–I don't know where she came up with that name–and left six months ago. I didn't try and find them because I was afraid Jacob or Minnie would tell the law." She paused for a moment, and then said softly, "Then you came along, and I thought maybe I could start a new life. I knew Jacob and Minnie could take care of Martha." She sighed and looked at the tall boy, "I'm sorry, Jacob. Where is Minnie? Let's go and get her, wherever she is, and go home. Nicholas, I'm not going to kill you. And you can take the horse, the dog, and the other boy. I have no idea who he is."

Nicholas looked at Jacob, waiting for his reply to his mother, knowing that it would change the situation for Harriet. He stared at her, and as he patted the horse on his nose, he said in a voice that brought chills to Nicholas. "Minnie's dead. She was raped many times by Andrew. I killed him. Let's go home."

Her whole body shook as she stood up, went to Martha, and with tears streaming down her face, picked the child up and put her over her shoulder. As she stared off at the boy who sat near the woods, her voice quivered, "I'm sorry for everything. You are a kind person. Good luck to you, Nicholas." Jacob led the way as the three disappeared into the woods and headed for the road to Dillsburg. Nicholas peered through the darkness at the boy with no name.

34.

Letter to Mother

✩✩✩✩✩✩✩

By the time Nicholas returned to the battlefield from burying Billy and the captain, he knew what he was going to say if asked if he had seen the captain or the rebel prisoner; however, no one ever asked him, and he never had to tell it. The upper command had their own way of explaining or justifying disappearances. While they never told the troops what had actually happened, the word was that someone was killed. Nicholas was more than happy to have any story circulate about the disappearance of the captain and the reasons for it.

By the time the survivors were able to march to Washington, Nicholas's anger ha begun to surface. The young man with the disposition of a kitten was slowly turning into someone even he didn't recognize. He was quick to pick fights or quarrel at the drop of a hat.

In one instance, shortly after arriving in Washington, he was approached by a young lieutenant and given an order to assist in moving the remains of a barracks that had been torn down. Nicholas didn't recognize the man and knowing he had not fought with him at Gettysburg, refused. He told him he was not feeling well and no longer felt required or obligated to help. An argument ensued, and Nicholas was pulled away from the officer by one of his comrades. The lieutenant stepped back and advised him that his time at Gettysburg did not entitle him to any special privileges with respect to military decorum.

Nicholas replied scornfully, "I have seen your kind, and they are all dead. Some at the hands of the enemy, some at the hands of their own men."

The young officer gulped, "We'll see. I know that we cannot physically fight, but as they taught us at the Point, there is surely more than one way to win a battle, and believe me, private, I am by far smarter than you, and you will regret this encounter. Gettysburg will feel like a minor skirmish when I am done with you." Nicholas had again, be restrained by his friends.

Nicholas's dreams were vivid, most times waking him with a scream. Faces of men he had killed and men he had seen killed appeared in them. Atrocities that he had witnessed committed by others and other atrocities he had been a part of by being in the wrong place at the wrong time, played out again and again in his mind. He tried to avoid confrontation by waiting patiently to muster out and return to Herronville. He was sure that his anger would subside when he returned to his loved ones and to Ella, the woman he had intentions of marrying, the woman he had known and loved since he was a child. However, his letters to her had gone unanswered, and he fretted that she had found another man. Her name was never mentioned in letters from his mother.

Because he was so distressed that he had no idea what was going on with Ella, he sat down and decided to write to his mother once more. Even though he knew he would probably be home before she received it.

November 1863
Dear Mother:
This will probably be the last letter you receive from me before I stand on our doorstep in Herronville, as I will soon receive my discharge and look forward to being with you and father again as a family. I cannot lie, I believe I have changed, and not for the better. The war has taken a toll on my head, and hopefully I will return to being myself when I get back in familiar surroundings. I need to

ask if you have seen Ella? I have not heard a word from her, or for that matter from you about her. I know that it is silly for me to ask you, as I will probably be home before you ever receive this letter. However, I think it only fair to tell you and father that I intend to ask her father, Alfred, for her hand. She has been on my mind constantly since I walked off the farm to join this army and this absurd war. I hope that you and father are aware that this war has been fought in vain and nothing will come of it. The president seems to have no idea what is going on upon the fields of battle. Does he have any idea of the death and limbs being lost? I too, have suffered an eye problem. I hope doctor Wilkins can fix it when I get home. How is father? I worry about his health, but I know he is strong.

The men are becoming very nervous in anticipation of being discharged. One man who was so distressed from his time in battle took his life in front of the formation. It was plain as the nose on your face that he wasn't right in the head. The Colonel acted mad because he shot himself. He told one of the Negroes to "clean that mess up and get rid of it!"

I better go to bed, it's getting late, and it is a bit chilly at night, but I have enough blankets. Did I tell you I have a horse? I found him on the field after the battle at Gettysburg. I plan on riding him to Herronville. I will see you and father before Christmas.

Your loving son,

Nicholas

PS. If you happen to see Ella, please give her my regards.

Nicholas folded the letter, put it into an envelope, and addressed it to his parents in Herronville. He handed it to the mail clerk the next morning in hopes of it being sent that day. The following day as the men gathered for the evening formation, the lieutenant he had words with on the previous day, strutted to the head of the men to give the orders for the next day. At the sight of him, Nicholas's body tensed, and the other men glanced at him, waiting for his reaction. The officer reached into his pocket and retrieved the duty roster and another paper. But before reading its contents, he addressed the troops.

"Gentleman, I have here something that might be of interest to you. It appears that one of us is having problems with his time spent at Gettysburg." And with that, he began to read Nicholas's letter:

November 1863
Dear Mother:

This will probably be the last letter you receive from me before I stand on our doorstep in Herronville, as I will soon receive my discharge and look forward to being with you and father again as a family. I cannot lie, I believe I have changed, and not for the better. The war has taken a toll on my head, and hopefully I will return to being myself when I get back in familiar surroundings. I need to ask if you have seen Ella? I have not heard a word from her, or for that matter from you about her. I know that it is silly for me to ask you, as I will probably be home before you ever receive this letter...

The reading did not receive the expected response the officer believed it would. Nicholas exploded and stomped forward toward the young lieutenant, violence in his heart. But, at the last minute, he was stopped and restrained by his comrades.

A sergeant who had been through several battles with many different divisions stepped forward and addressed the lieutenant. "Sir, you have dishonored yourself as an officer, and you certainly are not a gentleman. Several days ago, one of our own killed himself right where we stand today. It wasn't because he missed his family. The war has made us all revert to children. We stand in battle. We kill. We maim others. We look into their lifeless eyes and wonder who their parents were. We wonder why we are doing what we are doing! Private Haff is an excellent soldier, and if his biggest problem, which you have brought forth, is missing his mother, father, home, and girlfriend, then he is good with the Lord! And you, young man, you are not good with the Lord. Now, if you want to proceed with a complaint on me to your superiors, that is your prerogative. But you are no gentleman—in fact, you are not a man." The sergeant then turned and faced the men and barked, "You all are dismissed. And what you heard here should never be repeated. Dismissed!" He remained in place until all the soldiers left. He then turned facing the officer. "So, lieutenant, do you plan on pressing insubordination charges against me?"

"No, sergeant, you are dismissed," he replied, his voice quivering.

"That's good," he replied, "because the fact that I no longer value life should mean something to you. Insubordination means nothing to me. Leave the private alone." After taking several steps away from the lieutenant and without turning to face him, he added, "Sir."

As Nicholas trudged back to his tent, he stared up at the sky and muttered, "What kind of God are you?"

35.
Luke

Nicholas listened to Harriet and her children rustle through the brush as they walked away from the campsite. All that was left was Grant and Abner, his wagon, the dying campfire, and a boy with no name who didn't talk. In fact, the only time he heard a sound from his mouth was when he had screamed at Jacob to repent after Jacob was ordered by the old man, Andrew, to go outside and do just that. He stood for a long time, staring off into the dark woods, wondering what his next move would be. The truth be told, he had no idea how far Emmitsburg was, or for that matter if Beatrice would even be there. And if she was, had he overestimated her feelings for him?

"Maybe I should just hook ole Abner to the wagon and head back north to my mother," he said softly as he stared at the boy. The dying embers reflected a faint red glow onto the boy's face making him appear angelic. Still, Nicholas's gut feeling told him differently. He liked children, but other than in his own childhood had never actually been in the company of one for more than several hours. He continued to stare at him. Finally, he addressed him.

"What's your name?" he asked in a friendly voice. The boy stared back without replying.

"How old are you?" he urged. "Cat got your tongue?' he kidded with a smile. The boy sat on a log and put his head between his legs.

"Okay," Nicholas said, responding to the silence, "I'm just going to stoke this fire up. We'll decide in the morning a plan of action. There is a blanket or two in the wagon, I'm going to get one. Do you want one?" Again, no reply came from the youngster. Nicholas went to the wagon, grabbed two blankets, and handing one to his silent partner, told him, "You might want to snuggle up in that, but not too close to the fire. I don't want you looking like a roast of buffalo in the morning!" he laughed. The boy cocked his head, squinted his eyes, and laid down at his location, not moving any closer to the warmth of the fire.

"You're welcome," Nicholas mumbled sarcastically.

As the sun eased its way over the trees and began to shine on the ashes of last night's fire, Nicholas stirred and looked toward the boy half expecting him to be gone. In fact, he hoped the boy had run off. But to his disappointment, he was still there, wrapped in the blanket Nicholas had given him. Grant was snuggled next to him, snoring and twitching as he slept. Abner, too, was lying down, asleep. After stoking up the fire, Nicholas took the bag of food they had taken from the house, which contained several broken eggs, along with some of which managed to make the trip in one piece. He pulled out the frying pan that he had also packed up from the house and tossed in the eggs with some salted pork and began to cook breakfast. The delicious smell of frying bacon teased Grant awake, nose sniffing the air. A few minutes later, the boy also awakened.

As Nicholas walked over to Abner, he spoke to the sleepy boy, "How'd you sleep? You hungry? I got some eggs and pork cooking on the fire. Better eat. We might have a long day ahead of us!" Untying the horse, he wondered aloud, "What in the world am I going to do with that kid?" He slapped Abner gently on the rump, urging him to wander near the camp to chomp on some dried-up grass and weeds. "I'll find you some hay today," he promised the old horse. *God, please don't die on me, I cannot bury another horse.*

"So," looking toward the orphan, he asked again, "you hungry?"

Without saying a word and still wrapped in his blanket, the boy moved toward the sizzling pork. Nicholas sighed and watched him as Grant stretched his legs and let out a moan. The boy sat next to the fire, hair tangled, and his eyes wide open staring at the sizzling meat. Suddenly, he spoke. "You gonna leave me here?" he blurted out. "Ain't got no one to go with now."

Nicholas approached the boy, and squatting down, picked at the meat with a fork. And after some thought, he answered, "Well, depends. You gonna talk to me? If not, there ain't much use to me and you staying together. Hell. I can talk to Abner, that's the horse's name. Or I could talk to Grant. He's the dog." Nicholas smiled.

"How come you call them that? That's not their names."

Nicholas, cocking his head and squinting at the boy, asked, "And how do you know that's not their names? You a mind reader?" he added. The boy was silent. "Well, if you're so smart, what's their names?" he prodded.

"The horse is Whistles, and the dog is Spot. Even though he ain't got none." He swallowed his last words and then asked, "I talked. You gonna cook some more eggs now? I'm fucking starving!"

"Yep, but if you use that word again, you will not be with me. You'll be on your own. And how do you know the names?"

"Jacob told me but didn't want to say anything. He was afraid you killed his mom. Can we eat now?"

"Sure, let me put some more eggs in the pan."

The boy stared at Nicholas. "My name is Luke."

"Okay," he nodded, as he put eggs on a metal plate and handed them to Luke. "Well, that's interesting," he replied quietly. "Here you go. Eat up. We can talk later, Luke."

36.

The Sigh

☆☆☆☆☆☆☆

The night before, there was a drizzle of rain and, his bedroll was damp. The autumn sun was not strong enough to dry his blankets. He decided the drying of Luke's bedroll and clothing would steer their conversation away from their current situation, which he was beginning to think was dire. More importantly, he was conflicted over what his next move would be with Luke. He now felt embarrassed that he had even considered leaving the boy sleep while he slipped away. He had several options, and as he rolled them around in his head, he knew that in the end, he would take the boy with him. He believed that Beatrice, being the kind soul that he had remembered from their meeting at Gettysburg, would certainly welcome Luke with open arms after he explained the story of how he ended up as his keeper. He decided after they had eaten, he would hook the horse and wagon and continue on to Emmitsburg. And as he formulated the plan, he contemplated what to say to Luke when they spoke.

The sun hid behind the clouds, and the rain returned. It was heavier than the night before. "Luke, get up boy, you're gonna catch a death of pneumonia," he warned. "Here," he continued, pulling a dry shirt from the chest on the back of the wagon. "This will be too big for you. It'll be like a dress, but it's dry," he chuckled. "Put it on," he ordered the boy as he tossed it to him.

Catching the shirt as he sat up, he stared at Nicholas. "You ain't my mother, ya know. Don't tell me what to do."

Nicholas glared at the boy, "Ain't your father either, but I'm kinda stuck with you." The two stared at each other. "How old are you, boy?" he asked as he rearranged the clothing in the chest.

Luke stood up, picked up a stick, and poked at the fire, which was beginning to hiss at the raindrops. "Twelve," he mumbled.

Nicholas cocked his head, "You're kinda big for twelve, ain't ya?"

Luke folded his arms across his chest. "How old are **you**?" he snapped back at Nicholas.

"I don't think that matters. What does matter is that you are in my charge. Now, how the hell old are you? Cuz if you are twelve, I am gonna have to drop you off at the orphanage in Gettysburg I read about. I can't have you wandering around the countryside. On the other hand, if you are older, which I think you are, and I have no idea why you are lying about your age to me, we can travel together to meet my friend Beatrice in Emmitsburg. So, what's it gonna be?"

Nicholas began to stoke the fire in an effort to keep the damp logs from losing their heat. He decided it was better to stay at the campsite and dry their clothing and bedrolls before moving on. The rain had stopped for a time, and he needed to make decisions on the boy. He heard about the orphanage in Gettysburg but didn't know if they would take any more children. Plus, he had also heard that the treatment of the boys was not good, especially boys and girls from the southern states. He was sure that it would be overflowing with the children of the war dead. If he was unable to leave Luke at the orphanage, it would be his responsibility to care for him. Nicholas had a suspicion that something was not quite right with the boy. *Maybe the old man had hurt him?* Regardless, he knew he may be burdened with Luke until he could reach Beatrice, and even then, was unsure as to what her reaction would be.

The wood was damp and crackled and spit as it struggled to burn. Luke walked into the heavy brush to change into the dry shirt, then returned and stood with a stick in hand, poking at the fire. Nicholas worked at hanging the bedding on a makeshift rack next to the low flames to dry.

"I have a couple more eggs. You should eat them. They won't

be good for much longer. Maybe we will find a friendly farmer along the way and get more. The boy gave Nicholas his first smile and accepted his offer of the eggs. Nicholas retrieved the pan from the wagon and scrambled the eggs, also mixing in the small amount of pork that was left over from earlier.

The two sat on the damp ground, Luke eating the eggs and Nicholas watching him and tending to the drying clothes.

"You're a pretty good cook," Luke said.

"Thanks, learned to survive during the war. An egg, and maybe the chicken it came out of, made for a nice meal at times!" he said, nodding his head.

"We had rat meat mostly when..." he halted in mid-sentence.

Nicholas's ears perked up. "When what?" He had heard of the atrocities at POW camps, and the prisoners' penchant for cold rat meat. Luke did not at first reply. "When what, Luke?" he pressed. "Where did you have rat meat? Did Andrew feed it to you?" he insisted. "You need to tell me, Luke. Where did you have rat meat?" *Surely, this boy wasn't in a camp!*

Luke put his arms on his legs and placed his head on them. In a muffled voice, he said, "I was in the war. I lied about my age to join the confederacy. I was a drummer boy. Well, I was a drummer boy until I got captured by the Yanks at Chancellorsville and sent to Point Lookout. They was gonna send me home, but when they found out I wasn't eight, they kept me in the camp. That's where I met Andrew."

Nicholas heard about young boys lying about their age to join the armies on both sides. He had seen them die in front of him. He had seen them executed. Now he sat peering through the rain at the face of a young boy who, more than likely, had been severely abused by Union soldiers, and had seen atrocities not meant to be seen by anyone. After several moments, he asked with compassion, "So, Luke, how old are you? The truth."

Without hesitation, he answered, "Fifteen. And there is something else you need to know."

Biting on his lip, he asked the boy, "So, Andrew wasn't your father?"

Tears welled up in his eyes, "No, sir, he was not. My pa died in front of my eyes in Chancellorsville. I was drumming, trying to gather the men, you know, rally them. The men around me was doing good. We had chased all the Yanks off into the bushes and the swamps. At least we thought we did. My father and me sat down on a log. The smell of gun smoke was still in the air. He had his pistol on his lap and was packing his pipe. I was waiting for him to light it; I liked the smell of it!" he smiled. "And all of a sudden, a man walked up to us, gave us a wave and sat next to us. He asked pa if he could spare some tobacco. He sounded like a Yank but had on a gray jacket. It was all beat up, like everyone else's, so I figured he was a Northerner who came to fight with us. There were a lot of them. Not everyone in the North was against slavery, ya know. I guess pa thought the same as me. Anyway, he handed the guy his pouch of tobacco, and when he did, the guy pulled a pistol and shot him square in the head and laughed. 'Now bang that on your little drum!' he said to me, laughed, and walked away. I don't even know how I did it, but I grabbed my pa's pistol, and when he was walking away, I ran up behind him. He heard me coming and turned around. He still had that look on his face that he did when he laughed after he killed my father. I pointed the pistol at his head, and he laughed. 'Whatcha gonna do with that big gun, little drummer boy?' I didn't say nothin'. I just pulled the trigger. I think I hit him in the eye. I really didn't look at his face, but the back of his head was blown apart. It wasn't but a little while later in the day that I got caught by a Yankee and sent to the camp."

Nicholas, still visualizing the horrors Luke must have seen, just stared dumbfounded at the boy.

Luke tried to smile, but his lips quivered, and tears rolled down his face. "There's one more thing," he began. "My name is Lucy. I'm a girl."

Nicholas's eyes opened wide. He cupped his hands in front of his mouth, closed his eyes, puffed his cheeks, and let out a long sigh.

37.

Point Lookout

☆☆☆☆☆☆☆

When the young soldier was captured by the Union Army at Chancellorsville, he refused to give his name. He refused to say anything. He just sat– scared.

Before his capture, he watched as the Yanks killed his friends in front of him while he lay in the putrid water of the swamp feigning death, that is, until his hand cramped and twitched. And just as it did, a Union soldier stuck his bayonet into the mud next to his neck, "Don't move, Grayback, you'll be going with us now," he growled. The young boy's eyes moved to the right and stared at the blade. His body stiffened in terror at the implied threat. The old soldier laughed, "You'll be going off to Point Lookout. They'll like you there! They like young ones!" The soldier dragged the boy through the muck of the water. All the while, the young Rebel clung to his drum.

The blue back continued, "And you won't be needing that drum where you're going. You won't have the strength to bang on it after a week there." The boy never cried. In fact, he never made a sound.

When confronted by the Union captain and questioned, he merely shook his head. Then the frustrated captain snapped at a corporal. "Take this man and put him on the next shipment to the Point. Maybe he'll talk there when the men get to look at his young, bare arse," he said with a grin on his face.

Life at the P.O.W. camp was sadistic and inhumane, but the young soldier never budged. He refused to speak to anyone. He initially passed his time chasing and killing rats for the older prisoners who were too slow to do so. They would often give them a small bite of their pork rations and occasionally some of the rat's meat. In time, the young soldier learned to catch lobster from the bay and dig clams, which he would keep for himself to avoid eating the rodent meat.

His main goal was to stay alive. He had watched as men were shot by the Negro guards; they were paid ten to fifteen dollars for anyone they killed who tried to escape. Most of the men he saw killed were not escaping but were close enough to the fence to be considered fair game. The murders were done to help keep the population of the prison to a minimum; however, the camp was still overcrowded, and diseases were rampant, especially after the Gettysburg battle when the conditions completely deteriorated, and most of the small privileges afforded to them were taken away. It was the population explosion and constant brutality that caused the boy to befriend an older soldier for protection. He was the youngest soldier in the camp, and it became apparent early on that he was fair game for sexual pleasure. After escaping several attempts by the other men to molest him, he was saved by a man he befriended whose name was Andrew Jones.

Andrew had fought in Chancellorsville, Gettysburg, and several other battles. While he was much older than most of the men, he was meaner than any of them, and they avoided him at all costs. One time Andrew had nearly beaten a man to death with a rock while he quoted the Bible, "So you shall stone him to death because he has sought to seduce you from the Lord your God who brought you out from the land of Egypt, out of the house of slavery."

After the beating, the two could walk through the compound without fear of attack. He was respected; however, soldiers still ogled the boy, and Andrew told him not to stray too far from him.

It was well into their friendship before Andrew Jones bothered to ask the young soldier his name. The little talking that had taken place between them before was usually answered with "yes" or "no" or a "thank you." One night as they sat in front of their tent, which was shared by fourteen other prisoners, Jones asked him where he was from and what his name was.

The answer was hesitant, "From Virginia. My name is Luke. You?"

The older man muttered, "It don't much matter, I'm from Charleston. My name has long been lost by most, except for the Lord. He knows who I am, and I know who he is, but you may call me Andrew. Andrew Jones. And you need to stay by my side, or you shall be punished by Jesus." Luke put his arm around the old man's waist and promised him his allegiance.

With the arrival of December, the weather changed, and the frigid winds blew hard into the camp off of the Chesapeake Bay. The minimal allotment of clothing that was supposed to be distributed to the prisoners was taken by the guards and other prison staff. Men stole from the other men. Blankets became a rarity, and promises of food and other necessities were made by the men to other men. The rations of food were mostly non-existent, and rats were also becoming a valuable commodity. As other men did, Luke and Andrew huddled for warmth in the one blanket they shared. It was the day before Christmas when the two men were hugging each other for warmth when Andrew placed his hand under the waist of Luke's pants in an effort to touch him and discovered that Luke was what he had always expected, a young girl disguised as a boy.

After the silence of the moment, Andrew spoke, "Leviticus says, 'You shall not lie with a male as a woman, it is an abomination!'" Then he added, "But you, my boy, will be my woman until I say otherwise, or I will toss you to the prisoners like a crippled rat!" He snickered as he slid his hand under Luke's rope belt and roughly penetrated the stunned girl's privates with his calloused fingers.

38.
Lucy

☆☆☆☆☆☆☆

In 1857, when she was seven, Lucy Barton watched and wept as they buried her mother Mary in the family cemetery on their small farm outside of Charleston, South Carolina. Henry Barton, her father, stood next to her and grasped her hand so tightly that he unintentionally bruised it. Her mother had been trampled by a bull as she and Jacob attempted to untangle the animal from the wire fence in which he had gotten ensnared. Her father was inconsolable, and his life, as well as Lucy's, would never be the same.

Henry did his best to farm his land, but after the death of Mary, his efforts were disappointing. He spent most of his time trying to raise Lucy as his wife would have wanted. Two years after her death, he met Pauline Hopkins, an unattractive, ill-tempered woman from the nearby village. Against his better judgment with hopes of giving young Lucy a mother, he married Pauline. All too soon, he realized he had been mistaken. Lucy, now nine, was not accepting her stepmother's attempts to raise her as a young lady or her discipline in doing so. Lucy did not fancy the frilly clothes and fancy shoes Pauline made and purchased for her. Instead, she was more comfortable wearing her farming clothes. And rather than learning the correct way to set the table, or to sit properly in a chair, she preferred digging in the dirt or dehorning the livestock. Her resistance to Pauline was instrumental in the collapse of her father's marriage. Two years later, after much political and religious wrangling, Henry obtained a divorce. He was again forced to make a decision on what would be best for Lucy.

Everything changed on April 12, 1861, when Confederate General P.G.T. Beauregard bombarded Fort Sumter in an attempt to prevent supplies from reaching the Union troops stationed at their camp. Henry, fearing the war to be inevitable, sold his farm for very little money. He and Lucy moved to North Carolina, where he felt they would be safe, believing the war would not advance that far north. In any event, the small amount he had received for his farm was insufficient to purchase a farm of any substance in North Carolina. As the war progressed, he realized he could not avoid serving his new country for long. He needed to find a caretaker for Lucy, and with the war beginning to rage, and with no living relatives interested in taking her in, he devised a plan. He would join the fight, disguise Lucy as a boy, and take her as a drummer boy. Lucy agreed to this plan, more in fear of being left behind by her father than facing the Yankees on the battlefield. In January of 1862, after months of practice, Lucy could beat a drum as well as any other young boy. Henry, along with Lucy, disguised as a young boy, traveled from Caldwell County to Raleigh and volunteered to serve in the 22nd Infantry Regiment. Henry insisted that his son, Luke, be allowed to stay with him and not be transferred to another unit. Staring at Lucy, the recruiting sergeant appeared skeptical.

"What's your name, son?' he barked.

She hesitated slightly and looked up to her father–this was the one obvious part of the plan they had not anticipated. Then turning to the recruiter, Lucy blurted out, "Lucy, Sir!" Her face turned red as she looked at Henry and immediately corrected herself. "**LUKE**, it's Luke, Sir!"

"So," raising his eyebrows, he asked, "Is it Lucy or Luke?"

"Luke, sir!"

"Last name same as your father's?" he asked.

"Yes, sir." Now shaken by her error, Lucy kept her answers short. She and her father had discussed her voice and decided it best not to speak too much because her voice would obviously be a sure giveaway.

After a long pause, the sergeant asked with suspicion, "So, **Luke**, how old might you be?"

Trying to deepen her voice, she replied, "Fifteen, sir."

"Hmm," he cracked a smile. "And you might not be a lass trying to join up with us? Because that happens, and we prefer men only."

"Oh, no, sir, I am a boy. A drummer boy!" she announced, her voice quivering while pointing toward the drum she had brought with her.

"I can see you have a drum. Do you know the commands? Pick your drum up, and let me hear you play what I ask."

Moving to her drum and strapping it on, she waited.

"Okay, play 'The Alarm,' 'Assembly,' and 'To Arms.' Play them in that order.

Lucy looked at her father. He nodded and held his breath as she began to bang on her drum. She was flawless. The sergeant nodded with satisfaction.

"Now, do 'Beat for Orders,'" he added with a smile. It was a more complicated call, consisting of peculiar rolls and taps. Again, Lucy was perfect.

"So, Luke, one more question," he asked with a chuckle. "If I were to take you over into those bushes," he said, nodding his head toward the wood line, "and asked you to pull your prick out, would you be willing to do that?"

Lucy looked at her dad, who hesitantly responded to the recruiter. "That isn't necessary. I can assure you. I will vouch for him being a male. I have washed him many times when he was a baby. He surely is a male."

The sergeant laughed. "Okay, he's your **son**," he said with mockery in his voice. I will take your word for it. Put your X's on this paper and come back tomorrow. Bring anything of a personal nature you may need. You will be given uniforms, and Luke, we will issue you a new drum. And may God bless the both of you." Henry and Lucy signed the enrollment form and walked away with smiles on their faces. The sergeant watched them, shook his head, and looking toward the sky, whispered, "Sweet Jesus, what will this war bring to us?"

39.

Vermont

On October 10 of 1864, Bennett H. Young sat on the bed in
the run-down hotel room, surrounded by a small ragged
group of confederate soldiers and others who had been
discharged from Lee's army. They all had battle wounds and were
suffering from fatigue but had decided to fight on and to take the
fight north. The lodging was on the border of Canada and America
and the closest point to St. Albans, Vermont, where Young's plan
was to unfold. In the room were only his five most trusted men. He
would discuss the operation with them, and they would disclose
it to the other men the night before the attack. Standing around
Young were three sergeants, a corporal, and one crippled veteran,
Edward Valentine, his trusted friend from his days in the P.O.W.
camp. Upon their escape, Young and Valentine traveled to Canada,
a neutral country. While Young remained in Canada, Valentine had
returned to America.

"So, gentleman, I assume that many of you are wondering
how I attained my rank of lieutenant, as the last time many of
you saw me, I was a private. My commission came as the result
of my proposed plan to assist President Davis in rebuilding the
treasury of the Confederate States of America, which is why we
are assembled here today. I don't have to tell you that the defeat at
Gettysburg was a major blow to our forces and has weakened the
economic situation of our country. While many believe the war is
lost, I, for one, do not, and fervently believe this war can still be
won. There will be more men coming here to support us; they are
on their way as we speak. Most of them are men who escaped from
Union camps and made their way to Canada. When they arrive, we

will meet again, and I will disclose the plan. You will be given your assignments at that time, and, on the nineteenth, we will attack St. Albans, Vermont."

The idea of attacking a small town in Vermont made the men uneasy. Many of them were fidgeting from side to side while others were rubbing their faces and wanting to know more. They were wondering what the point of the raid was but knew better than to ask questions until the details of the attack were revealed at the next meeting. So, they remained silent. They had all known Bennett Young as a Private in the 8th Kentucky Cavalry, but now were curious as to how, and why, he was in charge of what seemed to be a strange place to fight a battle.

Several days later, after the arrival of the others, Young convened the meeting. "Gentlemen," he began, "there will be a total of twenty-one of us to make the attack. I would rather call it a raid, as I don't expect much resistance from the good people of St Albans. In fact, if you prefer, call it a bank robbery," he said with a grin. "There are three banks in St Albans. We will rob all three simultaneously. Four men in each group and the others, Corporal Pell and me, will control the townspeople. I would like this to be a bloodless attack. However, if any interference comes from anyone, kill them, otherwise remain in control." Young then took the time to assign squad leaders and gave each one the names of their members. Edward Valentine was assigned the duty of overlooking the entire operation. He was the one man Young trusted to ensure the raid would not get out of control. He had, after all, masterminded the escape of several men from the P.O.W. camp, including his and Young's.

As Young concluded the briefing, he asked, "Any questions? We are going to be bivouacked in this area for a week, maybe more. If anyone asks you what you are doing here, tell them you are on holiday. Stay out of town and keep your mouths shut. If I find anyone has talked to anyone outside this group about our plans, I will have you shot. Better yet, I will shoot you myself. Questions?"

The group in the room was quiet for several moments until

Valentine spoke up, "Will there be any money in it for me? I ain't even in the army no more!"

Young was taken by surprise by his trusted comrade, "The money will go into the treasury of the Confederate States of America. I will ensure you get enough food and supplies for your horse. So, the answer is no."

Valentine clenched his teeth and nodded. "If Pell hadda told me that, I'd a stayed home."

Young stared directly into Valentine's eyes, "And I believe he told you that he had orders to kill you if you refused. I need you on this raid, but you're not essential at this point. You are disposable." Young continued his stare, as did Valentine. Valentine smiled and walked out the door.

By October 18, all 21 men had moved the 15 miles toward St Albans and were prepared for the attack on the next day. All of the squads were deep in the woods, separated from each other to avoid making too much noise. The next day at 2:30 pm, they gathered and formed one unit. Young, leading the men, entered St Alban's, and like clockwork, the men walked into the banks. Valentine rode from bank to bank, watching and ensuring each robbery went smoothly. Young and Pell held the citizens who had gathered on the sidewalks at bay. Suddenly, Young announced with an exaggerated Southern accent, "Everyone, remain calm. We just want your money!" The townspeople did not resist, with one exception. One of the groups, led by a former prisoner of war, held a group of bank tellers at gunpoint and insisted they pledge allegiance to the Confederate States of America. Instead of the raid ending as planned, the delay gave several citizens time to enter the back of the bank with rifles. During the fracas, one citizen was shot and killed.

Incensed by the defense by the citizens, Young ordered the town to be burned to the ground. In spite of that, the small amount of 'Greek Fire' brought by the raiders was insufficient to cause any major damage, and only one building, a small shed, was burned. As the men raced out of the village with Young leading the way, he heard shots ringing out from the rear. As he looked back, he saw Pell holstering his pistol and Valentine toppling from his horse. Pell looked down as his horse leaped over the body. The column never slowed down.

40.

Friends At Last

✰✰✰✰✰✰✰

Nicholas and Lucy's journey took two days to get to Gettysburg. If Abner had been younger, it would have taken one day, but Nicholas was fearful of injuring the old horse, maybe even killing him. He also thought it would give him time to assess the situation with Lucy and to mull over what to do with her. *She is certainly capable of taking care of herself. Maybe let her go on her own.* Then he thought of his fiancée. Ella and her tragic demise. "No, she would have helped her," he said quietly.

On the first day of the journey, both Nicholas, Lucy, and Grant sat on the seat of the buckboard as the wagon moved along the rutted road headed toward Gettysburg. Both were silent, lost in their own thoughts. The weather was changing quickly, so Nicholas covered their legs with a blanket he had in the back of the wagon. He peered at her out of the corner of his eye. *Why did I not see that she was a girl?* In fact, although her looks were not unlike Ella's, they did not compare in beauty to Beatrice. As the day wore on, the silence became deafening.

"So, Lucy," he began cautiously on the first day of their trip. "Or, do you want me to call you Luke?" he asked, trying to make light of an uncomfortable situation.

Scratching one of Grant's ears, who sat between the two, she replied. "Does it matter?"

"Well, I think it does. After all, we're going to talk, right? We can't just call each other, 'Hey!'"

Lucy paused with a slight grin. "No, I guess not. You think I look like a boy or a girl?"

Without hesitation, Nicholas replied, "Why, a girl! So, you are going to be Lucy. And when we get to Gettysburg, I will find you some clothes to wear. That way, others will know too!"

"Okay, what will I wear? I've had this uniform on so long, I don't know if I can wear a dress, and I never really liked them anyway," she said with a smile. "So, I'm not going to the orphanage in Gettysburg?"

He looked at her, lifting his eyebrows and shaking his head, he replied, "No, you're not going to the orphanage." He gave a weak snicker, "Unless you want to, but I don't believe they allow soldiers in there as orphans."

Only halfway to Gettysburg, and fearing Abner was wearing down, Nicholas turned him into a field and directed him to the wood line. After stopping the horse, he scouted the area for a safe place to camp for the night, hoping no one would chase them from their property. Lucy stepped down and unhitched the buckboard, then turned and rubbed the old horse's back, talking to him softly. From a distance, Nicholas could hear her voice, soothing Abner. *Her voice sounds different now. Soft.*

"Let's clear this area and camp," he called out to her. "This looks good. Doesn't feel like any rain tonight." Nicholas built a small fire, and Lucy got out a pan and heated up a small meal of salted pork and hardtack, the last of their provisions.

"Well, Lucy, I think you and me are gonna have to 'borrow' a chicken and some eggs from someone tomorrow, or we're gonna starve," he laughed.

As she licked the grease from her fingers, she spoke out loudly, "We ain't gonna starve. I can guarantee ya that. I'll get us a hen and her eggs. You don't gotta do it."

"Okay, you southern boys were much better at poachin'," he said with a fake mockery in his tone. "Oh, are you southern girls good at it too?"

Lucy laughed. "You betcha. I'll wring that chicken's neck so fast she won't know what happened!"

The two sat in the darkness, not talking, both staring into the crackling fire. Finally, it was Lucy who broke the silence.

"You ever been married? Got any kids?" Her aloofness and silence had melted away.

Nicholas softly bit his lip, "Almost once. But not really. No kids."

"That don't make no sense," she said, shaking her head. "You can't be **almost**, but **not really**!"

Nicholas smiled, "Well, it's a long story," he answered softly.

The sense of her youthfulness started fading away during their conversation. "Well, I got all night. We ain't going nowhere, are we? So, tell me, the long story," she almost pleaded.

He continued to stare into the fire. Visions of Ella appeared to him in the glowing embers. "I really don't want to talk about it. It's kind of a painful story." Then added, "I'd actually rather try and forget it."

"She die?"

He stopped staring at the fire and turned toward her. "Like I said, it's a long story. Let's get some sleep. We have to try and make it to Gettysburg tomorrow. And to tell you the truth, I'm a little afraid that Abner may be on his last legs."

Lucy scooted closer to Nicholas, "Sorry 'bout what happened to your woman. Was she pretty?" she asked without hesitation.

"In her own way, I guess," he mumbled, searching again for the image of her in the dying cinders.

"Do you think I'm pretty?" she asked, moving next to him and placing her hand on his thigh.

Nicholas was taken aback. He moved away from her touch, stood up, and with a quick reply, "Yes, of course, you are. And when we get to Gettysburg and get you some clothes, you will be even prettier." He paused, took a deep breath, and trying to lighten the situation, continued, "Now, you go to sleep. You have to catch some breakfast for us in the morning!"

Lucy stood up and stared at Nicholas. "I only wanted to be next to you. I didn't mean nothin' else," she said with a quiver in her voice.

He was embarrassed. "I'm sorry, Lucy. I thought maybe you wanted, well, you know to..."

Interrupting his words, she snapped, "You thought I wanted to fuck you! I had enough of that with Andrew, and I didn't like it. I just thought you liked me. Don't worry, I'll fetch us a chicken and some eggs in the morning." She threw herself on the ground, wrapping herself in her blanket and stared away from Nicholas.

He bent down, picked up his blanket, and put it next to her, then stretched his arm out and put his hand on her shoulder. "We are friends, Lucy. And I will always be there for you, just like your father would have been. I'm sorry."

41.
Millie

It was early in the afternoon when they arrived at the outskirts of Gettysburg. Nicholas pulled back on the reins, and Abner came to a halt. From the height of the seat on the buckboard, Nicholas surveyed the ruins of the battlefields. They were empty now, but in his mind, he saw the dead lying face down; he heard the wounded calling out for their mothers, and he saw the young soldier he had shot point-blank in the face. It was that shot that changed his opinion of the war and, ultimately, his life. As he looked off into the fields, his thoughts raced back in time.

That war, these people—**their** war. The lies that got us here. I wish I had hidden in the woods of Pike County.

Nicholas was drifting on his memories as Lucy stepped off the buckboard, announcing that she needed to stretch her legs and get some grass for Abner. Grant jumped down and followed her. He had shared their breakfast made of the chicken she had managed to steal from a coop in spite of the farmer being nearby. Her words interrupted his reminiscing for a moment before acknowledging her. "Sure, go ahead" Then he immediately found himself drifting once again.

Other than hunting squirrels, deer, rabbits and other game, Nicholas had never used a gun. In fact, unlike other Herronville and Pike County folks, he was not a fan of hunting, but it was how his family and others survived during the winter months. In the summer, his family feasted on garden-grown vegetables and fruits.

So, when he was taken into the newly formed regiment, the 151st PA Volunteers, he was not familiar with the weaponry used by the military. His knowledge of the army was limited, and his world was that of Herronville, Pony Lake, and an occasional trip to Milford with his father to purchase supplies. When he reported with the other men to Camp Curtin and mustered in, he was shocked at the size of the rifle issued to him, a Springfield, Model 1842. It was long and bulky and heavy. Nicholas, along with the other newly recruited men, was leery of the situation they were being put into.

The training, while not physically demanding, was mentally tedious. Nicholas abhorred the marching and disliked the target practice. The men complained daily about the food and discipline meted out by the officers and NCOs. According to an old man, Albert Forrester, a recruit from Warren County who had rejoined the army and proclaimed to be a veteran of several previous battles, he talked about being wounded and subsequently discharged. In spite of that, no one ever saw his wounds, nor did he lay claim to any particular unit to which he may have been assigned. It occurred to Nicholas that Albert may have been exaggerating his stories and exploits.

One particular night as they sat around a small fire, Forrester began to tell a story of his time in Fredericksburg in 1862. "We was getting slaughtered. Men falling like fleas off a dog's back! Men on both sides were layin' everywhere. Piled up like logs on a woodpile. Well, once we got the upper hand, we went into that town and burned and stole everything we could. Even forced me on a woman, or two. I killed a lot of rebels there, some young boys, some old men. But, just remember when you get on a battlefield, young or old, they can kill you just as dead."

The young men sat wild-eyed as they listened in a combination of horror and fear of what they might encounter in the future.

"What's it like to kill someone?" a young soldier asked. Nicholas looked at him with curiosity. *He can't be fifteen.*

"Ever kill a deer?" Albert retorted excitedly.

"Yeah, lots!"

"Well, times that by one hundred. Hell, a thousand!" The young boy's eyes glistened.

"I can't wait to kill me a reb," he said with a grin. "I'll just take my gun and put it at his head and **BLAM**, blow it right the hell off!"

The older man continued, "Anyone else here ever kill anybody?"

The men just stared, some in amazement, some in disgust, some, by their expressions, terrified. Others with a glimmer of doubt.

Nicholas spoke up. "Me? Well, I never killed anyone, and don't wanna kill no one. And if I do, I hope it's someone that needs killing. And, Albert, personally, I've had enough of your stories. I don't know if they're true or not, but I've had enough of them! But I know that if I **do** have to kill someone, I sure as hell ain't gonna sit around and brag about it. Good night all. Reveille comes early.

As he stared into nothingness, his eyes watered, remembering the men he had killed. He also remembered Albert Forrester falling on his face when his head exploded from a rebel's bullet at Gettysburg. *There were no good feelings about it. And no good feeling about killing a deer.*

Nicholas yelled, "Lucy, get Grant. Let's move on to the part of town where there might be a shop. I gotta get you dressed up pretty," he said, smiling.

Lucy picked up Grant, holding him with his back legs dangling, and set him on the floor of the buckboard then pulled herself up. "You okay?" she asked.

"Yep."

"Then why you cryin'? Your eyes are all wet."

"Long story."

Lucy looked at his profile, "You sure do have a lot of 'long stories,'" she said softly. And then, "Let's go," and she reached over and held Nicholas's hand. "It'll be okay."

Abner plodded along the rutted road. Nicholas knew the horse's days were numbered. For a moment, he thought maybe he'd either sell him to someone in Gettysburg or maybe, just abandon him and move on with Lucy and Grant on foot to Emmitsburg. Still, each time he looked Abner in the eyes, he seemed to sense that Abner knew of his plan, so Nicholas spoke to him like he used to. "Don't worry, I'll never leave you." But in his heart, he knew one way or another that he would.

As they moved through the town, or what was left of the town, he searched the streets for anything resembling a shop where he might find clothes for Lucy, but there was nothing like that kind of shop. People, still weary from the war, were milling around on the fields of battle. Some were digging up graves of soldiers mostly looking for silver or gold on the bodies of the dead. Others were looking to find graves where they could easily exhume a body, or a body part still suitable to be sold to medical schools for training. *They're like crows picking at last year's crop.* Most of anything valuable had already been robbed shortly after the war. The body snatchers continued to stalk the fields which had already been taken by other grave diggers after the bloody battle. It was difficult for Nicholas to look at the fields. The site of them saddened him as well as enraged him. For most of the ride, he turned his head away or conversed with Lucy.

"Ya know, Lucy, I have about two dollars. Maybe we can get a little grub for ourselves and Grant. You can take Abner out into a field and let him munch grass and get him watered. We don't really have that much farther to go."

Lucy smiled, "So, I guess I ain't gettin' no new dress," she laughed. "That's okay, I wouldn't look good in it anyway," she said, forcing a smile.

Nicholas jumped off of the wagon, "I tell you what. You unhitch the horse, take him out into a field, and feed him good. Stay with him. Those diggers will take him if you don't watch out for him. Then come back into town and find me. I'll try to find us and Grant some food. Lucy nodded her head, walked to the front of the wagon, and began to take the harness off Abner. Nicholas whistled to Grant and walked into what was left of the small village.

Nicholas scoured the main street, hoping to find someone willing to sell him some food to feed the three of them. When he had passed through the town on his way home from the war, the people had been friendly. Now they were indifferent, not cordial, and most of his, "Good Afternoon" salutations were not returned by the town folks. As he turned the corner toward the seminary, a woman sat on her porch, rocking.

"Good morning," he said, tipping his hat.

She stopped rocking, "Okay, but it's afternoon," she said with a shallow laugh. "I guess I can't blame you for not knowing the difference. It all seems the same anymore, don't it? The war changed it all—everything," she said with sadness as she looked out onto the now barren battlegrounds.

Nicholas nodded his head in agreement. "It sure did. I know it changed me!" He wondered why he had responded like that and quickly changed his tone, "Ma'am, might I ask you a question?"

Without hesitation, the woman answered, "Millicent Cron, or Millie, and of course, you may, but I know what you're going to ask already, but go ahead."

Nicholas stepped back, "And how do you know that?"

"Cuz, I saw you come down the road with your boy in the wagon, that old horse pulling you. You know that horse don't look too good. Is he okay?"

Nicholas chuckled, "Yep, I think he's okay, but not really okay. And that boy, well, it's a long story, but he's a girl."

Somewhat appalled, she asked, "So, is she a Lobster Kettle?"

Nicholas was speechless, "A Lobster Kettle? What is a Lobster Kettle?" he asked with a grin on his face.

The woman gave out a hearty laugh, "You know, are you having a 'brush' with her!"

Nicholas blushed, "Of course not! She's only fifteen! She was a drummer for the Confederacy! I would never 'brush' with her! And shame on you for suggesting it!" he said, reprimanding her. "But I do need to feed her and my dog. That's what I was going to ask you, but I will look elsewhere. Thank you just the same."

Millicent stood up from her rocker, "Come into the house," she said, squinting her eyes. "You certainly are a different kind of man. I will give you some food. It won't be much, but I have some meat and bread."

Nicholas, still taken aback, replied, "I have two dollars. I am not looking for a handout."

"And you're not getting one. I need some things done around here. You can do them for me." She held the door open for Nicholas, "Dog stays outside. There's a rope by the tree; tie him there. I'll get him a bowl," she said, staring at Grant, who was staring back. "Yep, you are different," she mumbled.

42.

The Candyman Returns

☆☆☆☆☆☆☆

It was snowing on the night of January 20, 1865, when Sidney Pell pulled his horse to a halt in front of Beatrice Valentine's house in Emmitsburg. He dismounted, walked onto her porch, and knocked on the door. He could see the light of a lamp shining through the window. After rapping several times on the door, Beatrice's oldest son, John, answered.

"Good evening. Is your mother at home?" he asked the boy. "Tell her Sidney Pell is here. If she has a moment, I'd like to speak to her."

The boy's eyes widened. "Ma!" he yelled excitedly. "The rebel with the candy and who took Uncle Edward with him is here!" He dashed toward the rear of the house, announcing it several times.

Trying to keep the heat from leaving through the front door, Pell took it upon himself to enter the house and close the door behind him. The mouth-watering aroma of a cooking roast wafted past his nostrils. He hadn't had a home-cooked meal in a very long time. A couple of minutes later, John reappeared, followed by his sisters, Esther and Ruth.

"My mother said to tell you that she will be with you in a minute. I think she has to brush her hair. She looks terrible," he blurted out.

"She does not, John!" Esther said, coming to her mother's defense. "She's just been working all day cleaning and such."

Pell laughed softly.

The youngest child, Ruth, poked her head around her older siblings, and asked, "You have any candy, Mr. Pell?"

Again, he chuckled, "Well, I don't know. But if your big brother were to go out to my horse and look in my leather pouch, he could find something y'all might like. Go ahead, John. Name is John, right?"

"Yes, sir, Mr. Pell. It's John. I was named after a John in the bible, I think."

"Well, John, you better get outside and get that candy before it disappears!' Ruth's eyes widened as she watched her brother sprint out the door.

Before John could return with the sweets, Beatrice came from the rear of the house and stood in the hallway.

"Good evening," she said, her face beaming, smiling broadly.

There was an embarrassing silence before Pell tipped his hat and offered a greeting that was more of a stutter than the eloquent one he had planned. What was supposed to be something like, "Good evening, Beatrice, it is a pleasure to see you again. As I promised, I have returned, and your brother-in-law will not," came out as, "Evening, Beatrice. John said that you look terrible, but I disagree."

Beatrice burst out laughing. "Well, I am flattered that you disagree with my son." Again, her face glowed. "And where is my favorite son?"

"Getting candy from Mr. Pell's horse!" Ruth chimed in loudly.

"Hmm," Beatrice said with a smile, "Mr. Pell's horse has candy? He must be a magic horse!"

"No, mother! It's in a pouch on the horse!" she giggled.

Within moments, John returned with a bag of candy. It was easy to see that the bag was well worn, and the contents were more than likely a bit stale, but no one would care. Pell and Beatrice stared into each other's eyes, neither having to say a word. It was apparent both of them were happy to see each other again. The silence was broken by John.

"Can we have some of the candy now, ma?"

Beatrice's eyes never left Sidney's gaze. "Yes, all of you go upstairs and take the candy with you. Mr. Pell and I have things to discuss. Go ahead," she said.

The three of them began up the steps, when suddenly, Esther turned to Pell, "Is my uncle coming back?"

He looked to Beatrice for help in answering.

"I don't know," Beatrice said sternly, "Now, go upstairs, or the candy will go in the cupboard until tomorrow!" Not having to be told twice, John and Ruth scurried up the steps. However, before she went up the steps, Esther, turned and looked at her mother and Pell. "Good-night," she said with a knowing smile.

Beatrice led Sidney into the parlor and lit a lamp. He walked over to an overstuffed chair, but Beatrice directed him to the sofa instead. "That will be more comfortable. I am sure you are exhausted from your journey." He graciously accepted her offer and made himself comfortable.

Beatrice immediately began the conversation she had wanted to have with him since the evening he and Edward had ridden off into the darkness.

"I didn't know if you would really come back. To be truthful, I didn't believe you when you promised me. I didn't believe much of what you told me. And, I am going to be blunt. Is he dead? Is Edward Valentine out of my life, and my children's life?"

Sidney leaned forward on the sofa, "First of all, Beatrice, I would never lie to you. I am a man of my word and honor. My word is my bond." And without hesitation, he added, "He is dead. I am sure of that."

Beatrice sighed, "You are sure?" she asked with great anticipation. "Did you see him die?"

"I did. There was a small skirmish, and he was shot dead," he added solemnly.

Tears welled up in her eyes. "I am grateful. I will tell them he was shot in battle. Regardless of his incivility towards us, I want them to grow up with dignity for the dead. I took them to Gettysburg when Lincoln gave his speech. I don't know if they understood any of it. In fact, I think Ruth slept through it," she smiled, "but maybe one day they will remember that they were there. It really wasn't much of a speech, but he made his point, I guess—the dead need to be honored.

Beatrice stood up and went into the kitchen and prepared Sidney a cup of coffee. Returning to the parlor, she set it on the table in front of Pell and casually asked, "Can you tell me about it? About what you and the others did in Vermont?" When Pell looked off to the side, she continued, "I read about it at the telegraph office. It said you all got caught. I was sure I would never see you again," her voice quivered.

"Well, we never really got caught. We made it into Canada with about eighty-eight thousand dollars from the three banks we robbed. Unfortunately, the United States government wanted Canada to send us back to them," he said with a small laugh. "When they refused to extradite us, they settled for the money to be sent back. We gave them about sixty thousand and told them that was all we got. We were allowed to return back to the south, the rest of the money with us, and now here I am keeping my promise to you," he said as he looked into her eyes. "I'm back."

Beatrice, though unsure why, felt herself blushing, a warmth filling her up. "So, what will you do now?" she asked, trying to change the subject of the conversation.

He suddenly smiled, "I figure the war is coming to an end soon. I am going to probably go back to Kentucky and farm tobacco. Maybe find a woman and fall in love, get married," he said with a gleam in his eyes. "I don't really know," he said, rubbing his chin as if in deep thought. "How about you? What are your plans when the war ends?"

"I have no idea. But, if you come and see me when it's over, I'll let you know." Then she quickly added, "How would you ever afford a tobacco farm?"

As he stood up preparing to leave, Pell's face lit up. "As I said before, not all of the money was given back to the banks."

Beatrice's face became blank. She looked up at him, "Are you saying that you, and the others, stole the rest of the bank's money?"

"Let's say, we confiscated it," he said, trying to make light of the situation.

Beatrice became silent. After several moments, she spoke, not harshly, but with great seriousness. "Mr. Pell, I am conflicted."

"How so, Beatrice?"

"Should I not be concerned with your moral character? You have sat here and admitted to stealing money from a raid. Money that belongs to the Union. I admit I am in great debt to you, and I also admit that I am attracted to you. From time to time, I have found myself thinking of you these past several months, hoping you would return. But now..."

Sidney stopped her. "If it is the matter of the money keeping you from wanting me to court you, I will gladly give it to a comrade. I am clever enough to make a living with my hands and provide for you, that is if our friendship should blossom into romance." Pell reached his hand to her, and after a brief gaze into his eyes, she reached out and grasped his tightly. There was silence until Beatrice spoke.

"Okay, Mr. Pell," she said with a wry smile, "I shall give you a chance to prove yourself as an honorable man."

He lowered his head and kissed her hand. Looking up into her eyes, he said, "I am no longer a part of the military. I have resigned. I have seen enough. I will find work in Emmitsburg and court you properly if you would allow it."

Beatrice's smile widened. "We shall see, Mr. Sidney Pell. We shall see!" She stood, grasped his hand, and escorted him to the door. As he walked toward his horse, she closed the door, put her back against the cold wood, smiled, and repeated, "We shall see, Mr. Pell."

43.

A New Friend

☆☆☆☆☆☆☆

Nicholas occasionally looked out the window, watching for Lucy. There wasn't much to the town, but he figured he would eventually see her. Millie was not like Harriet. She was older, and certainly not attractive by anyone's standards. Still, Nicholas liked her. If anything, she reminded him of some of the women from Herronville—pleasant, but maybe a bit too inquisitive. And as he had found out during the brief conversation on the porch, she apparently had a dirty mind.

He saw Lucy at a distance and poked his head out the door, whistled to her, then waved her to come to the house.

"When you're done whistling, come into the kitchen, and I will make you some sandwiches. And there is a bone here for your dog," Millie offered. "What's her name?"

"Grant," he said, as he moved toward the kitchen, still looking back for Lucy.

"Not the damn dog, the girl. And how the hell did you end up with her?"

Nicholas sniggered, "Well, the dog, whose name is Grant, was given to me by a woman who was going to kill me. And Lucy, that's the girl that you thought was a boy as did I, well, I kind of inherited her from an old, crazy man who was also going to kill me, at least I think he was. But then, the son of the woman who wanted to kill me, well, he killed him. And Lucy was his. I guess you'd call her his 'Lobster Pot.' She didn't want to be his girl, but he protected her while they were in a prison camp in Maryland. So, anyway, that's how I got the dog and the girl. OH! And the horse, Abner, he also belonged to the woman who wanted to kill me." He finished the story with a quizzical look on his face. "Did any of that make sense to you?" he asked apologetically.

Millie stood with her mouth open, staring blankly at him. By this time, Lucy was standing in the doorway, having heard it all. Both women's eyes were wide open. The silence was broken by Millie when she burst into a deep, baritone, laugh.

"I don't understand one damn word you said! So, let's start over. Why don't you start by telling me your name!" she said, shaking her head and smiling. "I know Grant and Abner, and this pretty girl must be Lucy. Now, who are you?" she smiled.

Embarrassed, Nicholas, who had taken his hat off when he entered Millie's house, gave a half-hearted bow, "Nicholas, Nicholas Haff, ma'am. I apologize for not introducing myself. My mother would be unhappy with me. She taught me manners," he declared.

"Well, Nicholas, where do you hail from?" she asked with a smile.

"Herronville, it's in Pike County," he said.

As quickly as she had smiled, she became serious. "Did you fight here in these fields?"

"Yes, yes, I did," he replied, taking a heavy sigh. He didn't want to talk about the war. He heard and saw the war every night in his sleep.

"Pike County boys," she added as she put her hand over her mouth. "Were you with those boys who were slaughtered?"

He wanted to avoid the question. He only wanted to have a bite to eat and to feed Lucy and Grant. However, he didn't want to be rude. He already felt as if he had made a fool of himself telling the story of Lucy and Grant.

"Yes, ma'am, I was with them. They were brave men."

Millie's mood was somber, and tears welled up in her eyes. "Those boys, you boys, never had a chance. You were slaughtered like pigs. Doubleday," she spat his name out, "well, let me just say that you could have picked a better name for your horse."

Nicholas, not wanting to disparage the great general, nodded in agreement, "Yes, we lost most of our men. I was only saved because..." he stopped short of telling her the reason he had lived, and also of the young rebel boy he had killed in a battle. "Ma'am, I don't want to seem rude, but I prefer not to talk about the war. It makes me uneasy. So, I think Lucy and my animal friends will just move on. But I do appreciate your hospitality." In an effort to lighten the situation, he added, "And maybe I will change Abner's name to 'Abe.'"

"**Bullshit!**" she barked. "You'll stay here and eat. Then you'll see if you can fix the handle on my well pump because both of you need a good cleaning. Neither of you smells any too good. And Lucy, we haven't really met yet, and even if I am a good bit bigger than you, after we eat, you and me are gonna go upstairs and get you some clothes and turn you into a girl. If they don't fit, I'll fix 'em up so they do. Nicholas, take this bone to your dog. After we eat, go get that old nag and bring him here. I have some oats in an outbuilding. He looks like he could use a meal. Now, take the bone out and come back, and we'll eat."

Millicent insisted that they stay and rest for two days. Because she was so easy to talk to, Nicholas bared his soul to her. He told her about his time in battle, the death of many of the men he had fought with at Gettysburg and Chancellorsville., his love of Ella in Herronville, and her death. He also told her about Beatrice, how he was headed to Emmitsburg to find her, and of his intentions of courting her, perhaps even one day raising a family. Millie listened intently, never responding with other than a nod of the head, or a "yes" or an "Oh my" and a smile.

During their short stay, Millie began to transform Lucy into a proper girl. She was not entirely comfortable in her new garments. Still, it was plain to see that she would blossom into a beautiful young woman. Nicholas imagined her mother must have been a pretty woman, as well. When Lucy saw Nicholas, she would feign a curtsy, and Nicholas would tease her and call her "your majesty"!

The weather was cold the day before he had planned on leaving. Millie went to the room he was occupying, knocked on the door, and asked him to put on something warm. She wanted to walk with him. Agreeing, Nicholas and Millie walked toward the seminary, an area he knew only too well. She rested against a wall, the same one that many soldiers had used for cover as they watched their comrades as well as rebel soldiers slaughtered.

"Nicholas," she began, as she reached to hold his hand, "As you are probably quite aware, I have become very fond of you in a very short time."

Memories of Harriet flashed through his mind, and Nicholas quickly pulled his hand away and stood up.

Millie laughed a soft laugh, "NOT THAT kind of fond. Sit back down, Nicholas."

He squirmed as he tried to hide his embarrassment and attempted to offer an apology.

Waving off his stammering, she continued. "I am sorry for you and your time in the war. For everything you and the others endured. I watched as the bodies were taken to the seminary. I watched it all. I only hope–I pray– that all the blood that was shed will someday make this great country greater. We will never know. But I am sorry what you went through." She hesitated, possibly waiting for a response, or waiting for her words to make sense to the young veteran. "I have a couple of things I want to say to you, both might be difficult to swallow, but I have to say them. Nicholas was peering into the fields. He only half-heard what she had said. He was looking at the battlefields. *I was here! Right here!*

She stared at him, understanding what he was seeing. After all, she witnessed it for three days out of her window and off her porch. "Nicholas, did you hear anything I said?"

He shook his head. The battle stopped, and she appeared. "Yes, I'm sorry I was just..."

"I know," she interrupted. "but I have to say this now, and please don't be upset," she pleaded.

He gave a forced smile, "Go ahead, I might as well have one more bad memory of this place."

Again, she reached for his hand, but this time he did not pull away. "I know that you are in love with the idea of Beatrice. And believe me, I want it to happen for you. Just be sure that you know that it might not happen as you want it to." She paused, waiting for a reaction or a response that did not happen.

He sat with his head cocked as she continued, "You don't know anything about her situation. She could be remarried, maybe moved. Any number of things could have happened since you saw her for that fleeting moment. I want it to happen for you, but if it doesn't, well, there are others who will love you."

Without looking at Millie, he responded, "It'll happen. She'll be there."

She sighed, "Okay, Nicholas, and I will pray that it does."

"Don't pray, Millie, it doesn't work," he mumbled. He could feel his anger building, and he needed to control it. *This woman has been good to you. Thank her and move on.*

"Well, that discussion will have to take place at another time," she said sheepishly. "But in the meantime, I am going to be blunt with you. Lucy needs to stay here with me. She is young, and if everything with Beatrice falls apart, well, what will you do with a fifteen-year-old girl? I can use the help, and she needs my assistance in learning how to become a woman. We can discuss it with her tonight. If she is adamant about not staying here, then you can take her, but I believe that it would be the best thing for her. I can teach her to cook, to sew, and well, to take care of herself as a woman."

Nicholas was silent for several moments, and then his chest heaved with a long sigh. "I have no particular hold on Lucy. Hell, I've only known her for a short time. I just know that she, like all of us, has seen terrible times. She saw her daddy killed, she's been raped, beaten, you name it. And to tell you the truth, if Beatrice isn't there for me, I don't know what I will do with her; in fact, I don't know what I will do with me. So, if she agrees to stay with you, I think it's for the best. If she wants to stay with me, well, I'll just have to figure out how to turn a fifteen-year-old boy into a girl," he laughed, somewhat sadly.

44.

Memories

☆☆☆☆☆☆☆

Millie, without any parting words, nodded her head as she turned and walked away back to her house. Nicholas sat alone on the wall, staring at the chips of stone and rock still lying on the ground from the volleys of bullets and cannon fire that had hit it not that long ago. He began walking toward the battlefield where he had fought. *Back then, there was so much smoke and confusion, I didn't know where I was.* He surveyed the landscape, and he recalled the sounds of the battles reverberating in his ears.

When they were ordered to move to McPherson's Ridge from the relative safety of the Lutheran Seminary, Nicholas swallowed hard, believing it would be the end of the war for him. And while it wasn't the end of his life, the Confederate troops, strategically placed in trees, took careful aim and began to kill the men to the left and right of him. Inexplicably, he was not hit, which gave him no solace at the time. Under the command of Lieutenant Colonel McFarland, the men fought nobly until they became outnumbered and flanked by a brigade of North Carolina infantry led by General Pettigrew. The result was disastrous for his unit, and he, along with the remaining men, were directed back to the safety of the seminary. There they, along with other regiments, dug in to prepare for the next wave of the Confederate attacks.

Unknown to the men in Nicholas's company, the Confederates had outflanked them, and the Federal troops to their left had retreated leaving them alone. McFarland, in an effort to save his remaining forces, ordered a retreat to the heights, south of the town. During the retreat, Nicholas watched as McFarland was shot in both legs. He stood motionless as Private Lyman Wilson pulled, dragged and carried McFarland to the Seminary for treatment. Nicholas did not help.

It was on July 3, when General Doubleday, ordered the remaining men of the 151st to assist in repulsing General Picket's charge. It was during that attack that Nicholas killed his final man and became too mentally distraught to fight on. He later learned that of the 478 men who mustered in with him, only 111 remained.

The battle raged in his head as he walked in a daze through the fields. Recently dug and dug up graves were scattered for miles. He didn't recognize anything except the seminary. As he looked back at it, the sight of the building still brought him comfort. It had been the only place where he felt safe during the three days of the raging battle. He wanted to find the fields where his comrades had fallen and died, but he couldn't recognize the places anymore without the smoke of cannon and the noise of gunshots and screaming. He sat on an unmarked grave, not even sure if anyone was still lying beneath and gazed onto the fields.

From out of nowhere, a late afternoon thunderstorm rolled across the fields. A wave of anger swelled inside him, and tears rolled down his cheeks as he spoke softly. "To all of you responsible for the death of these men and boys, may your bodies suffer, and pain inflict you and your families until the day you and them die. Lincoln, no one will remember what happened here! No one will truly know the pain that happened here! No one will ever truly know about the men who screamed for their mothers as they lay bleeding to death! No one will care! Where was that caring God that everyone speaks of?" He looked around, and then more loudly said, "Nothing good will come of this, nothing."

Still unable to find landmarks where he fought and where his friends died, he turned, put his hands in his pockets, and walked toward the seminary and on to Millie's house. He hoped Lucy would accept Millie's offer to stay with her. In his heart, he knew it was the right thing to do.

45.
Emmitsburg At Last

☆☆☆☆☆☆☆

Nicholas's planned departure was delayed until the next day, as Millie, Lucy, and he discussed Lucy remaining with Millie. What Nicholas thought would be an easy conversation, ended up being a four-hour argument. Lucy, at times, reverted to her battle-hardened personality, cursing at Nicholas and Millie, calling them "dirty Yankees" and wishing she had killed him when she had first met him. Then, she would apologize and beg Nicholas to take her with him. Nicholas, on edge, not knowing what the results of the meeting with Beatrice would be, insisted that she stay with Millie. Promising her that if the reunion with Beatrice was as he hoped it would be, he would come back and take her with him to Emmitsburg. Millie, on the other hand, stayed silent during this exchange. "Let's see what happens," is all she said in response to his promise to return for Lucy. It was finally decided, with very little agreement from Lucy, that she would stay with Millie until Nicholas returned for her.

Lucy's response to the plan was simple and angrily to the point. "I will stay here for one week, and then I'm coming to find you in Emmitsburg. How hard could it be to find a Beatrice, especially one named Valentine!"

Nicholas and Millie looked at each other, both knowing Lucy was bound to end up in Emmitsburg. She had been through so much in her young life already. A short trip alone to Emmitsburg would be easy.

It was very early in the morning when Nicholas hooked his wagon to Abner and woke a sleeping Grant who had been relegated to the porch. Millie stood next to him as he finished buckling the

219

leather straps to Abner.

"I hope Abner makes it all the way. He's an old guy," she said with compassion as she stroked the animal's face. "Go slow with him," she added with concern.

"I will," he replied. "I think there are still fourteen or so miles left in him," he said, also with concern.

He looked to the upstairs window. A lamp was lit in the room where Lucy was staying, and he could see a silhouette behind the lace curtains.

"I guess she ain't coming down to say good-bye," he mumbled.

"She'll be fine," Millie said in a consoling voice. "Goodness, you've only known her a very short time. You go and see what goes on with Beatrice. Come back if you need to." she added with a tone in her voice that said, 'Don't get your hopes up.'

Nicholas shook her hand and thanked her, helped Grant up onto the wagon, and took one last look at Lucy's room. "Thanks again."

He shook Abner's reins, and the old horse began to plod off. It was several moments when he heard Lucy yell, "Nicholas, wait!" A slight tug on the reins is all it took to stop Abner.

"Here! she said as she reached into her pocket. "Take this. It was my mother's ring. I know if you have it, you'll have to bring it back to me! It's all I own. I'll see you soon." Her voice quivered as she turned and quickly retreated to the house.

Nicholas attempted to holler and stop her, but nothing came out of his mouth. He sat, staring at the small gold ring. He tucked it into his pocket and said, "Giddy-up."

Most horses could have made the trip in three hours. It took Abner seven. He needed to rest. His ribs were beginning to show, and Nicholas knew that his days were numbered. He dreaded putting another horse down, especially Abner, who had been through so much with him. *They are such noble animals, not like a pig.* However, when he saw the steeple of the church in Emmitsburg, all of his thoughts turned to Beatrice. She had told him she lived next to the church. All of his anticipation now turned to anxiety and fear. His thoughts became jumbled, and they all ran together like a hail of bullets coming at him.

Maybe she remarried; maybe she's dead; maybe she won't like me. What if she thinks I'm crazy? What if she moved away? "Maybe I should turn around, go get Lucy and go back to Herronville," he said under his breath. He looked at the back of Abner's head that was bowed down as if in prayer. He shook the reins and directed the animal toward the church.

As he approached the building, he could see children in the yard. "Don't stop. Not yet." He passed the house. He thought he recognized the kids, all of them waving, while the boy yelled, "Hi, Mister!" Nicholas waved back, wondering if they recognized him. He would go to the outskirts of town, feed Abner and Grant, eat the food Millie had given him and, camp out for the night. *Tomorrow will bring a new day.* He reached into his pocket for his knife and felt the ring.

"What am I supposed to do?" he asked himself, confusion in his voice.

46.

Beatrice

☆☆☆☆☆☆☆

When Nicholas awoke, there was no food for him or for his animal companions. Worse yet was his urge to break campsite and point Abner toward Herronville and forget about the folly he now believed he was on. He had become completely befuddled by Millie's words as they had spoken at the wall near the seminary: *Millie is right! I don't know anything about her situation.*

The words resounded in his head. "She is right. I **don't** know anything about her situation," he repeated out loud. "Those children, those children won't remember me. Hell, she might not even remember me!" *What was I thinking? Did the war make me this crazy? A lady puts a patch on my eye, and now I show up wanting to court her?* He sat for hours, not bothering to start a fire, but rather stirred the ashes of the previous night with a stick. Grant ambled over and leaned into him, staring at him.

"There's no food," he said with no compassion in his voice, not bothering to look at the hungry dog. His emotions began to overload his mind. *What am I going to do? I can't just walk up to her house and say, Hi, I'm Nicholas Haff. Do you remember me? I met you when Lincoln said his stupid speech at Gettysburg! You fixed my eye when it was filled with pus.* He stood up and became animated, acting the scenario out loud. "You don't remember me? Why I laid right next to you in the grass while that ugly monkey gave that speech that meant nothing! And you tried to convince me that he was a great man! Remember?"

After he wore himself out, he gave a deep sigh and looked at Grant, "I'll kill us a rabbit or a squirrel. Too bad we ain't like Abner.

We could just eat some grass." When he turned to look over at Abner, the horse was gone. He had tied him to a small tree with rope enough to graze. He rubbed his temples, and tears formed in his eyes. Grant looked up at him, his soft brown eyes filled with understanding, or so it seemed. Nicholas responded with uncertainty in his voice, "Come on, Grant. We have to go for help. Let's go see what happens when I knock on her door. She fixed my eye; maybe she can fix this. Hopefully, we'll spot Abner on the way." Somehow, he knew he wouldn't find him, at least not until he walked back into the woods near his campsite. Either way, he would eventually have to find another horse.

It was a mile or two before he saw the house and yard where he had seen the children playing the evening before. As it first came into view, he felt another surge of panic flow through his body, and he stopped walking. He sighed deeply. He wanted to sit and think his plan out, which was not really a plan, but a plea for help. He had no money, no horse, and he now believed no chance to court Beatrice, which he realized was a fool's quest at best. He remained motionless for several moments. "Keep moving, soldier," he mumbled. "C'mon, Grant." Ten minutes later, he and the dog stood on the road staring at Beatrice's house. "It's next to the church, just like she said it would be," he said, looking at Grant and stalling. Grant looked at the house and then at Nicholas. "Let's go, boy."

As he approached the house, the door opened, and a boy appeared in the doorway. He recognized him. *I think his name is John.*

"Hey, mister," he yelled at Nicholas. "Can I help you?"

He stared at the boy for a moment. "Hi," he returned the greeting. "I was wondering if you might be able to give me and my dog a bit of food. I'm afraid that we've run upon some bad luck. And I'm also afraid my horse has either run away or maybe died in the woods. He was very old and frail." Then he gathered the courage to ask the question he wanted to. "Also, is your mother at home? I don't want her to see me out here talking to you and be scared that something bad is happening."

John shuffled his feet. "Okay, she's home, I'll get her. And I'll get you and your dog some food. Is he a friendly dog?" he asked.

"Thank you," his voice replied with a quiver. "I really appreciate it. He's friendly. His name is Grant." The boy turned quickly and disappeared into the house, leaving the door open.

It seemed to Nicholas that the boy must have forgotten him, when in fact, it was only minutes when he returned with a basket filled with food. "Here," he said, handing the basket to Nicholas. Grant jumped on to Nicholas's leg begging for food. As fast as he could, Nicholas set the basket on the porch, reached into it, and tore a piece of meat from a roast that was meant for him and gave it to the dog. "My mother said to give this to you. She's very busy right now and cannot come out."

His heart fluttered with anxiety. He gave his thoughts some time to make another plan. *Sometimes, like Pickett, you just have to charge.*

"Are you, John," he blurted out.

The boy, taken by surprise, blurted back, "Yes, sir. Yes, I am."

"Well, John, do you remember me? I was at Gettysburg when..." then he hesitated, "when President Lincoln gave his speech. Remember, your mother fixed my eye?"

John's face lit up. "I remember you! You were that soldier! You and me went to the pond and got water! Wait here! I have to tell my mom! Come on the porch," he yelled excitedly, and turning around, added, "And your dog!" The door slammed, and without hesitation, Nicholas and Grant climbed the steps and sat down, waiting for Beatrice. Nicholas began to gnaw on the rest of the roast he had shared with Grant.

When Beatrice appeared, Nicholas swallowed hard. She was as beautiful as the first time he had seen her, and his heart pounded. She smiled at him, the same way she had when she had told him to sit next to her during Lincoln's speech.

"And I believe you are the young soldier I met at Gettysburg," she said with a singsong in her voice.

His mouth was parched. He tried without success to moisten it. "I am, and you are Beatrice, the kind woman who fixed my eye. Thank you!" he replied.

Beatrice grinned, and nodding, responded, "You're quite welcome. How is your eye now?"

"It's fine. Well, as fine as it's going to be. The doc in Herronville, that's where I live, well, where I used to live. That is, I lived there until I came here. My mother still lives there, she's old now," he rambled. Saving him from any further embarrassment, Beatrice interrupted him.

"So, what brings you here?' she queried with a smile and wide eyes after listening to Nicholas's humorous story of Herronville. "And I must apologize, I cannot remember your name. Nathan?"

He swallowed hard. "No, ma'am, it's Nicholas," he replied, glancing down at Grant. "Nicholas Haff."

Realizing that she had hurt his feelings, she quickly added, "How stupid of me, how could I ever forget the name of such a handsome, well-mannered young man. So, what in the world are you doing in Emmitsburg?"

He had not planned on this type of encounter. Beatrice stood, waiting for his answer. And after a long pause by Nicholas, she asked him if he and Grant would like to come inside, saying she had a chore or two to do.

Upon entering the house, Nicholas looked around and noticed the well-made pine staircase. "This is a beautiful home."

"Why, thank you, Nicholas." Then, "How long will you be staying in our town?"

Nicholas scratched his head. "I don't really know. I think my horse died or is lost. I'm not sure."

"Oh my! I am sorry!" Excusing herself, she walked toward the parlor and then speaking loudly, "Well, you are welcome to stay in our barn for as long as you like. I am sure my husband will be glad to help you find a new horse. He is doing labor work, but he will be home this evening. Even though he was a Rebel, I think you two will hit it off just fine! I remember you were very good with my children. They will be glad you are here!" she laughed. "His name is Sidney. I am no longer Beatrice Valentine. I am Beatrice Pell. And in seven months, there will be a little Pell!" she announced with glee.

When she returned to the living room, Nicholas and Grant were exiting the front door and jumping down the porch steps. Running to the door, she yelled his name, beckoning him to return. He never looked back, and when he approached the road, he turned left and headed toward the town of Emmitsburg. All of his earthly belongings were left behind with Abner.

The walk to Emmitsburg was not far, but his mind was having a battle of its own. *I should have known better.* Stopping, he looked back toward Beatrice's house. *What was I thinking? Why would a beautiful woman like that want to be my wife?* He had not felt this kind of emptiness in many years, not since Ella's death. He immediately dismissed that thought and tried to focus on what lay ahead. He had no money and no horse. He only had the clothes on his back and Grant, who kept looking to him for food. "I know boy. I'll find us something when we get to Emmitsburg," he said, reaching down to scratch the dog's head. He didn't want to go back to his wagon. If he did, he would have to pass Beatrice's house, and he didn't want to go there and find Abner dead. He knew, in his head, he had died. He had seen enough dead horses.

He and Grant moved about town. *Maybe I can get a job to make some money. Maybe I could go back and ask Beatrice for some.* The thought made him laugh. He realized that his situation was bleak. He and Grant sat on the side of the main road in town, gazing at the buildings. There weren't many, and none had been affected by the war, as the town was divided in their loyalties, some men fighting for the North, some for the South. Suddenly, his eyes saw a sign in the window of a building, and a thought flashed through his mind. It was the telegraph office. He stood up and crossed the road to the building, "C'mon, Grant. I think I may have found a solution to our problem."

He walked into the office and looking at the man behind the counter, asked, "How much to send a telegram to Gettysburg, sir?"

The operator smiled. "Why, it's a dollar, young man."

Nicholas put his hands in his pockets. "Well, I don't have a dollar."

"Then how did you think you could send a telegram. They aren't free, you know," he replied with a smile. "Who is your friend there?" he asked, looking at Grant.

"Huh?"

"The dog, what's his name?"

"Oh!" Nicholas responded," He's Grant. Yep, he's my friend. Seems like my only friend, right now, anyway."

The man studied Nicholas's face. "Hmm, hard times hit you? I assume you were in the war. No one would name their dog that if they weren't. At least I don't suppose they would. He looks hungry. In fact, you both do. I have a sandwich here," he said, reaching under the counter. "Here ya go, mister."

Nicholas stared at the brown paper containing the sandwich.

"Your name, sir, what's your name? Not Ulysses, I hope," the telegraph man chuckled.

Nicholas stopped staring at the sandwich. "Oh, I am sorry, sir. My name is Nicholas. Nicholas Haff. And I was in the war. I passed by here once on my way to fight in Gettysburg. Of course, we didn't know we were gonna fight for three days. But then when we got there, well we fought and my unit, well, we didn't do too good. And when I mustered out, I came by here and heard Lincoln give that little speech that he gave up there. I met a woman, her name was..."

"Nicholas! Slow down, you're going to break your tongue! You eat your sandwich, and I'll get Grant some scraps from the butcher next door. I will be right back," he said with a grin.

Nicholas gulped the sandwich down, sharing one bite with Grant and hoping he would be able to send a telegram. Within several minutes, the man returned with enough meat and bones to keep Grant busy for hours.

"Thank you, sir," he said as he wiped his mouth. "This has been very kind of you."

The man removed his glasses, "You're surely welcome, Nicholas," he said softly. "I had a boy in the war as well. His unit didn't fare too well, either. He died," his voice quivered. "So, anyway," he began taking a deep breath. "I take it you need to send a telegram. I also take it that if you don't have a dollar, you are flat broke."

Nicholas looked down at the floor, "Yes, sir, I am."

"Nothing to be ashamed of. Many people are broke these days. And the Carpetbaggers aren't making it any better. But I tell you what. I have a cot at my house, and I need someone to chop wood for the winter. I'll pay you two dollars a day, and you can send as many telegrams as you like for free. And Grant is welcome in my house. The missus will love him."

Nicholas mulled the offer for only moments, "I accept your offer, mister." The man stretched his arm out and shook his hand. "Mr. James Bradford. Call me, Jim."

"Thank you, Mr. Bradford, uh…Jim. You will never know how much I appreciate what you are doing for me."

Bradford sat down behind his desk, "Well, let's send your first one!" he exclaimed, rubbing his hands together. "Go ahead, who is it going to and where?"

Nicholas took a deep breath, "To Millie Cron, Gettysburg…"

47.

The Speech

☆☆☆☆☆☆☆

In January 1874, to his dismay, Nicholas was elected commander of his local G.A.R.. His duties included attending and speaking at the organization's eighth national reunion in Harrisburg, PA, on May 13 of the same year. Although he was only thirty years old, his body was weathered from war and stress. And yet, other than having eventually lost the sight in one eye from washing in polluted water, he was healthy. His memory of the war from the previous ten years remained perfectly clear. It was still very disturbing at times, and left him suffering from sudden fits of anger and rage, but he had learned to deal with it.

Nicholas had never spoken to an audience, let alone the large gathering of men who would attend the convention. For three months, he contemplated the different topics that would be interesting to the veterans, knowing that they would be eager to hear of his thoughts and experiences during the war. Some members of his post suggested he address the sacrifices of their fellow comrades, the pain and suffering they endured, while others told him to lobby for benefits they believed were due them. After much soul searching, Nicholas decided he would use his time on the stage to declare his admiration for those who died on the battlefields. He would tell the gathering of men, never to forget those who sacrificed so much. He would also say it was time to start paying homage to those men from the southern states, and that it was time to forgive each other. And finally, he would speak of his unit's valor at Gettysburg. He would read the names of those who gave the ultimate price from his unit, the Pennsylvania 151st Infantry Volunteers.

He arrived by train in Harrisburg on Tuesday, May 12. On the following day, much to his relief, the group he was to address was much smaller than he had anticipated. *Maybe two or three hundred?* He sat and attentively watched and listened to the other speakers before him. Most spoke of their own heroism and not of their fellow soldiers. He surveyed his veteran colleagues who sat on the grass. Most of them were older than he, a few younger, some missing limbs, some rambling to themselves. Others were attentive and had tears in their eyes as they remembered the battles in which they had fought. Some of those battles were won, some were lost. But all had one thing in common–the men suffered from their experiences in the war.

It was late in the afternoon when the Master of Ceremony announced his name and the unit he represented. The man beamed as he beckoned Nicholas to the platform, "Next to address you," he bellowed, "is Private Nicholas Haff. He was a member of one of the most honored regiments at the great Battle of Gettysburg, the 151st Pennsylvania Volunteer Infantry." When the unit was named, men stood and cheered. They recognized that the unit had been destroyed at Gettysburg. They knew there were very few of them left to speak about their exploits. His eyes watered, and he took a deep breath as he stepped onto the platform. The men continued to cheer. As the audience began to settle, Nicholas pulled his poorly written notes from his pocket and began to read them to himself. After several moments, he tightened his jaw and returned them to his pocket, ready to begin:

"Thank you, sir," Nicholas said, nodding at the man who introduced him. "Gentleman, fellow veterans, friends," he gulped as his mind raced, reaching for the correct words to address the crowd. "I am honored and humbled to have been elected by members of my G.A.R. Post, some belonging to the 151st, some to other regiments, to speak to you on this occasion." Again, when the 151st was mentioned, the men cheered loudly, giving him time to gather himself and his thoughts. He stared ahead at a veteran with no legs and one arm. Nicholas watched him slap the stump of his leg in an effort to recognize him and his unit's valor.

He continued, "I am no speaker, but will do my best to honor my fellow veterans of the 151st and all who fought during the bloody and terrible war. I remember as a younger man, I heard Lincoln speak at Gettysburg. It was a short speech, and, personally, I didn't think he was a very interesting speaker or even gave that good of a speech, so if I do as good as he did, I guess I'll be okay." Most of the crowd broke into cheers, others laughed, some sat on their hands. Nicholas smiled, and then with a somber attitude and saddened voice, he asked, "Do you all remember the day you watched your first man die on the battlefield?" he paused. "Or maybe you never did see anyone die, but surely you had friends who died. Do you remember it? And it didn't have to be a Union soldier. It could have been a Confederate soldier," he stopped, taking a deep breath. "Do you still see their faces? I do. And when those faces appear, not only do I think of them, but of you too. I see your uniforms, torn and ragged, the dirt on your faces, sometimes the blood on your faces." His voice began to quiver. It wasn't the speech he had written. This was what was coming from his insides. He wanted to stop, but he felt he would dishonor those who had sent him.

The audience sat quietly, some looking at the others as if waiting for them to answer. "We all saw and heard the same things; I think we did, anyway. The screams of the dying and wounded. Some calling their mothers' names, some their wives', some their daddies' names. Some call for Jesus, but none of them come to help. That's what I hear." He continued to look at the soldier with the amputations. "And when people come to me and ask me what the war was like, or worse, when they ask me 'Did you ever kill anyone,' and if I did, what it felt like. I can't answer. I want to say that it felt like I wanted to be back in my mother's arms, listening to a lullaby. Like I wanted to take all of the dead men home, Confederates and Union soldiers, home with me, and let my mother sing 'Rock-a-bye Baby' to them. That's how I felt!" His tone became more somber, and his voice cracked as he repeated,

"That's how I felt." Never taking his eyes off the crippled soldier, he took a deep breath. "To all of you, I say that the men lost during the war were killed because of their commitment to their cause." Nicholas thought deeply about what he was about to say. He took a deep breath and began. "And I don't hate any of those men we fought against. They, too, had their own cause. They, too, had their own families, and they, too, are being mourned. They also will have reunions, and word has passed through the crowd today that next year a reunion of the Blue and Gray will, for the first time, be held in New Jersey. Some of you were angry when you heard it. I believe we need to go there. We need to heal. We need to be one country again." He scanned the crowd. "As you heard earlier, or may know, my regiment did not fare well. Bodies were splattered on the walls and fences of Gettysburg. It is my understanding that we suffered the second most casualties at Gettysburg. I doubt those men will be remembered after we are gone. I originally was going to read the names of those killed. Their names are in my pocket on paper. I shall leave these names unread and nameless as those who laid dying next to us on the fields of blood. It would be unfair for me to ask you to honor only them." He stared back at the amputee, saluted the audience, stepped off the platform, and walked through a silent crowd to catch the next train north.

Epilogue

☆☆☆☆☆☆☆

In the Spring of 1875, after a hard winter, Nicholas began to prepare his homestead farm in Herronville for the upcoming season. He had converted the one-time cattle farm to a dairy business along with some pigs and chickens that he sold and slaughtered for his family's food. The little town of Herronville was growing. The original Haff family had settled in the village in the 1840s and began to purchase large quantities of land to keep those who came after from encroaching on them. Nicholas, also, to prevent strangers from becoming unwanted neighbors, was able to convince his extended family and friends, to purchase all of the property along the north shoreline of Pony Lake. This was the part of the lake, which held a special place in the hearts of all the townspeople. Young love had blossomed there, and the history of special events was sealed in the citizens' minds. The big rock located along the shore was where he and others had held their first loves' hands and sneaked a kiss from them when they were young. Ella Samter, his childhood sweetheart, gave him his first kiss on that very rock. It was also the place where his father, Jake, had swum naked and was spied on by his mother, eventually leading to their marriage. And it also held the sad memory of Ella's father being found on the shore with a bullet hole in his head, a suicide according to Doctor Wilkins. Now, he and the others owned the area and all of the memories that lay on the shore and in the waters of the lake. Anyone else who wished to fish, swim, or conduct any recreation would be compelled to do it on the south side of the lake.

The summer was good to the Haff family. He and his wife worked hard to raise their cows into a healthy herd. They were producing so much milk that regular customers could not purchase all of it. He bought two new horses and a wagon, making weekly trips to the towns of Hawley and Honesdale, Pennsylvania, some twenty and thirty miles from Herronville. When his wife was left on her own with their six-year-old daughter, she kept herself and the girl busy tending to the chickens, milking the cows and slopping the pigs. She also took advantage of Nicholas's time away to teach their six-year-old to read and write, but her efforts to teach her to milk the cows were fruitless. She was an odd child when it came to taking care of the farm animals, as she had little interest. She only wanted to take care of the family horse and dog. Even though the new additions were not at all similar to his previous ones, Nicholas continued to refer to them as Grant and Abner, which caused the girl to constantly correct him by saying, "Daddy, the horse is Junior, and the dog is Ulysses. Can't you remember that?" Then she would giggle.

The townsfolk were very helpful, especially Floyd Wilkins, who had delivered Nicholas's daughter. He was the son of the older Doctor Wilkins, who had treated Nicholas's eye up until there was no more hope to save his vision. Old Doc Wilkins passed away in the summer of 1873.

While the summer had been good to the Haffs, autumn, as it does with most things in nature, took Margaret Haff, Nicholas's mother. The woman who had spied on his father, and who had taken such good care of him during his illness was gone. It had been a long time coming, and Nicholas's wife, in addition to her other chores and responsibilities, tended to her with the utmost care. Nicholas would often stand in the doorway of her bedroom and marvel at Lucy's kindness to Margaret. The night of his mother's death, he wrote in his diary.

October 20, 1875

Dear Diary,

Tonight, my beloved mother, Margaret Haff, passed away. While I have no belief in a higher power, I do have a belief in my wife, Lucy. She is a special person, having overcome the perils of war, rape, and starvation, to become the kindest, most caring person I have ever met. She watched as her father died at the hands of an uncaring savage, in a war I participated in, but a war that made no sense to me. As a young girl, she dressed as a boy to join her father in that war, and she paid dearly. Somehow, this woman, throughout it all, has become the most caring, kindest person I have ever known. Diary, I know I am repeating myself, but one day someone, probably an unknown person to me, will read this, and I want them to know that Lucy Haff was a person with an extraordinary gift of kindness. She sat a vigil with my mother as she lay dying, speaking the most comforting words to her as she patted her head and assured her that the life ahead of her would be far greater than the one she was leaving. Can anyone do more for a dying person?

So, as I grieve tonight for the loss of my mother, the woman who, along with my father, that made me the person I am today, I think that my deeper sorrow is more for my wife, the person who cared so deeply for my mother and cared for her with such tenderness, that of which I have never witnessed, even on the battlefield. I cannot pray, I do not believe in prayer or a God, but I am sure that my mother's spirit will be with her until Lucy's final days.

On the day of her burial, Lucy stepped to the grave, and with a silent prayer, tossed a bouquet of flowers, tied with a ribbon that discreetly held the ring she had once given to Nicholas. As the flowers fell onto the wooden casket, she whispered, "I know I will see you again."

The snows of the winter of 1875-1876 came early, and by Thanksgiving, there were several inches on the ground. It was after a heavy snow in the middle of December that Nicholas stood with an ax in his hand surveying the white pines framing Pony Lake; he was looking for the perfect tree for Christmas.

"So," he said to the passenger on his shoulders, "Which tree looks good to you from up there?"

The six-year-old, hanging on for dear life, replied, "I don't know, Daddy, I've never picked one out before! Maybe we should have brought Mommy!" Nicholas laughed at her shrill voice.

"What makes you think Mommy could pick a better tree than us?"

Squatting down, Nicholas said, "Hop down, Ella, you're getting heavy! Did you eat all of the chicken's eggs for breakfast?" he teased. "You know that old hen works hard to lay those eggs!"

Ella jumped off her father's shoulder. The snow was to her knees, and fresh white flakes began to fall. She looked up at the sky, stuck her tongue out, and tried to catch them on the tip.

Nicholas smiled. "You're gonna freeze your tongue off," he chuckled. "C'mon, let's find the perfect tree," he said, tossing a handful of fluffy snow at the little girl. The girl plowed her way through the snow toward a scrawny white pine.

"This one, Daddy! This is the prettiest tree in the woods! Chop it down!" she yelled, as she shook the snow off the soft green needles.

Nicholas never hesitated. "Okay," he said, smiling, knowing that his wife would grimace when she saw the tree they had chosen. "Here we go!" he yelled out as he swung the ax.

"Timber!" he barked out as the sapling tipped over.

"Timber!" she squealed, imitating her father.

"Okay," Nicholas said as he put Ella back on his shoulders and picked up the tree, "Let's get home before the snow covers us up, and we will be like Eskimos," he laughed, smiling at the girl.

When they arrived home, Nicholas's wife met them on the porch in the rear of the house. The snow was falling harder, having accumulated on the branches of the skinny tree. Ella got down from her father's shoulders and stood proudly next to her mother.

"Look, Mommy, isn't this the prettiest tree ever? I picked it out, and Daddy chopped it down with two hits of his ax!" she beamed.

Nicholas and his wife smiled at each other. "Well, I can believe that he did. It's quite a beautiful tree, and I bet I couldn't have found a better one," she said, putting her arm around her. "We will decorate it tonight and drink eggnog."

"Will we put the candles on it?" she asked, wide-eyed, "I don't remember last year too much, I was just little then!"

Nicholas laughed, "We will put candles on it tonight. But I think right now, we should take the tree inside before we all look like snowmen!" he said, shaking the snow off the branches.

That evening, Nicholas made a stand for the scrawny white pine and placed the Christmas tree near the fireplace. The candles were placed in small candleholders and set on the scrawny branches, then carefully lit by Nicholas. The candles, along with the paper stars, moons, popcorn, and other glittery Christmas decorations that were made during the week by Lucy and Ella, completed the prettiest tree ever.

DAVID HESS

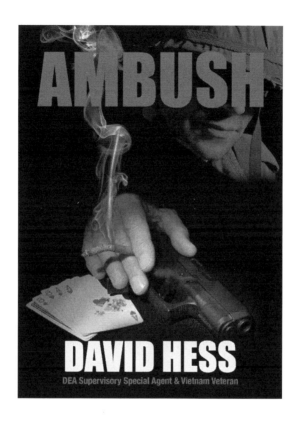

Read the first chapter in David Hess's novel Ambush that introduces us to the character Von Crocker. Learn about the events of Crocker's past that have shaped him and that he makes reference to in Gamble.

AMBUSH

1.

Seattle, Washington
March 10, 2003 - 10:00 a.m.

DEA Group Supervisor Von Crocker stood in the rain, occasionally peering toward the motionless figure of the drug dealer his agents had shot moments before. The head of the man's body was lying against the partially opened window of the vehicle. He had remained in the vehicle after being shot. In fact, he was able to drive his SUV several hundred yards before his adrenaline stopped pumping, and his girlfriend managed to stop the vehicle. Squinting and wiping the rain from his eyes, Von Crocker listened to the dead man's female partner scream obscenities as she lay turning the pavement red from the blood that flowed from her stomach. The wound was the result of one of the bullets that had hit her after passing through her drug-dealer boyfriend.

Crocker never liked dead bodies. While a soldier in Vietnam, he had always turned his head rather than look into the face of a dead enemy soldier. Now, rather than focusing on the face of the dead man, he gazed at the face of his watch. Although only minutes passed, it seemed as if his watch hands had stopped. He was nervously waiting for his team of agents to make their approach to the vehicle and the body inside in order for them to secure the area for what would surely be a long, tedious investigation.

The sight of the dead body and all of the activity surrounding the situation caused him to flashback to his days in Vietnam, and as usual, to memories of his friend and mentor Charles Slater. Smiling, he remembered sitting on his bunk in 1969, watching and listening to a drunk, animated Slater tell him about the time he had spit on the umpire's shoes.

"Did I ever tell you the story about the time I spit on the

241

umpire's shoes? I was in the Little League. We only had three teams. Our town was small, really small; none of the teams had names. We would just say 'The guys from Wooden Heights,' or 'The Pike Street Kids.' Marty Brennan played on our team. Marty used to play with dolls—and I don't mean G.I. Joe dolls. His father thought if he was on a team, he might stop doing that, but he didn't…"

Crocker recalled Slater's chuckling and his exaggerated animation and humor during his narrative. Inasmuch as Slater didn't talk too much, his behavior was out of character for him. Laughing wasn't something he did a lot of either, but on that particular night, Sergeant Slater was acting differently, and Crocker was finding that his fond memories of the story were better than focusing on what was happening around him at the moment. Slater had told him quite a story.

"…Anyway, I was about ten years old, and we were playing the championship game against Wooden Heights—I don't know why they called it that; there weren't any trophies or anything. The manager would take you for ice cream if you won. I loved baseball, and man, I was a good catcher. I didn't have any equipment though—just an old catcher's mask my big brother Mike gave me. Shit, I used to have to put electrical tape on the padding of the mask. If I didn't, it would scratch my face. A couple of times I actually caught games without wearing the mask—guess that's why I look like this. Ya know what I used for a chest protector? My mother took a pillowcase and stuffed it with feathers from an old pillow and sewed it shut. I would wear that under my shirt— the feathers used to tickle and scratch me, but my mother always made me wear it. I used to let the other catchers wear my mask, but no one wanted to wear the feather protector. I didn't have any shin guards though so my legs were always black and blue. Shit, I still have scars on them from being scraped so many times—but that's okay, I just loved to play ball…"

Crocker grinned to himself, enjoying revisiting the story in his head and visualizing a very drunk Slater balancing himself on one foot trying to show him the scars on his shins. *What a tough kid Slater must have been.*

"…So, we were playing for the championship, and I remember it was a hot, Georgia summer night—hotter than even this shit hole. The score was tied four to four; it was the bottom of the last inning, and I was at bat. I was so fucking nervous I couldn't stand it! I spit on my hands, rubbed them on my pants, and stepped into the batter's box. The very first pitch almost hit me, and I stared at the skinny kid on the mound. The second pitch looked like a watermelon, and I hit it like a rocket, over the fence. HOMERUN!!! As I rounded the bases, I could see my mother and father jumping up and down. Well, my mother was jumping and trying to hold on to her best red straw hat. My dad was just smiling and pumping his fist in the air. I knew they were proud. The whole damn team was waiting at home plate for me. Everyone was jumping up and down; I could hardly find enough of home plate to step on. Still jumping, we all headed to the dugout and then the umpire came running toward us. He took both of the managers off to the side and told them that I didn't touch second base then called me out! I was so fucking pissed! Our manager went crazy, and I thought I was gonna cry, but I figured we'd just beat them in the next inning. Until this day I know I stepped on the base—I'm a lot of things but a cheater isn't one of them. Shit, I'd fight you in a second if I knew I was right, but one thing my mother taught me was not to be a cheater or a liar, and if you're wrong—you're wrong. I still hate those kinds of people—liars and cheaters. Well, anyway, in the next inning their first batter hit one out of the park and we didn't score when we got up to bat, so that was the end of our championship…"

Crocker had always pictured young Slater as probably being a good looking, muscular freckled kid with intense blue-gray eyes that would penetrate whoever he looked at- like Superman looking through a wall. He always looked a person in the eyes when he spoke. It could be a warm friendly feeling or an intimidating jolt that couldn't be shaken off for a week.

"…Ya know what the best damn thing about that game was?

Marty Brennan got to play and he got a hit. I remember thinking how cool that was—of course everyone laughed when he got to first base because we all knew that he was scared. Hell, he was looking around like a bitch dog in heat! We knew he wouldn't know what to do or where to run if anyone else got a hit while he was on base. But no one did, and now I'm glad they didn't—it would have ruined his big day. I'll bet he still remembers that hit. Anyway, we lost the fucking game. I can still see my mother's face; she was crying and had tissues in her hand, waving to me. My father's face was beet red. I knew he was pissed, but he was too nice of a guy to say anything to the umpire. He loved baseball as much as I did. He would come home from the factory after working ten-hour shifts and play catch with me. So anyway, we had to meet on the infield and tell the other team 'good game.' As I walked down the line shaking all of the players' and managers' hands, I finally got to the umpire. I stared him in the eyes and said, 'Good game. I stepped on the base, asshole.' Then I spit on his shoes and said, 'Sorry,' and I was quickly escorted off the field by my manager…"

Crocker smiled sentimentally recalling Slater laughing the hardest he had ever seen him laugh, or would ever see him laugh.

The cold rain sent a shiver through Crocker. The soaking wet rain brought him back to the present. He looked at his watch again; only two minutes had passed since he began his daydream. Nothing had changed on the street. He was enjoying his daydream though, and he allowed himself to return to it. *Funny, how I can still hear Slater's laugh.* It was a hardy laugh and just like Slater—there was nothing phony about it. His memories returned.

"…But the whole night wasn't a complete disaster. Our manager put us all in the back of his old, red and white, 1952 Ford pickup truck to take us for ice cream. Before I got into the truck though, my mother, holding her red hat on her head, came running, yelling my name. She gave me a hug and two quarters, told me that she was proud of me, and then whispered that she saw me step on the base. As she was leaving, she said, 'Have a good time,' and kissed me on my forehead. She left a red lipstick print on my forehead but didn't tell me and laughed as she walked away. I saw it later and wiped it off with a napkin at the Dairy Cow. The Dairy Cow always had the best damn ice cream and it's still there! There's nothing better than a Dairy Cow sundae on a hot night in Georgia. I can't wait to get back. I swear that's the first place I'm going to go! I still remember that night like it was yesterday—hot as hell, and I had a root beer float that my manager bought for me, and then I took the two quarters Mother gave me and bought a medium chocolate cone. We proclaimed ourselves champions by the fact that we all agreed that I had touched second. Shit, I would have admitted it if I had missed it—that's the way I am—stupid I guess…"

Though Crocker had visited this dream many times, every time he did, he could still hear Slater's tone change when it got to this point:

"…On the way home, we all were in the back of the truck yelling, 'We won the game; we won the game,' even though we knew we really didn't; it was fun to yell it anyway. The hot, muggy air was hanging, almost like a wet blanket. The way it wrapped around my body and the ride in the back of the truck was a neat way to cool down and to keep the mosquitoes away. The manager drove everyone right to their houses, and as each player jumped off the truck, we would again scream, 'We won the game; we won the game!' I lived way out in the country and was always the last one to get dropped off. At the last player's house before mine, the manager told me to get into the cab of the truck with him. I remember wishing that I could have stayed in the back where it was cool. We didn't talk much, but as we got near my house, he asked me if I wanted him to drive me down the lane since my house was about a quarter of a mile from the main road. I told him no, I would walk—I always loved the smells and sounds at night when I walked down the lane—especially after dark. It was called Tulip Leaf Lane, but there were no tulips, just honeysuckle, with water lilies and Spanish moss in the swamp beside the lane.

When I got out of the truck, he asked, 'Charlie, did you step on the base? Tell me the truth.'

I looked him right in the eyes and said, 'Yes, Sir, I did.'

He said he believed me and said I was a good kid and never to compromise my principles. I didn't really know exactly what the hell he meant other than don't cheat or lie, but I knew it was good because he smiled, taking my hand and shaking it like I was a grown-up. I got out of the truck and began the slow walk home. I could see lights in the house; I perked up a bit. I was glad Mom and Dad were home—I still felt sad about losing the game. Mom always found a way to make me feel better whenever I was upset. I knew she would try to feed me, but truthfully, I wasn't feeling too good from all the soda and ice cream, but I was looking forward to her trying anyway like she'd done before I got in the truck after the game.

As I walked down the lane it was getting cooler, and I could hear frogs, crickets and smell the honeysuckle and moss. I even bent over, picked up a couple of stones and threw them into the woods to make the frogs stop croaking. Then I'd wait for them to start up again, and then throw another stone—I always liked to do that. As I rounded the bend, I could see my brother Mike's rusty pickup truck parked in the driveway, but Dad's Buick wasn't there. I could see Mike's silhouette in the doorway, and as I approached the porch he came out of the house to meet me in the yard…"

This was the part of the daydream Crocker hated. However he was unable to change it or stop here. It always had the same ending.

"…My brother came over to me, put his hand on my shoulder and said, 'Charlie, I don't know how to do, or say this,' he started crying. 'Mama and daddy were in a terrible accident—they ain't comin' home. They were killed by a train 'bout twenty miles away. I guess daddy didn't hear it or see it coming. The Sheriff called. He'll be here in a little while to talk to us and let us know what happened.' Mike suddenly bent over, sobbing uncontrollably.

"I stared at him and didn't say a word. I didn't know what to do so I went to my room and lay on my bed—just staring at the ceiling. When the Sheriff finally came, Mike called for me to come out, but I didn't want to hear anything he had to say. Instead, I stayed in bed, picturing mama in the stands with her fancy red hat and dad's red face, how he held his head and then yelled, 'No way—he touched that base!' I remembered her kissing me on the forehead and how she tucked the two quarters into my hand. I saw those things over and over all night long. I wanted those two quarters back. I felt sick to my stomach, remem-bering how I'd thrown away the napkin I'd wiped mama's lipstick off my forehead with, and I punched the wall. I wished I had kept the napkin..."

Crocker got that familiar lump in his throat recalling how Slater's blue-gray eyes burned into him. The vision of his friend as a young boy in such pain had haunted him for over thirty years. The daydream ended the same way every time, a drunken Slater looking into Crocker's eyes as he finished the story:

"...So that's the story of me spitting on the umpire's shoe; no one else needs to know about it—it's a stupid story anyway."

Crocker shook his head and came back to reality. The rain was coming harder and washing the woman's blood away from her body. His team had finally agreed it would be safe to approach the body and were getting into a tactical formation, the same formation every DEA agent is taught at the academy-The Snake Method. Supposedly it was the safest possible method to conduct a raid. It was also the easiest to learn and to use. Crocker was not into the tactics taught at the academy; he thought it was all nonsense. The woman was still screaming at the agents. "You fucking killed him! YOU FUCKING KILLED HIM!!!"

He rubbed the rainwater off his face. *Hell, no one cares if this guy is dead. It doesn't really matter. He's just another drug dealer thinking he could win. They never win. Maybe for a week, a month, some even a year or more, but they never make it all the way.*

Crocker was restless as he stood watching the scene continue to unfold. The team had obviously been confused about how to approach the SUV. They were focused on finding the best solution that would prevent anyone else from getting hurt. The woman who had been in the car with the drug dealer was making too much noise for them to hear anything other than her screams. As she lay on the rain-soaked street and still bleeding profusely from her belly, Crocker's hands shook while he watched her white clothing turn red. *If she would just shut up, maybe we would be able to get up there and help her; this is not good.* Her screeching was making everyone more cautious and more deliberate than was probably necessary. *Just shut the fuck up*!

Finally, what felt like an eternity, but was in reality only minutes after the shooting, she stopped screaming. Crocker could see she was still moving, and suddenly the silence quickly settled into sadness. Everything seemed to move in slow motion. The agents were approaching the drug dealer's body, the lead agent's shield held in front of him. Their posture, crouched over, was something he always found funny. *They look like Groucho Marx sneaking out of a restaurant without paying his check.* He nervously smiled as they made their approach on the lifeless figure in the SUV.

Suddenly, as quickly as she became quiet the woman sat up and began to screech, sending a chill up and down Crocker's spine.

Please shut up, please shut the fuck up! How the hell did all of this shit happen?

"Son-of-a-bitch," he muttered, as he continued staring at her blood-soaked blouse.

He could hear his heart pounding. It was really loud, and he knew its beats weren't in rhythm. The situation wasn't helping his atrial fibrillation, *AFib, another gift from the DEA! Just one more gift from an agency that never stops giving.* Too much drinking, carousing, smoking and lack of sleep had taken its toll along with his high blood pressure, anxiety, high cholesterol, several marriages, string of women, drinking and gambling problems. *Thanks for the fucking memories, DEA!* He reached into his pocket and pulled out a Winchester. *This is what I need.* He knew it would make the AFib worse, but he didn't care; he loved the little cigars. He stared at the Winchester, lit it and watched his team moving toward the vehicle. Trying to rub the AFib away, he massaged his chest. He took a deep drag on his smoke and said, "Christ, what the hell else can go wrong?"

"Fuck this!" he yelled at no one in particular. Ironically enough the woman shut up. *Damn, I should have done that an hour ago*, he chuckled.

The team moved quickly to reach the body before another round of chaos could erupt. The team leader opened the door of the vehicle, and after checking the body for signs of life, signaled to Crocker that the drug dealer was dead. *He's done selling cocaine, heroin, crack, meth, marijuana, ecstasy and anything else to those who chose to put the shit into their body. Fuck him.* "I hope he rots in hell."

Several ambulances had arrived at the scene and it was time for him to begin working.

"C'mon, heartbeat, get it together," he murmured to himself.

His first business would have to be a call to his boss. He took his cell phone out and punched in a number from his speed dial. He listened to the phone ring and ring before closing it and punching in another number. His boss, The Special Agent in Charge, the SAC, the Old Man as he was called, was not answering either of his phones. *Great, just fucking great! What an asshole! You're such a bald, short, self-centered, pot-bellied, ass-kissing man who never put a drug case together in your entire 32 year career. Everyone swears you got promoted by setting chairs up for meetings when you were a young agent in the New York Field Division. Can't even fuckin' bother to set up your voicemail or too dumb to figure it out. Special Agent in Charge, Michael Burne; SAC Burne— sack-of-shit Burne.* "What a joke this guy is."

As the medical personnel moved to assist the woman, the ear splitting screams resumed. "You fucking killed him! Why the fuck did you kill him? Why did you assholes have to shoot him? YOU FUCKING ASSHOLES!"

He found her words strange. He used those same words all the time, even liked the words, but now it just sounded all wrong.

He felt uneasy, like he was standing in front of his best friend's mother's casket telling him that he never really liked her. It was unsettling.

The view of the woman was being blocked by the medical team that was assisting her. And now, as he looked past the team, he could see the press arriving. *It is all complete now; the leeches are here.* They were the maggots of law enforcement, making their living listening to scanners and trying to beat the other media to the scene, sometimes even beating some of the police. It was upon seeing the media that his thoughts turned to his wife Carla. He needed to contact her; he didn't want her to find out about the shooting on the news. There were few people in his life that he truly cared about, but Carla was the one who had saved him from himself. He knew she was probably the only person that truly loved him; he also knew he was tough to love and to get close to. If it hadn't been for her, he would have long ago been fired by the DEA. She had been responsible for changing his coarse personality into one that most people found tolerable—at least at the DEA. He also knew she would be upset when she got his call. He slowly reached for his phone, and then returned it to his pocket.

He watched as the EMT's were finally able to put the woman into the back of an ambulance, but as they were driving away, he could still hear her screaming obscenities. Laughing nervously he shook his head, and as he watched the vehicle leave the scene, he lit another Winchester off the first one.

"Where the fuck is Burne? What the hell else can go wrong?" he mumbled as he stared at the body of the drug dealer lying on the wet ground. He pulled his phone from his pocket and slowly pushed the numbers that would reach his home phone.

Read the rest of Von Crocker's story in **Ambush**
amazon.com/author/davidhess

About the Author

David Hess is a retired Drug Enforcement Administration Supervisory Special Agent and a Vietnam Veteran. He served with the DEA for twenty-one years and was in Vietnam with the 173rd Airborne Brigade and 1st Field Forces. He attended Penn State University and graduated from the University of Scranton. He and his wife, Marlene, reside in Pennsylvania. He has published three previous novels: Ambush, Gamble, and Damaged.

Two of the short stories from DAMAGED were chosen to be produced and performed at Shawnee Playhouse as one act plays.
amazon.com/author/davidhess

Don't forget to write a review after you read. I really appreciate hearing what you think about the story and the characters. You are my best reason for writing, so help me to make it better. Go to the book on amazon, and under the customer reviews, there is a link to write your review.

No matter where I am or what's going on, I try my best to set aside time every day to answer emails and messages from readers. You can reach me at: dhessauthor@gmail.com

Find him on Facebook under David Hess Author
www.davidhessbooks.com
amazon.com/author/davidhess